HOLD
YOUR
BREATH

BOOKS BY HELEN PHIFER

DETECTIVE MORGAN BROOKES SERIES

One Left Alive

The Killer's Girl

The Hiding Place

First Girl to Die

Find the Girl

Sleeping Dolls

Silent Angel

Their Burning Graves

BETH ADAMS SERIES

The Girl in the Grave

The Girls in the Lake

DETECTIVE LUCY HARWIN SERIES

Dark House

Dying Breath

Last Light

STANDALONES

Lakeview House

HOLD YOUR BREATH

HELEN PHIFER

bookouture

Published by Bookouture in 2023

An imprint of Storyfire Ltd.
Carmelite House
50 Victoria Embankment
London EC4Y 0DZ

www.bookouture.com

ISBN: 978-1-83790-346-7
eBook ISBN: 978-1-83790-345-0

PROLOGUE

She strained against the ropes as they worked with their back to her, humming softly. She knew the song, it was an eighties hit that still got played on the radio, a lot. Dave liked to listen to some eighties radio station when he worked, but she couldn't remember the title of it. He'd listened every week for all the years they'd worked together, and yet she just couldn't think of the name.

She pulled against the ropes again. They were firmly tied to the examination chair she was lying on. She moved slowly without distracting them from whatever they were doing. But they had bound her so tight that she was only giving herself friction burns, and it hurt too much trying to twist them free. She could see everything, but couldn't scream for the awful, stinking piece of material that had been tied tightly around her mouth. It was cutting into the soft flesh of her cheeks. She would scream if she could, she would scream so loud that it would pierce their eardrums. It would serve them right. It was what they deserved, and probably not punishment enough for what they were doing to her. It came to her, they were humming 'Sweet Dreams' by the Eurythmics, a song her mum liked to listen to back in the day. She felt her heart break for her mum; she was in her sixties now and all alone, or she would be once they found her body.

With their backs to her they looked like any normal person, and it was hard to tell if it was a guy or a girl underneath the balaclava they were wearing. Whoever it was she had no doubt they were busy working on something that was important to them.

And she knew that it was going to be painful. Was this how she was going to die? Strapped to a hard chair in a freezing cold garage? She squeezed her eyes shut. They had seemed so kind, and they had nice eyes that you thought you could get to know if you had the chance. Now though, in this place they no longer looked as if you would kiss them under the mistletoe at the office Christmas party, after a glass or two of Prosecco.

They turned to face her, and their eyes smiled for the briefest of moments. She realised that she'd been rambling, trying to get lost in her mind, to distract herself from what they were about to do. Now their eyes were small, black glittering orbs that gave not one ounce of warmth. It was the eyes that terrified her because there was no feeling inside of them, only hate; and she knew if she stared at them for long enough, she would die a thousand times.

She decided he must be a guy, because a woman wouldn't be this cruel, surely? He hadn't spoken to her since she'd woken up, and she had no idea how she'd got here, what time it was or how long he'd had her tied up. It was hard to breathe through her nose now, and the panic inside of her chest made her feel as if she was suffocating, and her heart was thumping hard enough that she could feel every beat. The fear of not knowing if each painful breath may be her last was too much to bear.

There was no one to notice she was missing. Her mum had been struggling with depression since her dad had died six months ago, and they didn't always speak every day, even though they lived in the same house. Her best friend was on holiday. She would have known something was wrong if she were here. But while she was sitting on a chair in a cold garage taking her last breaths, her best friend was probably lying on a warm beach, drinking cocktails. Tears welled in her eyes, but she blinked furiously. She wasn't going to let him see her cry; she wouldn't give him the satisfaction.

He lifted a large roll of clingfilm and walked towards her. She tensed her entire body as he got nearer to her, and began to push against the restraints holding her down. A sound escaped from her mouth. It was a scream, but it was so quiet against the gag she was surprised he heard it.

'Don't panic, this won't take long. And when I've finished you will live for all of eternity. Your beauty will never grow old. You won't have to worry about wrinkles on your forehead or crow's feet. You'll be eternally young. Isn't that wonderful? Isn't that what all women dream about?'

She began to fight then, really struggle, but he didn't stop, and he began to unwrap the clingfilm, and as he began to wrap it around her face he whispered, 'Shhhh.'

She could barely breathe, but he kept on wrapping the plastic around her face across her nose, until she couldn't take in air through her nostrils, and then he lifted down the gag and she gulped in air. But too soon her mouth was quickly covered with the sticky plastic, and the panic set in.

As the world began to swim out of focus, she pushed against the ropes, but she was getting weaker. It was too hard to fight.

The last thing she saw were silver spots floating across the back of her eyelids. Where were her favourite memories? Wasn't she supposed to at least have those in her final moments of life?

She was being cheated and it was so unfair.

Death was nothing but blackness.

ONE

The CID office was as full as it ever was. DCs Amy Smith and Morgan Brookes were discussing whose turn it was to make the coffee, when Cain walked in carrying a medium-sized cardboard box. He had not long joined the team. Their sergeant, and Morgan's partner, Ben Matthews, was at a meeting about the rising violent crime rate and probably getting interrogated about the statistics and what they could do to reduce the problem. Morgan wouldn't want to be Ben; how could he explain the rise in murderous monsters? She supposed he could blame her. Sometimes it seemed like she was a walking magnet for every violent criminal this side of the north-west. He repeatedly told her she wasn't to blame herself, but she did and always would.

'Hey, Brookes, this parcel is for you. Have you been getting your Amazon deliveries dropped off at the front office? You know the big boss's boss won't be happy about it,' Cain said.

Morgan had given up arguing with Amy about brewing up, and had walked around the office collecting the empty mugs. She'd make her own, it would probably taste better than Amy's anyway. Turning to look at Cain she crossed the room to look at the box.

'No, I have not. Are you sure it's for me?'

'Last time I looked you were called DC Morgan Brookes, right? Or have you changed your name to Matthews and got married on the sly?'

'What are you talking about, don't be stupid.'

She looked at the box, it had a handwritten label stuck to it. The writing was neat, block capitals that she didn't recognise.

'I have no idea what that is.'

Amy came to have a look. 'Get you, looks like somebody is sending you gifts. Or...'

Morgan looked at her. 'Or what?'

'Cain did you check if it's making a ticking noise? With Morgan's luck someone has probably sent her a bomb.' Amy started to laugh, and Cain's face paled as he stepped away from the box. 'I'm joking, Cain, come on, who would want to blow our celebrity detective up?'

Morgan glared at her. 'That's not funny, not one bit.'

Amy shrugged and bent down, pressing her ear to the cardboard for a few moments, and then stood up. 'It's not ticking, so you can open it. Hurry up, the excitement is killing me.'

The door opened and in walked a flushed Ben, with a huge folder tucked under one arm, his cheeks red, his tie loosened, and his shirt buttons undone.

'What's all the excitement?'

'Morgan got a mystery parcel.' Amy was grinning at him. 'Unless you sent her it.'

He shook his head. 'Not me, sorry to disappoint you. It's probably a stack of Neighbourhood Policing Leaflets or something equally as boring. I wouldn't get too excited, folks. Morgan, why don't you just open it and put them out of their misery?'

Morgan grabbed a pair of scissors off her desk and slit the

red and white fragile tape, tearing open the flaps to see nothing but a sea of white foam peanuts. Everyone was watching her. A sense of dread filled her stomach, and she didn't want to put her hands inside to see what was buried underneath them, when she had no clue what it could be. She paused and looked at them.

'C'mon, Morgan, just get on with it.' Cain was nodding enthusiastically at her.

'You have a look if you're that bothered.'

He stuck his hands inside the box, and for a split-second she had a vision of him getting his fingers stuck inside of a giant mouse trap. He felt around then snatched his hand out.

'No idea what that is but it feels all slimy.'

Amy shook her head. 'Jesus, what a pair of wimps.'

She stuck her hand in the box and pulled out a face.

Morgan and Ben both jumped backwards. Cain let out a yell so loud it scared Amy, who threw the white rubberlike face she was holding onto the floor.

'What the hell is that thing, is it real?' Cain asked.

No one could answer, they all took a step closer, and Morgan began to laugh.

'It's a mask, you idiot. Okay, which of you smart arses thought you'd scare the shit out of me with a woman's face? This better not be my Secret Santa.'

All three of them shook their heads. Morgan tutted and took a step towards the strange mask and, picking it up, she put it on Cain's desk.

'That's one weird mask. It's only half of a face and it looks dead.'

'Cain you're even weirder than I thought. It's some crappy joke shop mask that hasn't even been finished off. Nice to know whoever sent this couldn't even buy the finished thing.'

Morgan tipped the box up, spilling the little foam peanuts all over the desk and the floor, to see if there was anything else inside of it. It was empty, no note, nothing. She began to scoop the peanuts back into the box before the inspector walked in.

She left the mask sitting on the desk and took the box out to the bin in the kitchen area. When she came back in someone had propped it on the filing cabinet behind her desk, with a Post-it note stuck to its head, the word 'Barb' written on it.

'You are so childish at times,' she said to them both.

'And it's your turn to brew up, Morgan. Fun's over, kids, let's get back to work before Marc comes in to have a pop at you all messing around on company time.'

Ben walked into his office and let the door slam behind him.

'Is he in a mood because someone sent you a present?' Cain's face was serious.

'No, he's in a mood because he's probably just been given a right telling off at the meeting, and Marc will be on the war path.'

Amy shrugged. 'I'm not sure how they expect us to come up with a way to stop the crime rate. It's not as if we are the ones committing the crimes, is it? We're just the silly buggers who have to clean up after them and work the crappy long shifts while we're at it.'

Morgan grabbed the mugs she'd put down to open the box.

As she left the office she glanced at the mask and shuddered. It was a creepy woman's face with her eyes shut. It looked as if whoever it was really was dead, like Cain had said, and it kind of looked familiar.

Thank God it was behind her. She didn't want to have to stare at that all day while she worked, and she wasn't going to admit to Cain or Amy that it freaked her out. They'd never let her live it down, and before she knew it there would be a whole collection of them staring at her.

The rest of the afternoon went by without incident. Amy and Cain, who had worked an early, had left for the day leaving her and Ben. He still hadn't come out of his office; she'd left him to it, and he was also due to finish soon, but she knew he'd do his best to hang around as long as he could because she was the only one working the late shift.

The desk phone in his office began to ring and she watched him through the glass as he answered it. His face was serious and then he lifted his left hand and ran it over his shaved head. Morgan knew this was bad news: running his hand across his head was how he coped with stress. She walked across to the window to see if Amy or Cain's cars were still in the car park, but they weren't: they had left pretty sharpish. Not that she could authorise for them to work overtime, but it would save calling them back out if they needed them, if she could have shouted them and waved them back.

Ben walked out of his office, and she turned to look at him.

'Hey, are you okay?'

'Patrol have found a body in a car by Thirlmere. It looks suspicious, and they need someone to go take a look.'

'I'll go, and if I need you, I can ring you if you're busy?'

He shook his head. 'We'll both go, save the time and effort.' He glanced at the mask propped on the filing cabinet. 'Barb?'

'Cain's idea of a joke. He's only just watched season one of *Stranger Things*.'

Ben looked even more confused. 'Oh, okay.'

Morgan reached out and took hold of his hand. 'Is everything okay?'

'Yes, I just get fed up with all the office politics and bullshit. I'd rather be out doing my job than trying to figure out how to stop things I have no control over, just to make headquarters feel better. I have no idea what the whole point of these monthly meetings are; it's always the same old.'

'Screw them, Ben. We do a great job. The whole team works tirelessly to solve some of the most horrific crimes in the country – you'd think they'd be happy we get the results that we do.'

He stepped towards her and pulled her close, hugging her tight for the briefest of seconds before letting her go.

'God, I needed that. It drives me crazy that we have to behave as if we hardly know each other all day.'

She smiled at him. 'It does. That's great to know, at least it makes you want me even more because you can't have me.'

He laughed. 'You're so bad, Brookes.'

'I know, that's why you love me.'

He nodded. 'It is, that and your fiery hair and fishnet tights with those Doc Martens; they're enough to drive a man my age insane. Come on, we better go take a look at that body, back to reality with a bang.'

'You truly know how to show a gal a good time. It was nice while it lasted though, wasn't it? Dealing with shed break-ins and agricultural thefts.'

Ben laughed so loud it echoed around the empty office.

They left the station, both tugging on winter coats to keep them warm. Morgan also pulled on a black hat, scarf and gloves, as the sun had set when the others left, leaving them about to go out into the dark and bitter cold, to go find a body in one of the area's top beauty spots, two weeks before Christmas.

TWO

It wasn't hard to find the lay-by the car was in, because Morgan knew it well. It was where she had run away from a killer a couple of years before, when she had not long become a detective. A police van was parked next to a Vauxhall Astra that was illuminated blue with the flashing lights. The reporting officer, Amber, climbed out of the van. Morgan hadn't seen her for a while, not since Cain had come to work with them anyway. He and Amber didn't get on too well, and she knew he'd been glad to escape from her.

'Amber.'

'Morgan.'

Ben paused at the back of the unmarked car they'd arrived in.

'We better suit and boot, Morgan. Amber have you touched anything?'

'I touched the door handle, knocked on the window then I realised something was wrong and put some gloves on. I opened the door and felt for a pulse before requesting ambulance who are still travelling.'

He nodded. 'Good, what have we got then?'

'Female deceased. She doesn't look old enough to have had a heart attack, and there is no rubber hose leading into the car, and no empty blister packs of tablets lying around either. I don't think it's suicide.'

'Thanks, we'll take a look.'

Morgan, who was now an expert at crime-scene attire, was suited and booted before Ben had put one leg through the paper overalls. She walked towards the car and looked around it before opening the passenger door, not wanting to disturb the body.

Amber was right, it didn't look as if this was a suicide. The woman, who only looked to be in her twenties, was sitting with her head slumped to one side. Amber passed Morgan a torch, even though the internal light had come on when she'd opened the door, and she shone it on her face. It had taken on the waxy, yellow pallor of the dead. Her eyes were wide open, and there was something on her eyelashes that looked white and sticky. Morgan shone the torch in the footwell and then into the back seat.

Ben peered over her shoulder.

'Yep, she's dead all right. I wonder what happened?'

Amber sighed. 'Since I joined, I've been to one drowning and two suicides here. It gives me the shivers every time I drive past on patrol and there are families eating picnics, staring down at the lake and taking selfies.'

Morgan didn't add her own experiences. Amber had only been a Response officer for twelve months. 'It's such a beautiful place though, the view of the lake down below surrounded by the trees, it does make you want to stop and take a moment.'

'Yeah, if you want to top yourself with a view, it is. What are we doing about her?'

'Have you run the number plate?' Ben asked.

'Yes, the car belongs to a Ms Jasmine Armer of Millfield

Gardens, Keswick. Her DOB is seventh December 2002. No intelligence, no PNC record, not even a fixed penalty notice.'

'Good job, she's only twenty, although I don't suppose we can confirm it's her just yet. Have you requested CSI?'

Amber rolled her eyes, and Ben glared at her; Morgan looked away.

'Yes, they're on the way from Barrow. Wendy is on holiday for a fortnight.'

'Oh right, thanks.'

Ben walked away, leaving Morgan to shut the car door and then follow him. He leaned towards her and whispered, 'Is she always so arsy? She's worse than you.'

'Yes, why do you think Cain was so eager to join us.'

Ben nodded. 'Why do I get all the people with attitude? Is having a bad attitude all part of the recruitment process now, I wonder? What happened to being sensitive and making people feel better?'

'You can handle them, it's what you do.' She didn't say that he could deal with her on her worst days. She nodded at the car. 'What do you think?'

'I don't know, we need the forensic pathologist, Dr Donnelly, to call it. Until we know more, I'm going to treat it as a suspicious death. I'd rather that than miss anything. We can't revisit the decision once the body is moved, and we could lose vital evidence. If it's not suspicious, then so be it. But she looks too young to have died of natural causes.'

'I know, it's so sad. Dying out here on your own.' Morgan felt a full body shiver run down her spine just thinking about it.

Ben pulled out his phone and rang his friend, Declan, the pathologist, to give him a heads-up, before he got the official phone call from headquarters, notifying him that he was needed. Morgan loved how close Declan and Ben were. They had been friends before she came along but, lately, they'd been spending more time together, which was good for Ben and The

Black Dog, where they preferred to drink. She didn't want him relying on her to keep him company. She wanted him to feel able to spend time with his friends and not have to choose between her and Declan. She knew that when she was alive, Cindy, his wife, was the opposite; she had been possessive of Ben, but then again, she hadn't had the luxury of working with him like Morgan got to. She loved Declan as much as Ben did. He was such a good gossip and went through boyfriends like they were in short supply. Ben also encouraged Morgan to spend time with her friends, but she only really had Emily, Amy and Wendy. She preferred to read or listen to podcasts on her days off. It was nice having the occasional meetup for cocktails and coffee, but she liked to keep it at that.

Amber had got back into the van, keeping the engine running and the heating on full. Morgan guessed there wasn't much point in freezing to death while waiting for the rest of the team to arrive. Before she got back into the car she had a walk around the parking area, shining the torch onto the floor, checking to see if the victim had perhaps taken something and discarded the evidence before getting back into her car. She couldn't see anything, not even an empty crisp packet. Nine times out of ten you could guarantee there would be an empty packet of Monster Munch or Hula Hoops blowing around somewhere on the floor, but it was litter free. There was a wooden gate that opened onto a path which split into two ways. One path took you on a walk down to the lake, which was actually a reservoir, but everyone called it a lake because Reservoir Thirlmere didn't quite have the same ring to it. She walked down the steep path a little bit before she heard Ben's voice calling her back.

'Morgan, get back here. We'll let the dog handler take care of that.'

She stopped, shone the torch a little further and decided that Jasmine hadn't been down here at all. Not that she knew this for certain. Who knew what had happened. Did the poor girl kill herself or was she killed? Morgan had a gut feeling that she was already dead when she arrived here? If that was the case, who had killed her, and brought her body here and dumped her?

THREE

Morgan stared down at the blackness of the body of water below, it was a steep descent to get to it and the water's edge was surrounded with tall trees and a stony shore. With Helvellyn overlooking it, there really was no place quite like it for the wonderful views. It was such a beautiful place on a warm sunny day. Tonight, though, it was dark and the looming mountain behind them along with the shadows made the whole place take on a totally different vibe, it felt sinister and not a beautiful tourist spot.

It was like waiting for a bus. Both Morgan and Ben had got back into the car to warm up while they waited what seemed like an eternity for someone else to turn up, and then one after the other they arrived: Cassie with Brock, the search dog, Claire, the CSI from Barrow, who was on duty, and Declan.

Morgan and Ben got out of the car, keeping a distance from Claire, who was even stricter than Wendy when it came to securing a crime scene.

Declan strode across towards them.

'What have we here then, suicide? I suppose if you're going to do it a nice view would help.'

Ben shook his head. 'I don't think so, but it's not my shout, that's your decision to make.'

Declan arched an eyebrow at Morgan. 'Well, I never, what's happened to you? Has the Ben I know been abducted by aliens and replaced with one who doesn't profess to know everything?'

Morgan stifled a laugh and elbowed Declan; Ben shook his head.

'It's not obvious is what I mean.'

Declan smiled at his friend. 'Winding you up, mate. Have you got any spare overalls? I forgot to replenish my stock in my haste to come and assist you.'

Morgan opened the boot and fished out a pair that would fit him, and she passed them to him. 'Need anything else?'

'Nope, just these thanks. Christ it's freezing out here. Was her engine running when they found her?'

Morgan shrugged. 'Let me check with Amber.'

She left Declan getting changed and knocked on the van window.

'Declan wants to know if the engine was running when you found her.'

'Nope, it was cold. She's been here awhile, or the car has.'

Morgan relayed the information back to him. Claire was ready to begin processing the scene, but she waited for Declan to look first.

'What's the plan?' he asked Claire and Ben.

Ben answered. 'We've already touched the passenger door and opened it, so you might want to open that one to take a look. Claire can check for prints on the driver's door before we disturb it.'

Claire nodded. 'Sounds good to me.'

'Any identification?'

Ben answered. 'Yes, a driving licence for a Jasmine Armer. Still need to verify this is actually her.'

All of them stood back and watched as Declan approached the car. He opened the passenger door. Morgan had passed him her torch, although the interior light came on when the door opened.

He leaned in. 'Good evening, Jasmine, I'm so sorry to have to do this but I'm Declan, the forensic pathologist, and I'm going to be taking care of you from now on. I promise you're in safe hands and no one else can hurt you, my lovely.'

Morgan's eyes filled with tears; it got her every single time. She used a gloved hand to blot at the corner of one eye and noticed Ben turn away. All of them were shuffling from foot to foot to try and keep some semblance of body heat inside of them. Every time they spoke cold plumes of white air blew out of their mouths.

Declan opened his case and took Jasmine's temperature; he lifted her hands which were by her side and looked at her fingers, then pushing back the sleeve of her jumper, her wrists. Then he bagged them up, carefully wrapping each one in brown paper bags and securing them with a rubber band. When he'd finished, he straightened up.

'There's no blunt-force trauma from what I can see, but it's not the best place to conduct an examination, especially with her fully dressed. Her clothes don't seem to be in a state of disarray. There is something on her eyelashes. I've taken a scraping of it to send off for analysis; there are also some petechial haemorrhages in her eyelids which are indicative of asphyxiation. Her hands look clean, but there are deep red marks around her wrists, so she was bound at some point. This isn't natural causes that's for sure, unless she tied herself up, then suffocated herself and removed the bindings after she'd died.'

Ben nodded. 'Damn, I was hoping for a natural cause of death.'

'For whose sake, Jasmine's or yours?'

'Both.'

Declan nodded at Claire. 'You can take over now. When you're finished processing the scene, get Jasmine sent to the mortuary, where we can take care of her. The inside of that car is colder than the fridges. She's going to be frozen solid by the time she arrives. Rigor is setting in, so she's only been dead somewhere in the region of two to six hours I'd estimate.'

Ben waved at Cassie, who was standing by the rear of the dog van.

'Cassie, you're good to go.'

She let Brock out and they began to search the area.

Declan turned to Ben and Morgan.

'Why leave her here on show in her own car? Whoever did this didn't try to hide her body.'

Morgan was staring back at the car. 'Whoever did this is proud of it, they wanted us to find her and fast. They had no intention of hiding her body. They want us to know who she is. Why?'

Declan shrugged. 'I'm afraid that's for you both, my super detectives. I can only deal with the medical evidence.'

She smiled at him. 'I know, I'm just thinking out loud.'

'And I love it when you do. I like watching the cogs in your brain come to life, Morgan. You are a living, breathing work of art. I'll see you at my place tomorrow, bright and early.' He winked at her, and she smiled.

He stripped off all the protective clothing, dumping it in a brown paper sack and left them to it, driving away.

Morgan turned back to where Ben was talking to Claire, and she hoped that they found whoever had done this and fast. It was so sad and unusual; killers usually liked to try and keep their bodies hidden for a little bit of time. This though, it was so brazen and so open. Imagine if it hadn't been Amber driving past. A family stopping to take in the view in the morning could have found her, and then the poor kids would be traumatised for life. It proved one thing: whoever did this had no empathy for others whatsoever.

FOUR

A couple of hours later Ben finally gave permission for the body to be moved. The undertakers had arrived thirty minutes before and were standing next to the private ambulance, bitching about how cold it was and how they were going to get her out of the car without breaking her legs.

Morgan hoped to God that they didn't break her legs, but the only other option was to get the car lifted and taken somewhere undercover; or maybe the fire service could come and cut the roof off the car, but then they might lose valuable forensic evidence. Ben had requested a full forensic lift for the car once the body was removed.

Morgan could no longer feel her toes or her fingers and thought that she might actually have lost the tips of them to frostbite. Ben was even worse; he had a pair of double latex gloves on, which she supposed were making his hands sweat even if they were being kept warm.

The dog hadn't found a trace of anything on any of the paths leading down to the lake, which she supposed was good. It narrowed the crime scene down, although this was the secondary scene. Now they needed to find the primary scene.

Ben's face was red, the tip of his nose even redder with the cold. Claire had filmed, photographed, sketched and logged everything that she could. She gave Ben the thumbs up, and he nodded at the waiting undertakers, both dressed in paper suits. They were still complaining about how they were going to get the body out of the car.

The older of the two announced in a deep voice: 'We're going to need a hand with her, boys and girls, no way we can get her out if she's in full rigor.'

'Is she in full rigor?' Ben asked.

No one could answer him. The undertaker walked to the car door and yanked it open. Claire grimaced.

'Glad he checked it was okay to open it...'

He lifted a finger and jabbed it into Jasmine's arm.

'She's bloody stiffer than Smithy here after his daily dose of Viagra.'

Morgan knew that Ben was going to explode when she saw that his fists had bunched, and his face was a mask of pure anger. He strode across to the guy who had the car door wide open.

'What's your name?'

'Mick.'

'Mick, do you see that drop down to the lake?'

He nodded. 'Yeah, what about it?'

'If you carry on being disrespectful, I will stick my boot up your arse and drop kick you over that wall and down that embankment without a moment's regret.'

Mick looked both offended and angry, and seemed to realise the predicament he'd put himself in.

'Sorry, mate, forgot myself for a moment there. Funeral humour, you know the kind. You must use it yourself. Keeps you sane, doesn't it?'

'Apology accepted, and yes, we all do but there is a time and a place and now is neither. Just do what you must, and we'll help.'

Morgan heard the guy who was still leaning against the private ambulance with blacked-out windows let out a small snigger, and she stared at him, stopping him in his tracks. He turned away and began to get the trolley and a body bag out of the back, pushing it towards Mick.

'We can't bag her in the car like that, it's impossible. We're going to have to get her out and then bag her on the trolley.'

'Fine, just do what you have to.'

Morgan stood by Ben's side, ready to help manoeuvre Jasmine's body out of the car. As it turned out they managed to manhandle her the best they could, and get her onto the trolley without their help, but her legs were set at the knees.

'Wrap her in a sheet and put a bag on top then seal it with a couple of tags, if you have to, but do not touch her legs.' Ben's voice was firm, and Mick nodded.

'Whatever you say, guv.'

They did as Ben suggested and tied the two bags together with cable ties the best they could. Ben walked with them to the back of the ambulance, where he supervised them putting Jasmine in as carefully as they could.

'Take her straight to the mortuary at the Royal Lancaster Infirmary, please.'

The two men nodded, and after securing the trolley, they slammed the doors shut and got in.

Morgan bet they had never been so scrutinised at a body removal before.

As they drove off, Claire gave Ben a round of applause. 'Well said, boss, what a pair of arseholes.'

'I'm too old, too cold and too sickened by this to put up with their crap.'

He turned to look at Amber, who was still sitting in the driver's seat of the van, looking all toasty and warm. He knocked on the window, waiting for her to roll it down.

'What time are you on till?'

'Midnight.'

'Good, then you can wait for recovery to come for the car. I want a full forensic lift.'

'I haven't had my tea yet.'

'Neither have we and we've been working since eight this morning. You're on a late shift, so if you can get someone to take over that's your shout, but if you can't you're going to have to wait for them. We need to go and defrost.'

Amber must have sensed that Ben was in no mood for arguments.

'Yes, boss.'

He nodded, beckoned Morgan and walked towards the car, where they both stripped off their protective clothing then got inside. He turned the engine on and cranked the heating on to full blast. She tugged off her gloves and pressed her frozen fingers against the heaters.

'I've never been so cold. That guy's face when you threatened to drop kick him over the wall was the funniest thing I've ever seen.'

Ben smiled at her. 'Enough was enough, I shouldn't have said that.'

'Yes, you should, he was out of order being so rude. That poor girl has only been dead a few hours, and before that she was a living, breathing soul. Maybe he'll think first in future.'

'I doubt that, men like Mick don't think before they speak. Christ I'm cold, my teeth won't stop chattering.'

The pair of them sat in the car, hugging the heaters, trying to defrost their fingers and toes, before Ben drove them back to the police station at Rydal Falls. Morgan knew that once they'd had a warm drink, they were going to have to visit Jasmine's next of kin and tell them the tragic news that their daughter was never coming home. Then ask them to come and identify her body at the hospital. She wished it didn't have to be like this.

That Jasmine hadn't run into whoever it was that did this to her, and she didn't have to go and pass on a death message that would turn the recipient's life upside down forever.

FIVE

Even after a mug of hot chocolate, Morgan's feet were still numb. She sat at her desk and unlaced her boots, then removed her socks. By the time Ben had come back from speaking to Marc she had both bare feet pressed against the radiator and her hands tucked under her armpits. The pair of them walked in and did a double take.

'Sorry, my feet don't smell but I've lost all feeling in them. I need to warm them up.'

Marc nodded. 'You'll get chilblains.'

'What, what are those, should I be worried?'

He laughed. 'They're small red bumps on your skin that itch like crazy.'

Morgan dropped her feet to the floor. 'Oh, they sound fun, just what I need.'

Ben's cheeks were still red along with his nose. 'Have you turned the heating up, Morgan?'

'As soon as we came in, and I made you a hot chocolate too. It's only that instant stuff Amy uses but it's okay.'

Marc pouted. 'Where's my hot chocolate?'

'I didn't know you were here; do you want one?'

He shook his head. 'No, I'm capable of making my own thanks, but if you're offering?'

She stood up. 'I'm offering, besides walking around might bring my circulation back to my feet.'

She left them to go and boil the kettle. When she'd arrived at the office, she had gone onto Facebook, to check if she could positively identify Jasmine Armer, and she had. She lived in Keswick. Morgan had looked through the many pictures of her with her mum and friends. Quite a lot of her dad, too, and messages saying how much she missed him, and she wished he was still here. Morgan didn't particularly like using social media, but it served a purpose in situations like these. Tomorrow Jasmine's feed would be filled with RIP messages and people saying they can't believe she's gone so soon. It was so sad, so unnecessary.

As she waited for the kettle to boil, she wondered who had killed her and left her so exposed.

Back in the office with Marc's drink, she found both men were hunched over a computer. She put the mug down next to Marc, and he thanked her, not paying the slightest bit of attention.

'What are you doing?'

'Checking Jasmine Armer's Facebook.'

'Already done it, it's her.'

They turned to her, and she smiled. 'Brains before beauty. What are we doing now?'

Ben crossed the room and leaned against the radiator. 'We're sealing off the entire lay-by and surrounding area until Al and his team can do a search, when it gets light. I know the dog didn't pick anything up, but I still want officers on foot searching the paths and area, in case there's something he didn't pick up on.'

'Amber will be pleased.'

Marc shrugged. 'Who's Amber?'

'Response officer, as angry and moody as Morgan sometimes.'

Morgan glared at Ben. 'Pardon me, I am not.'

Ben smiled. 'No, I take that back: you're not that bad, sorry.'

'Apology not accepted this time, boss, what a cheek. I made you hot chocolate and you insult me.'

She tutted and sat down at her desk, turning her chair back to the radiator and sticking her cold feet back onto the warm metal, deciding to risk the chilblains, to get some life back into them.

Marc smiled. 'We're a bit thin on the ground for staff, so I'm going to have to see if South can spare us a few bobbies. It's not too bad now: it's so late and so cold I can't see anyone being out and about, plus it's a bit out of the way. Is the area taped off?'

'It should be. I radioed Amber, who is on scene guard, and told her to tape the whole of the lay-by off. I don't want some random walkers parking there and trampling over potential evidence. I'm going to need someone to take over from her for the rest of the nightshift, then again someone on earlies, until the whole area has been searched.'

'I'll speak to Mads, see who he's got spare and get them to share it between them. It's the best we're going to do this time of night. Half of the station are on annual leave or off sick with the flu.'

Morgan didn't say anything, but if her toes didn't stop burning soon, she might be off with foot loss, not to mention how much the ankle she'd hurt a few months ago was throbbing like it had been hit with a hammer because of the cold.

Marc left them, taking his mug with him to go and speak to her old patrol sergeant, Mads, raising it in her direction, and she smiled at him, glad he was being a lot more chilled than his usual full-on self.

'Sorry, did I upset you?'

'I am not like Amber, so yes, you did.'

'I didn't mean it, of course you're not, that was a terrible bad joke.'

'Had we better go visit Jasmine's mum and see if she can come and identify her daughter? She still lives at home, so she might be waiting for her to get back, she'll be worried sick.'

Ben sighed. 'I suppose we should, this never gets easier, does it?'

Morgan shook her head. 'Absolutely not and I suppose in a way it's a good job it doesn't, because then it would mean that we didn't care about the victims we have to deal with. I know I'd rather feel sick and nervous than not give a damn about their families.'

'Ah, proof that you are nothing like Amber. Do you remember how awful she was at Emma Dixon's crime scene? You told me Emma's friend slapped her across the face for being so rude.'

Morgan did remember, she remembered the names and scenes of every single murder victim she attended. They were etched into the small box of memories she kept in the back of her mind.

'Her address on her driving licence is Riverdance House, Millfield Gardens, Keswick.'

'Riverdance? Do you think she's Irish?'

'I guess we'll never know unless we go speak to her mum.'

She plucked her socks off the radiator, where they were toasty warm, and bent down to tug them onto her feet, over the skull and rose tattoo on her right foot that trailed up the back of her calf. Then she pushed her feet back into her Docs. She made up her mind to buy herself a pair of fur-lined pull-on boots for the winter months.

Standing up, Ben was smiling at her. 'Are you ready?'

'Not really but let's do it.'

Morgan glanced at the clock on the wall: it was almost ten, they should be clocking off now and going home to maybe eat some supper, have a glass of wine. She would read for a little while, and Ben would lose himself in some TV show, something light and funny – old reruns of comedy classics were his favourite after a tough shift. Somehow, tonight she didn't think they'd be doing any of that. They'd be lucky to get home, have a hot shower and climb into bed for a couple of hours, before an early start to go back and search the scene before Jasmine's post-mortem.

They had a killer to catch.

SIX

Ben parked the car outside the garages at the back of Millfield Gardens, and they got out and walked to find the house called Riverdance. It was an end of terrace with a small, overgrown garden. It was even frostier now. Morgan glanced up at the sky and saw the stars above twinkling; the moon was almost full, and it illuminated the narrow path to the house. She loved watching the moon and stars. Some people loved the daylight but not Morgan, she had always been drawn to the darkness: it made her feel alive. Not tonight though, tonight she felt dreadful about what they were about to do.

Ben reached over to open the gate, and she grabbed his arm and whispered, 'There are no lights on, do you think we should wait until the morning?'

'What if her mum hears something about it and we didn't have the courtesy to inform her first?'

'I don't know, it just doesn't feel right.'

He shook his head. 'Tell me a time it ever felt right telling someone tragic news.'

He pushed the gate open, and she followed him, still convinced that they should wait – but he was in charge.

Ben knocked on the door, hammered really, and she glared at him.

'Morgan we can't sugar-coat this, no matter how much we try, better to get it over with.'

'You could have at least knocked a bit nicer.'

A light came on in the hallway and a shadowy figure moved towards the glass front door.

'Who is it?'

'Police, can we speak to you, Mrs Armer?'

The key turned inside the lock and the door opened a little.

'Police? What's wrong? Why are you here so late?'

Morgan stepped closer. Tugging her lanyard with her warrant card on it from out of the inside of her jacket, she passed it to the woman, who took it from her and read it out loud.

'"Detective Constable Morgan Brookes, Cumbria Constabulary".' She handed it back through the gap. 'And you are?'

Ben did the same: passing the card he kept in his wallet to her. 'Detective Sergeant Benjamin Matthews, Cumbria Constabulary.'

She passed it back and opened the door.

'What do you want, am I under arrest?' She laughed as if it was the most preposterous thing she'd ever said out loud.

'We need to talk to you about Jasmine, can we come inside?'

At the mention of her daughter's name, the woman's face paled but she took the safety chain off the door and let them into the cramped hallway. Then she led them into the lounge where the TV was paused on a rerun of *Benidorm*. She turned on the light, making both Morgan and Ben blink at the brightness.

'Sorry, I sit in the dark to try and save electric. Now, what's Jasmine done and why isn't she here to tell me herself? Has she been arrested? I told her time and time again that ex of hers was bad news. I knew he was selling coke, and she said that he wasn't, but what's a young lad like him doing driving a flashy BMW, when he only works as a farm hand? Bad news he is. I bet he's had her bloody dealing for him. Well if that's the case, she can get herself out of the shit. I'm not helping her. I can't afford that or a fancy solicitor.'

Morgan realised she was rambling, but wondered who Jasmine's boyfriend was and if he had killed her. Ben glanced at Morgan, and she knew he wanted her to be the one to break the news.

She inhaled.

'Mrs Armer.'

The woman held up her hand. 'Judith, please, or Judy but not Mrs Armer; it breaks my heart every time I hear it. I think of my poor Craig, God rest his soul.'

Morgan tried again. 'Judy, I'm afraid Jasmine isn't in the cells, she hasn't been arrested.' She passed the driving licence towards her. 'Is this your daughter?'

She stared at the piece of plastic with the small, not very clear photograph on it, and nodded.

'Yes, that's my Jasmine. Why have you got this, did she lose it?'

Looking as if he was in physical pain, Ben shook his head.

'I'm sorry, Judy, there is no easy way to say this. A patrol came across your daughter's car earlier this evening. We believe your daughter Jasmine was inside.'

He stopped, unable to carry on.

'What my colleague is trying to tell you, Judy, is we found your daughter, and I'm so very sorry to have to tell you this, but she is deceased.'

Judy stood up, then sat back down, then stood again and rushed to the window to stare outside. She turned to look at them.

'Dead, is this some kind of joke? Do you think it's funny to come here and tell me rubbish like that? Of course, she's not dead, why would she be? Where was her car?'

'Thirlmere, the lay-by that leads to the walks down to the edge of the lake and around it.'

Judy walked back to the chair in slow motion and sank down onto it.

'Did she kill herself? Please God tell me she didn't go there and kill herself, just like Craig did?'

Morgan felt fingers of icy cold run down her back. 'We don't believe that she took her own life, but we won't know what happened for definite until the post-mortem tomorrow. Judy how did Craig die?'

'He went there and took all of my sleeping tablets; God knows how long he was there, but it was long enough to fall asleep and fucking die, the selfish pig. Now you're telling me my precious baby girl has done the same?'

'When was this?' Ben asked.

'Six months ago, to the day. Please tell me that you're mistaken and that my girl isn't dead.'

Morgan could see he was struggling to speak.

'Would you be able to identify Jasmine?'

'Of course, I would, I know what my daughter looks like, I know every part of her from her hair to her toes. I spent hours staring at her when she was a baby; she was such a precious little bundle of beauty.'

'At the mortuary.'

At this, all of the fight that was inside Judith Armer seemed to deflate. She seemed to shrink in on herself in front of their eyes.

'When?'

'Tomorrow?'

She shook her head. 'Now, I need to know now if you're telling the truth, or you've made a mistake.'

She picked up her phone and dialled a number. It rang and rang.

Morgan heard a high-pitched voice say, 'Hi, if I think you're important I'll ring you back, otherwise send me a text.' She smiled to herself; Jasmine seemed like Morgan's type of girl.

Ben was flapping. 'Erm, I don't think it would be a good idea to go now, Judy.'

'Why not?'

'Because she will have not long arrived at the mortuary.'

'And, if she's dead it's not going to matter, is it? I have to see her with my own eyes, otherwise I can't believe you. I watch enough TV to know that cops get things wrong all the time. You could have the completely wrong person, and I'm not going to get too upset until I look whoever you have at the mortuary in the eyes.'

Ben stood up. 'Excuse me, I'll ring them and let them know we're on our way.' He hurried outside, leaving Morgan looking at Judy, who was wearing a red fluffy onesie with sparkling Christmas balls on the front of it.

'Do you want to get dressed? It's cold outside, so make sure you wrap up warm. Is there someone we can call to come with you?'

Judy shook her head.

'I don't want anyone. I haven't got anyone, I'm okay on my own.'

Judy left Morgan sitting on the sofa, wondering how awful this was going to be for all of them, but especially Judy who was in complete denial.

She stood up and walked to the mantel where there were framed photos of Judy, a man who must be Craig, and Jasmine. She picked one up, all three of them were smiling, and it looked as if it had been taken at Center Parcs, outside one of the lodges. There was a photo of Craig on his own, where he looked happy, with a big cheesy grin on his face and crinkly blue eyes. It just showed you never knew what was going on inside a person's mind.

'He was always so jolly, the one telling the jokes, playing stupid tricks, the guy his friends would swear never complained about anything, was always happy,' Judy said, watching Morgan at the mantel. 'That's why his death came as such a shock. Not once did he tell me he felt suicidal. He left that morning to go to work with his packed lunch and a promise he'd be home later, said we'd go out for tea if Jasmine was home on time. I sat and waited for him, and Jasmine came home from work, then went to see her friends, said to let her know when he was home, asked where we were going to eat, and she'd meet us there. He never came home. By the time he should have arrived here he'd been dead for several hours.'

Morgan felt a deep sympathy for Judy that she couldn't begin to express. 'I'm so sorry.'

Judy shrugged. 'Shit happens to the nicest people. I didn't believe it. How was I supposed to believe it when he was so happy all the time? That's why I have to see if you have the right girl, because surely this can't happen to me twice. I can't lose my husband and my child in the blink of an eye.'

Morgan wished she could say no, it couldn't be right, that it wasn't fair, and life wasn't like that, but she knew better. She had delivered a death message to a grieving parent who had died of a massive heart attack in front of her at the shock of his daughter's death. She had attended a family all slaughtered in their own home, so yes, unfortunately it did happen, and she had witnessed all kinds of horrors first hand that she would change if only she could.

Judy grabbed her coat off the hooks on the wall in the hallway and pointed to the front door. Morgan went outside and she followed her. Ben was already in the driver's seat, warming the car up, his face a mask of sadness that hers echoed entirely.

SEVEN

The drive to the hospital mortuary was excruciatingly painful. Judy stared out of the window the whole time. It wasn't until they were on their way that Morgan realised that they were going to have to drive straight past the crime scene, and she began to panic. As they got nearer, Ben looked at her, and she knew he was thinking the same thing: he should have gone the other way, past Penrith. She hoped to God that Amber had turned off her blue flashing lights; she shouldn't have them on now, as there was no need. She tried to engage Judy in conversation, but she didn't answer and kept staring out of the window. The cars headlights picked out the reflective yellow and white of the van in the lay-by, not far from Jasmine's car. Judy slammed her hand against the window.

'Stop.'

Ben carried on driving.

'Please stop, is that Jasmine's car?'

Morgan turned to her. 'Yes, it is and that's where we found her, but it's a crime scene and we can't let you in to go and take a look. You wouldn't want to comprise any evidence we may be able to collect.'

'Evidence? I thought you didn't know how she had died?'

'We don't.' Morgan could have kicked herself. 'We have to treat it as suspicious until we know for sure what happened.'

Judy sighed and leaned back against the seat, closing her eyes.

'If it is my daughter at the morgue, I want to see where she died on the way back home, crime scene or not. I won't touch anything, and you can't stop me, because if you don't, I'll just get a taxi to bring me here once you've gone.'

Morgan smiled to herself, she couldn't blame her, she would probably be the same if their roles were reversed.

'Judy when did you last see Jasmine?'

'I think it was last night before she went out to the gym.'

'Did you see her when she came home?'

She screwed up her eyes to think about it but shook her head.

'No, she wasn't home by the time I went to bed.'

'What about today, have you seen her today?'

'No, I assumed she'd gone to work before I got up.'

'Where does she work?'

'She's a dental nurse at New Smile Dental Surgery in Windermere.'

Morgan knew that was her first port of call when she was back on shift in the morning, to speak to Jasmine's colleagues, to see if she turned up for work today. It would help them narrow down the timeline leading up to her death.

The hospital car park was empty, as was the on-street parking outside of it, and Ben parked as close as he could get to the entrance of the mortuary. Susie, the mortuary technician and Declan's right-hand woman had phoned while they were on the way, to tell them she would hang on for them to arrive. Morgan loved Susie; she was a lifesaver. It meant they could go in through the mortuary entrance and not have to walk along what felt like miles of underground tunnels to get to it. Ben buzzed the doorbell, and Susie, with her lilac and turquoise hair and freshly shaved undercut, opened it.

'Hi.'

'Thanks, Susie, we really appreciate this.'

She smiled at Ben who shook his head.

'If you follow me to the viewing room, she's as ready for you to look at as she can be. I'm so sorry, but she only arrived a short time ago.'

Judy never spoke a word, she followed behind Morgan until they reached a room with a couple of bland, beige sofas inside, a coffee table with leaflets strewn all over it, and a large box of tissues.

'I won't be a moment. I'm afraid she's not in a very comfortable position, Mrs Armer, but we will make her cosy after the post-mortem and make sure she is.' Then she ducked out of the room before anyone could ask her questions.

Morgan knew that Susie wouldn't have been able to touch the body, except to remove the bag that was on top of her. The brown curtains on the other side of the viewing window were closed and, for a moment, Morgan wished that Judy would change her mind, but she didn't; she stood with her face pressed to the glass waiting to look at her daughter.

The curtains moved to one side and there was the body, her knees still bent as if she was sitting behind the wheel of the car. Susie had left the bag on and it was beneath her, but had covered Jasmine with a sheet as best as she could, so that only her face was exposed.

Judy uttered a small 'Oh.' And kept on staring, shock etched across her face.

Ben asked, 'Is that your daughter, Judy?'

She let out a long sigh as silent tears rolled down her cheeks. 'Yes, it is. Can I go and see her? I have to make sure she's not breathing in case you're wrong.'

Morgan shook her head. 'After we've examined her, then of

course you can, but right now we need to make sure we do everything we possibly can for Jasmine. I know this is difficult for you, but Jasmine isn't breathing, Judy, the paramedics and the pathologist checked her over, to make sure. We wouldn't have put her in there if she was breathing.'

Judy nodded. 'I know, I couldn't see Craig either, I just had to ask. Can you take me home now?'

'Of course.'

Morgan led her out of the room into the corridor, leaving Ben to talk to Susie.

'Would you like a drink?'

'Have you got neat vodka?'

'Unfortunately, not.'

'Then no, just get me home so I can have a drink. My whole life is over now, I have nothing left.'

She didn't make eye contact with Morgan; she was staring and in complete shock. Morgan knew that when it hit her it would hit her hard. She was obviously a tough woman who had known nothing but sadness and tragedy the last six months, and she felt helpless to know what to do or say to her as Judy's empty eyes shone with silent tears.

Ben drove home a different route so as not to drive past Jasmine's car a second time, but Judy didn't notice. She sat in the back of the car silently sobbing into her hands. Morgan turned back frequently to pat her knee, not knowing what else to do. By the time they had dropped Judy at home and Morgan had escorted her inside, it was way past midnight.

'Judy, is there anyone I can contact to come and sit with you?'

'I don't want anyone.'

'There will be a family liaison officer to assist you. Do you want me to get them to come here now or in the morning?'

'I want to be alone; I don't want a stranger in my house tonight. I'm not in the mood for conversation.'

'I understand. Please call me if you need anything.' She passed her a card with her details on. 'My mobile is on the back; I'll leave my phone on, okay.'

Judy nodded, and Morgan left her alone.

As she got back into the car Ben shook his head.

'We need to go home, now, the scene is covered, the body has been identified, so there isn't very much else we can do. There are no urgent CCTV enquiries to carry out because nowhere is open to ask. First light we'll hit it with everything we have and round up some troops to help.'

'I'm not arguing with you. I'm tired and cold. I just want a hot shower and my bed. There's always some awful tragedy for some poor family.'

He didn't answer her, there were no answers to give that would make a difference.

EIGHT

Morgan drove to work on her own. She normally car shared with Ben, but they both knew it was anyone's guess what today would bring – they'd need separate transportation. She wanted to go to Jasmine's workplace as soon as it opened. Ben knew this, as she'd told him before she'd fallen asleep and he'd murmured *whatever* on the verge of sleep himself.

She had no idea why she felt so compelled to be the one to visit the dental surgery, when she hated going to the dentist herself. The smell alone was enough to make her palms sweat and her stomach churn. Give her a doctor's any day over the dentist.

There was a briefing planned for nine, and Morgan could see that the station was far busier than usual as she walked in. Task force officers had been called in from Barrow, and Morgan had walked through a sea of men in black to reach the stairs up to the CID office. Marc, Amy, Cain and Ben were already gathered in the blue room, the station meeting room. It hadn't been blue for at least ten years – it was a tepid pink colour – but like certain things the name had stuck. Just like Mads was actually called Paul, but Morgan didn't think she'd heard one person call him by his real name. Then there was Ben, who older in service colleagues referred to as Benno. He called her Brookes, and occasionally Cain did too, which she didn't mind. It was better than the grim reaper, she supposed, which was how she felt sometimes, always on hand to deliver death messages. It should be section staff that delivered them. She had done her fair share when she'd been a Response officer, but the terrible ones, the murders and sudden deaths that were questionable always seemed to fall to her and Ben these days.

As she made herself a coffee, she wondered how Judy was this morning. She had a bad feeling about the woman, and she knew what that meant. After she'd been to Jasmine's place of work, she was going straight there to visit her. A search team would be going to the house to go through Jasmine's bedroom, to look for anything that might be relevant, and Morgan wanted to make sure Judy had someone to be with her. She had refused last night but she didn't want her to be alone. Ben would organise a family liaison officer to be on hand, but she still needed a friend.

Morgan took her seat around the long, oval table and sipped her drink while everyone else filed inside. When the room was full, and everyone was there, Ben stood up.

'Morning, thanks for coming. This is on first appearances: it looked like a tragic, sudden death. The victim, Jasmine Armer, was found deceased and had been for some time in her car at the lay-by looking down onto Thirlmere on the A591. The Home Office pathologist, Dr Donnelly, attended and on his initial inspection he found what he is certain are rope marks around her wrists, taking us from sudden death to homicide. The post-mortem is scheduled for eleven. I'll attend that with Morgan, if she's free; if not either Amy or Cain can come along.'

Amy pointed her finger at Cain. 'He's lacking experience in that department; you'd be better taking him.'

Cain muttered 'Arsehole' under his breath and both Morgan and Amy smirked at him. Ben ignored them.

'Morgan is going to visit Jasmine's place of work and speak to staff there; we don't actually know if she arrived at work yesterday. Her mum said she left to go to work yesterday... no' – he checked his notes – 'the day before but has no idea if she made it. At the present time we don't know how Jasmine spent her last hours or what she was doing, who she was with, and we need to narrow that down. I want an hour-by-hour timescale, if possible, so we can pinpoint when she went missing, and speak to the last people who saw her alive.

'I need a couple of officers to search her room in her home, so for now, Cain and Amy, I want you to attend the home address and conduct a full search.

'My favourite task force officers, I would like you to do fingertip search of the lay-by where the car was located by Amber yesterday afternoon. The dog did a search and didn't pick anything up, but I still want the paths and surrounding area checked. I don't think the lay-by is the primary crime scene, I think that is a dumping spot, but we can't rule it out.

'It's worth bearing in mind that the lay-by was the same place her dad, Craig Armer, took his own life, six months past to the day. Which I think points to the killer knowing Jasmine, or someone who knows an awful lot about her.'

Marc was nodding his head at everything Ben said.

'Is there anything you want to add boss?'

'Yes, the place where the body was found: I think this is further proof that whoever did this wanted her to be found relatively quickly. It's a well-used parking place that leads down to the water. He left her there on display. It was only a matter of time before a member of the public found her. What kind of individual would do that?'

Ben looked up from his notes. 'A serious, dangerous killer who had a lot of nerve if you ask me, someone who might go on to kill again, if we don't apprehend them soon. This might well be the start of a series, although I'm praying that it's not.'

'I agree with you. I think we have to work on the probability that he might kill again. The quicker we catch them, the safer the streets will be. Apart from that I think you have it covered, Ben.

'Al, while Ben is unavailable at the PM do you want to run any findings by me until Ben gets back?'

Al nodded. 'Yes, boss.'

Ben smiled. 'Thanks, I'll get the PCSOs to canvass the shops and businesses surrounding Jasmine's place of work, see if there is any CCTV footage of her leaving. Amy, can you get some photos of Jasmine off her mum?'

'Would it not be better to get some off her social media? Her mum probably only has school photos. If I go missing and you asked my mum, she'd give you one where I'm missing my front teeth and have a bowl cut.'

Cain sniggered, and Morgan smiled. 'Amy has a point; how many times have we asked for photos that mislead everyone because it's not what they look like at the time they went missing?'

'Fine, you can print screen a couple of her latest ones, Amy, before you go to her house. I think that's it for now, keep me updated, or Marc if I'm unavailable, and stay safe out there. The roads are a bit icy and it's still bloody freezing, so make sure you wrap up.'

Everyone nodded. Morgan stood up and squeezed past everyone because she didn't want to get caught up in polite conversations. She needed to get out of here.

Rushing into the office the first thing she saw was that bloody mask staring at her... or was it? There was something so creepy about it. She walked closer to it and realised it was the eyes. They were closed. The mask had eyelids; most masks had openings so you could see through them when you wore it. She stepped closer. It looked like one of those death masks they used to make hundreds of years ago; but why the hell would someone send her something like that? It had to be some sick joke; someone was being a smart arse.

The door was thrown open and it slammed into the wall, making her jump back.

'Oops, I got to calm down with the door pushing. I forget that this one flies open, there's hardly any wall left behind it. What's up with you, are you feeling a bit more love towards Barb?'

'No, it's creeping me out. It looks as if whoever this is, well, you're right, it looks like they're dead.'

Cain walked to where she was standing and studied the mask. It had been painted white or the material was white, there was no colour to it.

'Nah, it's just weird. Probably off that place where they sell all sorts of strange stuff online. My mate's wife got a dead bird off it, came in a big box, stuffed and glued to a piece of wood with two bags of mini Haribo next to it. I mean, come on, who's going to eat those sweets after that? What a waste of good gummy bears.'

'Etsy.'

'No, she's called Heather.'

'I mean the website, Cain, it's called Etsy. It's a marketplace where you can pretty much buy everything.'

He started laughing. 'Yeah, well weird masks and dead birds, what else can you get off it? Are you sure there was no gift note in the box? Sometimes they get hidden in the packaging?'

'You really didn't send it to me?'

He looked shocked. 'No, why would I? It's weird and funny but I'm not going to waste my money on crap like that. If I was going to buy you something it would be a signed Ted Bundy book, or one of John Wayne Gacy's paintings.'

Morgan was mortified. She didn't know if that was

supposed to be a compliment or that it just proved how odd Cain thought she was.

'Wow, thanks, Cain. That's very kind of you. I'd like that, you know, to add to my collection of other signed books by the most depraved men in the world, or to hang on my bedroom wall to give me night terrors.'

'See, people know you're a bit out there, Brookes. That's why someone sent you a creepy mask. It's probably worth a bit of money. Nobody makes them any more; at least I wouldn't think there is any call for them, when you can just visit your dead gran in the Co-op funeral home and take a quick Snapchat with her.'

He walked out, leaving Morgan staring after him. She grabbed her coat, took a quick photo of the mask and followed him out. She had to get out of here. The words 'death mask' were now embedded in her brain, and she knew she was going to have to do some research after she'd visited New Smile. The only time she'd ever seen something that resembled one was when she did her yearly first aid course at headquarters. There the instructors would drag out the Resusci-Anne doll for them to practice CPR on. The guy told them the same story each year: the doll's face was that of a real sixteen-year-old girl who'd thrown herself into the Seine, and drowned. She had been pulled from the river, in Paris, with that sad smile on her face. The mortuary technician had decided she was so serene that he took a cast of her face and made a mask of it. Morgan knew that death masks had been around since the Egyptian times, but she hadn't realised they were still a thing.

NINE

New Smile had a full waiting room. As Morgan walked in the smell of whatever it is that dentists use to make the scent cling to your clothes filled the entrance like some awful plug-in air freshener. The reception desk was at the back of the room, behind the plastic screens that had been erected across it to stop the spread of Coronavirus. A woman sat there in cropped white hair and a smart black suit. She looked up from the computer and smiled at Morgan.

'Can I help you?'

Morgan pulled her lanyard out and flashed her warrant card at her.

'Is it possible to speak to you and the rest of the staff about Jasmine Armer?'

The woman's lips parted, forming a perfect O. 'Is she in trouble? I just assumed she was sick; in fact I rang her yesterday and it went straight to voicemail. I was about to phone again.'

A tight knot clenched inside Morgan's stomach at the realisation she was going to have to do this all again. She had just assumed they would know. How, she had no idea.

'It's a little more serious than that. Please, do you have somewhere a bit more private where I can speak to you?'

Every person in the waiting room had stopped reading their phones or flicking through the magazine they were holding, and she knew they were all waiting for her to continue. Who didn't like a bit of drama?

The woman nodded. 'Of course, sorry. Please come through to the staff room, it's the second door out in the corridor.'

Morgan turned around and all the eyes that had been boring into the back of her head dropped instantly back to what they were doing moments before she'd walked in. The woman, who introduced herself as Nancy, was standing at the door holding it open for her. Inside the room was a small kitchenette. A coffee machine with an almost full filter coffee pot warming on the plate made it smell a whole lot better than the waiting room.

'Can I get you a coffee?'

Morgan realised she must have stared a little too long at the coffee and smiled.

'That would be wonderful, milk no sugar, thank you.'

Nancy poured her coffee and handed her the mug.

'Please sit wherever you want.'

Morgan chose a chair at the table, thinking it was more formal and suited what she was about to do.

'Nancy, who is in charge of the surgery?'

'Me, well, I'm the manager. I take care of the day-to-day running of things.'

'Do you want to take a seat?'

Nancy shook her head. 'I have to watch the desk. I'm a girl down today because of Jasmine not turning up. I had to ask my apprentice to go up and help Mr Barnard. What's happened to Jasmine? I can tell it's serious.'

'An officer out on patrol yesterday found Jasmine's car near

Thirlmere. There is no easy way to say this, she found Jasmine dead inside.'

Nancy let out a shriek and clamped her hand across her mouth. Tears filled her eyes, and she began to cry; the tears rolled down her cheeks in floods, completely taking Morgan off guard. She had thought Nancy wasn't the sort of person to show her feelings, turns out she was wrong.

'I'm sorry for your loss.'

Nancy kept shaking her head. 'How, I mean just how and why? Oh no, did she do it on purpose? Her dad did the same thing about six months ago.'

'We don't believe she did, but until the post-mortem later this morning, we can't say. I'm terribly sorry but I have no further information that I can give to you just now. I really need to ask you some questions about Jasmine, and when you saw her last. Do you think you can help me?'

Nancy nodded. Reaching out for a roll of kitchen paper on the table, she tore off a piece using it to dab at her eyes and then blow her nose.

'I'm sorry, it's the shock. I can't believe it, does poor Judy know?'

'Yes.'

'That poor woman, first her husband and now her only child. I can't imagine how she'll get over this. How do you, you just wouldn't, would you?'

Morgan had lost her mum to suicide; her dad, Stan, had been murdered, and then she'd found out that both her brother and biological father were serial killers. This was where her empathy came from; she knew the full range of emotions that different deaths brought, the guilt, the shock, the sadness, the grief, the anger, the loss and the realisation that the one person you always took for granted would be there for you was no longer alive.

'It's going to be devastating for her. Nancy, can you tell me when you last saw Jasmine?'

'Not yesterday. She didn't turn up for work, but teatime the day before. She was still here when I left for the day, she was cleaning up the surgery and waiting for a delivery from the denture clinic that was important for Mr Butler.'

'Was it like Jasmine to not turn up?'

Nancy shook her head. 'First time since she started working here three years ago. She's such a dedicated, loyal, hardworking girl.'

'Who else was here when you left?'

'Jasmine, and Mr Barnard, who was finishing up for the day.'

'I'll need to speak to him. Is he available?'

'I'll grab him when his client leaves. He has a break for fifteen minutes.'

'Thank you, how many other staff work here?'

'Three nurses and three dentists. Mrs Porter is fully booked today – this is her first day back since having Covid; and Mr Butler, he'd already left the day before yesterday. Lisa and Sarah were working but they'd also finished. We don't really work late on a Wednesday, everyone is usually out of here by four thirty, late nights are Friday.'

Morgan had taken out her notepad and was scribbling it all down.

'So, I need to speak to Mr Barnard first. Everyone else had already left or weren't here, is that correct?'

'Yes.'

'I will still need to speak to the other staff, Nancy. Did Jasmine have any bother with patients, friends? Anyone upset her or did she tell you she was worried about anyone's behaviour towards her?'

Nancy shook her head, but her eyes glanced towards the door as if to make sure no one else had walked in to hear their conversation. Morgan knew there was something she wasn't telling her.

'Did she get on with all of the staff, ever mention any problems?'

Nancy bit her bottom lip. 'Not a problem as such.'

'But?'

'She had a bit of a crush on Mr Barnard. Most of us do but we've had to get over it.'

'Why is that?'

'He's one of those drop-dead gorgeous guys and charming too, but he's happily married, has two teenage boys who are the apple of his eye, and he idolises his wife.'

'How do you know Jasmine had a crush on him?'

'She couldn't work with him; she would get too flustered around him. It was painful to watch. I had to put her with Mr Butler so she could concentrate on her work and not her feelings.'

'Did she not have any feelings towards Mr Butler? You know what us young women are like, we can get a bit carried away.'

Nancy laughed. 'Wait until you meet Mr Butler, even his wife doesn't have a crush on him.'

Morgan smiled. 'Okay so it was just Jasmine and Mr Barnard here on Wednesday. Do you have CCTV?'

She nodded. 'We do, internal and external; even though we are situated in a beautiful part of the world we still get our fair share of angry customers, you can't be too safe.'

At this Morgan felt a rush of hope that maybe she would see Jasmine leave with someone. Or perhaps even Mr Barnard hitting Jasmine over the head with something and carrying her out to the car, case solved.

Nancy stood up.

'I'll send a message to Mr Barnard to come and speak to you when he can, and I'll show you the footage.'

'Thank you so much, Nancy, I appreciate your help.'

Nancy stared at her, and her bottom lip began to tremble. 'I almost forgot why you are here. Poor Jasmine will never walk through the door again.'

Morgan nodded. She followed Nancy back to the rear of the reception area that wasn't as busy now that the woman with her three kids, and the elderly couple sitting by the window had been called in.

There was a large monitor on a shelf on top of a CCTV unit, and she watched with bated breath as Nancy expertly brought up the day and time of everyone leaving on Wednesday.

They watched as first one, then another nurse waved goodbye and walked out of the front door on the last day Jasmine worked. A portly man with a briefcase, and a coat that was too small – he jammed the zipper hallway up and couldn't get it any further – was next out of the door, and Nancy whispered, 'Mr Butler.' Nancy could be clearly seen on the different monitors as she moved around the building, tidying the waiting room, locking the front door, washing cups in the staff room; then a young woman came running down the stairs, and Nancy whispered, 'Oh Jasmine.'

Morgan felt her heart begin to pound in her chest, a part of her wanting to see Nancy leave and Mr Barnard attack the pretty girl who was chattering away to Nancy in the top left-hand corner of the screen. Another part of her wanting Jasmine to leave without a hair on her head being harmed, and Mr Barnard doing the same.

Nancy was putting on her coat and laughing at something Jasmine had told her.

'She wasn't unhappy, she never mentioned problems with anyone,' Nancy muttered.

'Did she have a boyfriend?' Morgan asked.

'Not that I know about. She said she was too busy for immature boys and wanted a man. Her last boyfriend was a bit of a card. He got sent to prison for drug dealing.'

Morgan thought about what Judy had said. 'How long ago was that? Judy thought that she was still seeing him.'

'I think poor Judy sometimes gets a little muddled. It's been getting worse since Craig died. Jasmine said she was worried about her mum and didn't know what to do. I think it's the grief myself, it affects us all in a different way.'

'What was his name?'

'Dan Bailey.'

Morgan wrote it down so she could check him out back at the station.

On the screen, Nancy waved and Jasmine let her out of the door, locking it behind her and leaving her and Mr Barnard alone. Jasmine had taken a seat behind the reception desk and was scrolling through her phone. They watched as an exceptionally good-looking man come down the stairs, his phone clamped to his ear. He stuck his head in the waiting room and waved at Jasmine. Covering his phone, he said something to her, and she nodded, the smile on her face almost spread from ear to ear, then he was gone, too, and Jasmine was on her own.

'Who was she waiting for?'

'A package from the denture clinic in Kendal. The guy said he was running late and would be there as soon as he could. It was for one of our very important clients who had an early appointment on Thursday morning.'

'What's the name of the clinic? That guy may have been the last person to speak to her.'

'Fix It Denture Repairs. I think the guy delivering them is called Joe. He's a nice guy, always friendly and helpful. He would only have been here seconds.'

Morgan didn't say anything, but seconds was all it took to make a decision that would alter the course of a whole lifetime.

The pair of them waited and watched until finally there

was a knock at the door and Jasmine stood up, and tucking her phone in her pocket, she rushed to open it. Smiled at the guy delivering the package, took it from him and then shut the door as he exited. She took the package to the reception desk and left it on there. Tugged on her own coat and turned all the lights off, letting herself out of the surgery, setting the alarms on her way and locking the door behind her.

Morgan felt deflated. She had been sure that either the denture guy or Mr Barnard were going to be on camera doing at least something suspicious.

Nancy glanced at her. 'I'm sorry, that's all there is.'

'What about the outside cameras? Did they pick up Jasmine leaving?' Someone could have been waiting for her outside, if they knew the cameras were on inside, Morgan thought.

Nancy switched view to the outside camera, which showed a screen so blurry they couldn't make out anything. She tapped the keyboard and switched it off then back on again.

'The outside camera was like this on Wednesday teatime, that's strange.'

'Is it working now?'

Nancy switched to live view and they could see the entrance to the surgery and the front of the street outside.

Morgan felt a spark of hope reignite again inside of her chest.

'Who has access to the cameras?'

'Me, and that's it. The doctors here may be great at fixing your crooked teeth, but they don't know shit about technology. They drive me insane at times.'

'So, no one here has access to the cameras from home or anything?'

'Absolutely not, except for me, and I had no reason to hurt Jasmine. I just wouldn't and couldn't do anything so terrible.'

Morgan believed her.

'Can you rewind it to the point where it is working?'

Nancy did, and it was around 12.30 when the camera went blurry.

Morgan watched as the camera went from clear to blurry in less than a minute. There was what looked like a pink splodge on the screen and then it was gone. She knew someone had messed with it, that same someone had also put it back online, so Nancy hadn't realised there had been a problem. They were clever, whoever they were: they knew the blind spots and had approached at an angle they wouldn't be captured on. They also needed a ladder to reach it.

'Do you have a window cleaner? Was there one here on Wednesday?'

'We do, but no, they come once a month, on the first Monday of the month.'

'Where was everyone at 12.30?'

'Lunch, we close the surgery at 12 p.m. until 1 p.m. every day. Most of us go out for lunch, and the ones who don't go out would have been in the staff room, so they wouldn't have seen anyone outside on a ladder.'

Morgan took out her phone.

'That's really helpful, thank you, Nancy, please excuse me whilst I make a call.'

She rang Claire, who answered immediately.

'Hey, how much do you know about CCTV cameras? Is it possible to get prints off one?'

'It depends on the surface, but I don't see why not.'

'Can you come to New Smile, in Windermere? I think our guy may have messed with the camera outside.'

'For you, Morgan, yes, give me ten minutes. I'm on my way to the station anyway, I've just left the lay-by.'

'Thank you, Claire.'

TEN

Morgan smelled Mr Barnard before she saw him, his aftershave subtle but expensive. He was one of those rare men who thought he could captivate women just by being in his presence. She turned around and smiled at him.

'Detective Constable Morgan Brookes,' she introduced herself.

He nodded. 'Neil Barnard. What's this about?'

Morgan stood up. 'I think it's best we go to the staff room and talk.'

He gave Nancy a strange look, and she swiped the paper towel she was still clutching across her eyelids again. She stayed behind the desk, leaving them to it, and Morgan wondered how many times she was going to have to do this again today.

'I'm afraid I have some terrible news.'

'About Jasmine?'

Morgan, who had taken a seat, felt her back stiffen. 'Yes, how do you know?'

'News travels fast in this place. My patient told me the police were here asking questions about that pretty nurse, Jasmine, and it seems to be bad news.'

Morgan studied him. 'It's the worst news there could possibly be. I'm sorry to have to tell you this, but she was found dead in her car yesterday afternoon.'

Mr Barnard sat down and stared at Morgan for a few moments, as if trying to decide if she knew what she was talking about.

'Dead?'

She nodded.

'How?'

'We don't know for sure yet, but it looks as if it is suspicious.'

She scrutinised his face for any signs of emotion. His eyes looked down towards the table.

'You were the last person to see her before she left work. How did she seem to you? Was she worried about anything, happy, sad, scared?'

'Why would she be scared? I saw that you were watching the cameras. You saw that I left before her. Did she look scared to you, Detective?' He was leaning on the table, his hands palm side down, pressing against it.

Morgan shook her head. He was getting a little agitated with her questions, and she wondered why, if he was as innocent as he was making out. 'No, but looks can be deceiving. I'm just trying to get a handle on what sort of mood she was in when you left her.'

'Happy, I would say. Just her usual chatty self. She's always so friendly and a pleasure to be around. She didn't seem down or depressed, and she wasn't scared. She was quite literally the most perfect specimen of a human I've ever met.'

Alarm bells began to ring inside Morgan's head, huge clanging bells that echoed around inside her mind. She looked up from her notebook, narrowing her eyes, and stared at him.

'What did you talk about?'

'I asked her if she had any plans for the evening, and she told me she was going home for a long soak in the bath, a

Chinese takeaway and a glass of wine with her mum, if she was home.'

'What did you say to her?'

'I told her to have a lovely evening. Nothing more, nothing less, and then I went home to my wife and sons, to have dinner together. We had pizza from Gino's and shared a bottle of wine.'

Morgan nodded. It could have been her and Ben minus the kids, their lives sounded so similar.

'You can clearly see that I leave the building first, and if you speak to my wife, she'll confirm what time I got home, if you feel the need to.'

Morgan smiled at him, but there was something about the man sitting opposite her that prickled at her senses. The way he'd described Jasmine as *the most perfect specimen of a human* was not something she'd ever heard anyone ever say before.

'I don't think I need to do that just yet, but thank you. I'm just talking to everyone who saw Jasmine, to narrow down the timeline of what happened to her.'

'Of course, you are, sorry, I understand that. It's just such a shock. I really liked her, you know, she was one of the most efficient nurses and all round good girl.'

'Good girl?'

His cheeks began to blush. 'As in wholesome, kind, sweet, she never gossiped or talked bad about anyone here, not even Dave who is an arse most of the time.'

'Dave?'

'Dave Butler.'

'You can't think of anyone who would want to hurt her? She never discussed boyfriend/girlfriend troubles with you or any of the staff?'

He shook his head. 'Definitely not with me. I don't know about Lisa or Sarah. She was closer to them than she was to me. Is there anything else, Detective?'

Morgan shook her head. 'No, thank you for your time and I'm sorry for your loss.'

He stood up, gave her a half smile then left her sitting there, alone, with her cold mug of coffee and an urge to find out as much about Neil Barnard as she possibly could.

Next in were the two dental nurses, Lisa and Sarah. Morgan asked them about Jasmine, and neither could tell her anything. She'd had no boyfriend since Dan, no problems with anyone, was always happy, and they absolutely didn't know of anyone who would want to hurt her. The pair of them could hardly talk for sobbing, and Morgan felt terrible. She wished she'd come here with Ben or maybe Amy, to ease the burden of having to talk to everyone, but she'd offered so here she was.

Next in was Dave Butler, who was very quietly spoken, and she had to keep asking him to speak up. He said he didn't really know her as well as the others, but she was a nice girl and who the hell would want to do something like this? Then he began to cry, not just a few tears, he completely broke down and couldn't speak for sobbing. He had to excuse himself and leave the room. It surprised Morgan because Neil had said Dave was an arse. He didn't come across that way to her. He seemed like he really cared about what had happened, and looked so visibly shocked she'd wondered if he was about to have a heart attack. The last person to speak to her was Mrs Porter, whose ashen face told her that she already knew what this was about.

'I can't believe it, Neil told me about Jasmine, the poor, poor girl. Who would do such a terrible thing?'

Another alarm bell rang for Morgan. Neil Barnard was a gossip, and she hadn't told him Jasmine had been murdered. She told him she'd been found dead under suspicious circumstances, although she supposed he could have assumed because of the nature of her questions.

'I'm so sorry, we don't know what's happened yet, we're trying to piece together her last movements.'

'How was she murdered?'

Morgan studied the woman in front of her. She didn't seem overly upset or on the verge of tears, she was holding up much better than the others had.

'Like I said, we don't know until the post-mortem later today.'

'Oh, I'm sorry, it's just I watch a lot of true crime documentaries, you know; I find it fascinating that such monsters can walk amongst us, and we wouldn't even realise. You don't expect it to happen to anyone you know.'

Morgan nodded, she also had a thing for true crime not to mention her career choice, although in her defence she had begun her time in the police as a Response officer, and had got thrown in at the deep end and dragged into a murder investigation on her first day out on independent patrol.

'Did Jasmine ever mention if she was having problems with anyone, anything?'

She shrugged. 'Not to me, I know she is a—' She stopped herself and tried again. 'She was a sweet girl, but we didn't really click, you know. I think she found me a bit intimidating. I get a little overenthusiastic at times, and I don't have time for anyone making mistakes when I'm working.'

This was interesting, everyone else had gushed about how wonderful Jasmine was, yet this woman was telling her she doesn't suffer fools.

'Did you and Jasmine not get along?'

'I liked her, she liked me, but I think she felt a little intimidated by me, maybe even a little nervous around me. She could be a little spacey at times. I'd be elbow deep inside a patient's mouth and she'd be staring out of the window at the birds, you know, that kind of thing. I didn't dislike her, and I wouldn't wish any harm on the girl, I'm just saying we weren't best buddies or anything like that.'

Morgan found the woman's honesty refreshing. Most

people instinctively gushed about how wonderful the dead person was, choosing to ignore their imperfections. They didn't want to be suspected. 'Mrs Porter—'

'Alesha, please. My wife calls me Mrs Porter when she's in a bad mood with me.'

Morgan smiled at her. 'Alesha, do you know if any of the others had any problems with Jasmine?'

'Not that I'm aware of. I saw Dave before. He was crying his eyes out. I guess he liked her but as a daughter kind of thing. He's a big softie. He's going through a bad patch with his wife, and they never did have kids.'

'Neil said Dave was an arse.'

'Neil is an arse; God that man is so full of himself it makes me want to puke on his shoes. He thinks he's better than Dave, than all of us, but he's not. He's arrogant and I'd rather work with Dave any day.'

'Is there anything you can tell me that might help me piece together Jasmine's last hours?'

'I'm afraid not. I've been ill, today is my first day back and holy shit what a day it's turned out to be. I kind of wish I'd pulled one last sickie and not bothered coming in. Look I don't know what crap Neil has told you, but everyone here is okay, on the level. We work hard and as far as I know none of us would want to hurt Jasmine.'

'Thank you.'

Alesha stood up. 'I hope you find out what happened and very soon, her poor mum must be absolutely devastated.'

Morgan nodded. 'I will, it's kind of what I do.'

The two women smiled at each other and then it was Morgan on her own once more.

A familiar face walked through the staff room door, and Morgan felt a sigh of relief cross her lips.

'Claire, you are a lifesaver,' she said, watching her colleague come over. Claire was looking serious, she was such a professional at all times when at a crime scene. Morgan knew however that she was completely different back at the station: she was the one person who could always make you laugh and crack jokes with her wacky sense of humour.

'I am, coffee is on you.'

'Always.'

'Show me what you have.'

Morgan took her outside and pointed to the camera above the door.

'I want you to dust it for prints, work your magic just in case someone messed with it the day Jasmine Armer died.'

'Are you giving me a bunk up?'

'If you want, or I can get you the stepladders I saw leaning against the wall in the staff room.'

'I'll take the stepladders, thanks.'

Morgan came back carrying them, with Nancy behind her.

'Please be careful, I don't want you to hurt yourself.'

Claire smiled at her. 'This is a breeze; you should see some of the places I have to squeeze in to.'

Nancy was standing on the front step of the practice, supervising them both, and her head kept looking left and right. Morgan got the feeling she was a little anxious about having a CSI van parked on the double yellows outside. Morgan passed Claire her camera, so she could photograph the dome camera, and then the dusting powder and brush. Claire deftly covered what plastic she could then lifted the prints that appeared.

'Not much, there's a couple of partials. I don't know if this is going to work or not. The glass cover is clean though, it looks much cleaner than the rest of the casing.'

'But worth a shot?'

'Always, Morgan, it's a bit strange how clean the lens bit is, and yet there are a couple of prints on the casing.'

Then she passed everything back to Morgan, climbed down and secured the samples in evidence bags, ready to be analysed back at the station, and put into the IDENT1 National Fingerprint database.

'Thanks, Claire, for getting here so fast.'

'No problem, I'll let you know if we get a match but don't hold your breath. It's probably prints off someone from the security firm who installed them.'

'Don't burst my bubble too soon, leave me with a glimmer of hope.'

'Sorry.'

Claire got into her van and waved as she drove away, leaving Morgan staring up at the camera.

'Is that it for now?' Nancy said from behind her. 'I really need to get back to work. I'm sorry I can't do anything else. Once these patients have been seen to, I'll go and visit Judy to see if she needs anything.'

'I'm finished for the time being. Thanks, Nancy, for being so helpful. It'll be nice of you to visit Judy, because I'm not sure if Judy has anyone. They have assigned her a family liaison officer to help her through the next few days, but a familiar face will be nice for her. I'm going to try and visit her when I'm through with my enquiries.'

Nancy's eyes began to water again, and she turned to go back inside, while Morgan stood on the step wondering how the camera had got so blurry on Wednesday, yet was working again now. Someone had caused it to go like that. She looked around for other cameras that may have caught whoever had been there, but she couldn't see a single one. Morgan needed to find someone who had seen Jasmine once she'd left the surgery, and she also needed to go to Kendal.

She saw a flash of yellow coming out of a shop and waved at Sam, walking towards her. Sam was one of the PCSOs on the team conducting the house-to-house enquiries in the area around the surgery. The only problem was it was mainly shops and flats. Opposite was a small park, so there weren't very many properties with a good view of the surgery.

'Hey, how are you?'

'Cold, you?'

Morgan smiled. 'Same, has anyone seen anything? Jasmine left the surgery at 17.25 on Wednesday, so can you tell the others we are specifically trying to find anyone else who may have been locking up their businesses and in the area around that time. Can you also ask if they saw anyone with a ladder around 12.30 on Wednesday outside the dentist?'

Sam was writing it all down on the blank questionnaire attached to her clipboard and nodding. 'Will do. This is terrible,' Sam said sadly. 'You know my daughter went to college with Jasmine. It's so hard to get your head around.'

'Oh no, I didn't realise you knew her,' Morgan replied. 'Do you want to go home, Sam, and have a bit of breathing space?'

She shook her head. 'Not really, I'd rather be here helping the only way I can to find out what the hell happened to her.'

Morgan got that, she felt like that most days, wanting to do everything possible to catch the bad guys and girls.

'I'll let the others know we have a definite time; it will make it a bit easier.'

She smiled at Morgan and began to type numbers into her radio set so she could call her colleagues and pass on the information. Morgan looked at her watch, she needed to get back to the station to go to the post-mortem with Ben, and tell him everything she'd discovered: that Jasmine was well-liked and had a crush on Neil Barnard; that Neil Barnard came across as suspicious to her in the way he talked about Jasmine. She couldn't rule out if the two of them were having an affair. She wondered if maybe she should speak to Mrs Barnard, to find out a little more about their relationship.

ELEVEN

Ben and Marc were watching the officers who were part of the task force team begin their painstaking search of the area surrounding where Jasmine's car had been parked. Her car had been moved to a secure garage the night before, ready to be forensically examined. Now, Ben was walking up and down the lay-by outside of the crime-scene tape.

'How did he get the car here and then leave? It's quite a hike from here to anywhere; the way we came was just a road with no pedestrian walkway. How far is it to the nearest village or town?'

Marc shrugged. 'I'm not from around here, I don't have a clue.'

'There's a hotel, Dale Head Hall, and a pub, The Kings Head, not too far away, as well as a camp site. They could have walked to any one of those. Maybe they left a vehicle there to get home with? We can check CCTV and interview the occupants who would have been here last night.'

Marc was pacing, and he turned to Ben. 'It was a lot of effort to leave her here, don't you think? I mean she clearly wasn't killed here, so he had to drive her car with her body inside it all this way from Windermere, if he took her from her place of work. Is that what we're thinking?'

Ben nodded. 'It was a lot of work and what would be the point? There were plenty of lay-bys nearer to Windermere that would have been just as suitable. Which makes me certain there is a significance to choosing this one. He had to have known about her dad's suicide.'

'It's a thirty-minute drive depending on traffic from Windermere to here. If Jasmine was taken from near her home address in Keswick, then that's around an eleven-minute drive. I think there are buses along this road. We need to check with Stagecoach and see if anyone was picked up from this area on Wednesday evening. And have someone follow the hiking trails to look for any debris, any recent boot prints.'

'Good shout, I like that. I still don't get it, though. Is the killer making a statement by leaving her here? Does he have an affinity with this particular area?'

Ben didn't know. His instinct told him that this killer was a sick bastard with an ego, thinking he was clever, leading them on this cat-and-mouse trail.

What Ben did know was that he doubted Jasmine would be his only victim. The location, the bondage, the positioning of the body... There were bound to be more. They needed to get his motivations figured out and put a stop to this in the next few hours. Ben was optimistic, or as much as he could be, but they didn't even have a concrete cause of death yet, so it was all still a bit up in the air.

'Boss, I think if we let the search teams do their job and concentrate on finding the cause of death it might be a good start.'

Marc stared at him. 'Are you saying you don't think it's suspicious now?'

'No, what I'm saying is let's find out for definite and then figure it out.'

Ben felt a wave of exhaustion wash over him, so bad that he felt like sitting down on the dry-stone wall in front of him and not moving. Each new case seemed to take its toll on him, as if it was sucking the life out of him. Maybe he could do with some of Morgan's Aunt Ettie's special tea to give him a bit of a pick-me-up; in fact he really might go and visit her. He hadn't really smoothed things over with her since he'd had her arrested last year. He'd meant to but something else always took precedent.

'So, what are you thinking?'

He jumped, startled, he'd drifted off. 'That we still need the area searching and that we need those post-mortem results ASAP.'

'Should we head back to the station so you can get a move on to the mortuary, then we will know for definite if we're wasting our time and resources when it was a sudden death.'

Ben knew he meant well, that he was doing much better at trying to fit in and not be too bossy or take over too much, but it was still there, that edge to him that couldn't help.

'Yes, boss. I think that's exactly what we should be doing.'

'Come on then, we'll leave the searching to these guys, besides it's too bloody cold out here.' His breath was all cloudy whenever he opened his mouth, which seemed to be quite often.

Ben's phone vibrated in his pocket, and he turned away to answer it.

'Anything?'

'A couple of interesting leads: one of the dental surgeons, Neil Barnard, was a bit odd the way he spoke about Jasmine. She was the last to leave the surgery and lock up. She waited for a delivery from a denture clinic in Kendal. There's nothing untoward on the internal CCTV, but someone messed with the external camera and then made it work again.'

'Really, that's interesting. It's not just a glitch or coincidence?'

'Erm, I don't think so, there's a slight possibility. I had Claire come and fingerprint it anyway just in case. Where are you?'

'On my way to the station, I'll meet you there.'

Marc was already in the car, engine running.

Ben waved to Al who was scouring the paths below, and he gave him a thumbs up, and then he got into the car glad to be out of the cold air and about to trade working partners for the most favourite one he'd ever had.

Marc parked the car and jumped out. Ben saw Morgan parked a few spaces away and smiled.

'Do you want the car, Ben?' Marc was dangling the keys from his finger mid-air.

'No, it's okay, Morgan has one, you keep it.'

Marc shrugged and began to jog towards the rear door that would grant him access to the station.

Ben got into the car, which was so warm with the heaters on full blast he had to unzip his quilted North Face jacket and tug off his woollen beanie.

'Am I glad to see you.'

Morgan smiled at him. 'Miss me that much? Did you not have a bit of a male bonding session with the boss, some quality time together?'

'You're funny.'

'So, I've been told. Seriously though, any news?'

'Not much happening our end, yours seems interesting.'

'There's this dentist, Neil Barnard, who the staff said absolutely loves himself. The way he spoke about Jasmine was a bit weird.'

'What like?'

'Well, he left before she did, but when he talked about her, he said she was the most perfect specimen of a girl. Don't you think that's a strange way to describe your colleague when you're married with kids?'

'I would describe you that way.'

'Well thanks, I should like to think you would, you're my boyfriend. No, you know what I mean though, it's odd.'

'Boyfriend? Is that the best you can give me, not lover, partner, love of my life?'

Morgan laughed. 'You know what I mean, you're all of those to me.'

'Glad to hear it.'

He realised then that he wanted more than anything to hear Morgan call him her husband. He loved her so completely that he never wanted to hear her call him her boyfriend ever again. The only problem was he was worried he'd scare her away, the age gap between them made him a little more old-fashioned than her. She probably wouldn't consider marriage this side of eternity.

'I think we need to look into his background, maybe speak to his wife and see if he did go straight home on Wednesday. For all we know he could have hung around outside, waiting for Jasmine. Plus, the receptionist, Nancy, claims Jasmine had a crush on him.'

Ben nodded. 'I have a problem with this whole scenario, though,' he replied.

'What?'

'How the hell did she end up at that lay-by? If she was murdered elsewhere, how did the killer get away?'

'There are plenty of places he could have gone. We can go speak to the staff of the pub later and ask if they know anything,' Morgan replied.

'I know, I said that to Marc, but it's just bothering me. I keep thinking about the location – is it something to do with her dad?'

'Maybe it's significant to the killer. Did the killer know the family? Has it got something to do with Judy? She's lost everyone in her family now, and it would have hit her so hard to know her daughter was there.'

'What in the hell could the poor woman have done that someone would kill her daughter in the same place her husband decided to end his life? That would be sick.'

'It is sick, whether that's the connection or not. Are we certain that he did end his life and it wasn't a murder made to look that way?' She reached out for his hand and her slender fingers felt warm in his icy grip. 'Are you okay, Ben, it's a lot and all this talk of suicide?'

She didn't finish her sentence, but he knew she was asking if he was coping. Cindy had ended her own life in their bathroom, and it had been hard to come to terms with. If he was honest, he didn't think that he ever would, but life continued on, the good days as well as the bad.

'I'm good, thank you for asking. Will you look into it? What was her dad called?'

'Craig, and yes, I'll take a look at the incident report when we get back.'

She drove out of the car park, and Ben began to google Craig Armer while Morgan drove them to the mortuary almost an hour away, if the traffic wasn't too busy.

TWELVE

The mask making was tricky, there was no doubt about it, and he had watched countless tutorials on YouTube, but after a few terrible attempts it got better. As he went about his work, he couldn't stop humming to himself. If he'd been whistling, he could have passed himself off as one of the seven dwarves from *Snow White*. It was like one of those ridiculous quizzes on Facebook, which dwarf are you most like, which cheese would you be, this is what you would look like as Barbie. Not that he did those silly quizzes, except he had done the cheese one because he was rather fond of cheese on crackers and a glass of red to relax after a busy day's work. The results had made him laugh; apparently, he'd be a Brie which was totally ridiculous. He was not hard on the outside and soft on the inside. Oh no, it was the opposite: he was soft on the outside and harder than a bed of nails on the inside. A few years ago, he had done the Hare Psychopathy Test on himself and hadn't been surprised to find his score was thirty-four. He had never felt real empathy towards anyone else. He had a string of one-night stands to his name; he was very impulsive; he was an aggressive child. He had no real long-term goals except to drive that cute detective, Morgan Brookes, absolutely insane.

It was her own fault that she had come to his attention in the first place. How many policewomen walked around in fishnet tights, cut-off denim shorts and Dr Marten boots in the autumn? He was being a touch judgemental about her, and he knew that, but she just didn't fit the profile of a cop that he associated with women in power. Granted that photo had been in the paper after the last case, and she hadn't been on duty when it had been snapped, but it had done something inside of him that he couldn't explain. He had spent hours searching for other pictures of her. He hadn't seen her in person, but that fiery red hair that was curled one day and straight the next, along with her long black velvety eyelashes and winged eyeliner stirred something deep in his loins that had no business being stirred.

He wasn't stupid, he hadn't printed and cut out the photos, sticking them on his bedroom wall like some lovesick teenage boy with a crush that was going to ruin him. He was far too clever for that. Instead, he had bought, for the first time in his life, a proper photograph album, from the little bookshop in Grasmere last time he'd been there. It had been in the bargain box, reduced; it was a dreadful orange colour, which kind of suited his need. He had spent hours painstakingly placing all the photos inside of it, in the order he felt they should go in. His favourite was one of her all fresh-faced, her hair in a tight bun, the smallest flicks of eyeliner and in full police uniform. She looked hot in that horrid, yellow body armour, and he didn't think there were a lot of women who could pull it off, but somehow, she did. Her face was so young, so innocent, her eyes full of hope and wonder. He had managed to copy and paste this one from the police website, which all but told him where she was living there was so much information on there. Then his second favourite was the one in the fishnet tights. She had tattoos on her legs that he had spent hours tracing with his fingertip. He knew he would very much like to see those vines and flowers in real life, run his fingers up them, but he knew that sometimes meeting a person face to face could destroy the fantasy you built up inside your mind.

He had a feeling that if anything it might be the opposite with Morgan. She might be so tantalising in reality that he wouldn't be able to stop himself. There was one problem with his fantasy revolving around her: the fact that she was always with that older guy with a shaved head. He didn't know how close they were. They seemed to work lots of cases together, and he was always described as her superior in the newspaper reports, but did the guy fuck her when they weren't at work? He didn't want to know this; he had put her up on a pedestal and didn't want that image ruined by the thought of her whoring her way through her colleagues to get her foot on the ladder and promoted. He liked to think of her as the innocent girl who had been thrown to the wolves in her early days, which according to the news she had, and had fought them with her bare hands to come out stronger than ever.

He wanted to make a mask of her perfect face, something he could stare at forever. He had been kind enough to send her his first acceptable attempt, and tomorrow she should receive the package containing his next, which had turned out so much better than he'd anticipated. He hoped that she like them. He wanted her to admire his work, to appreciate the trouble he was going to, so that she would live forever and be immortal.

THIRTEEN

Susie opened the door to greet Morgan and Ben at the mortuary. She smiled at them both, but it wasn't the huge cheesy grin she normally had.

'Hey, you two look fed up. This place is getting to be your second home.'

Morgan smiled back. 'Have you even been home, or do you sleep here?'

Susie laughed. 'What, in a spare fridge with the bodies? Naha, yes, I did go home because my dog gets all depressed when I'm away too many hours, and my girlfriend, Ella, can't cope with her when she's all sad and won't eat.'

'I didn't know you had a dog, what sort is it?'

'She's an Olde English Bulldog called Martha.'

'Cute.'

Ben rolled his eyes; he wasn't an animal lover, although Des's cat, Kevin, was slowly charming his way into Ben's good books, even though Morgan teased him about it. He would still deny it.

'We have a cat, don't we, Ben? Or we sort of adopted Des's, bless him.'

'Ahh, that's so sweet of you both. Hey, Ben, what books have you read this month?'

'*How to Kill Your Family*.'

'Ooh excellent choice, loved it.'

Morgan arched an eyebrow at him, knowing fine well he had not; she had been reading it and it was on the bedside table. When he'd first seen it, he'd sat her down and interrogated her for five minutes on her choice of book and if it meant anything. She had laughed too hard to be able to do anything other than shake her head.

Declan's voice boomed down the corridor. 'Susie.'

Susie shrugged. 'He's not so happy today. I think he split up with his boyfriend yesterday and he's been moping since he got in here. I kind of thought those two were serious about each other. I guess not.'

'The heart surgeon?'

'Ah huh.'

'Damn, I really liked him.'

'Yep, so did Declan.'

As they headed towards the changing rooms, the doorbell rang, and Susie opened it, letting in Claire, and another CSI that Morgan didn't know.

When they were all assembled in the mortuary, with Heart Dance playing softly in the background, Declan and Susie began their perfectly choreographed routine of dealing with the dead.

Morgan watched as Claire photographed and the other CSI, who had been introduced as Adam, began to bag up and label the clothing as it was cut from Jasmine's body. When she was naked, had been weighed, measured and ready for Declan's initial examination, Declan pointed to her wrists, where there were deep red marks along with some bruising.

'She was tied down. If you look at her legs there are similar marks, and bruising on her ankles. I highly doubt that she tied herself down, but I could be wrong. Have you seen those women who tie themselves into all sorts of knots with chains, ropes and belts? Then of course she could have taken part in some form of bondage session that went wrong. Scrap that, I don't know what I'm talking about. I'm assuming, and we all know what assumptions can make of a man.'

It was Susie who muttered. 'An arse.'

Morgan smiled then looked down at the notepad she was holding. Ben stepped closer to the body, which thankfully didn't smell because she had been discovered hours after her death and not days.

'Let's say this was bondage by mutual agreement. Why the bruises and scrape marks?'

'You're good, someone should promote you to detective sergeant. You're also right, those marks show us that she struggled against those ropes or bindings. Even if it started off as a mutual bit of fun, it didn't end that way for Jasmine, who had quite clearly changed her mind.'

'We have nothing yet to suggest this could be the sort of thing she was into. According to her colleagues, she was a bright, bubbly, lovely girl with no current boyfriend. Her last one got sent to prison for dealing, and I checked with the Intel department, and he's still there and not due for parole until March.' Morgan was looking at Declan as she spoke.

'Aren't bright, bubbly girls allowed to have fun?'

'Of course, they are, but I didn't get the impression this was the kind of fun she was into though.'

'Let's move on, shall we? We're getting way ahead of ourselves.'

Declan waited while Susie swabbed Jasmine's mouth and oesophagus, then using a needle he withdrew a sample of the vitreous humour from her left eye, to be sent off for testing, to check her blood alcohol levels. He also took a scraping from her left eyelashes, where there was still a little of the white gungy substance clinging to a few of them. When all the samples had been retrieved Declan began the external observations from right to left by starting to palpate her head for any fractures and pockets of swelling. Slowly making his way down the right then the left side of her body, he was diligent pointing out the abrasions and bruises once more.

Ben was watching closely. 'What was that white stuff on her eyelashes? It looked disgusting.'

'It did indeed. It wasn't semen, if that's what you are thinking. It has more of a thick, glutinous texture. It kind of looked like some form of glue or latex – it could even be alginate – but I'll have to get it tested.'

'Why is it on her eyes though, and nowhere else.'

'If only I could answer that.'

Ben smiled at him. 'Sorry, thinking out loud.'

Morgan looked up from the notepad she was scribbling her notes on.

'What's alginate?'

'Dentists use it all the time to take impressions of your teeth; it's excellent if you need a crown or a denture.'

'Jasmine is a dental nurse or was, she worked in a dental practice. Could she have got it while at work?'

'I suppose so, but this is quite a bit of the stuff. I would have thought she'd have tried to scrape it off, it would have driven her mad and hurt her eye.'

Morgan's mind was rushing at a thousand miles an hour. She could have picked it up at work but if it irritated her, she would have scraped it off; but what if her killer had it on him when he attacked her and it was transferred from him to her? That would mean he also worked in the dental surgery, wouldn't it?

Declan had one of Jasmine's eyelids peeled back. 'Petechial haemorrhages in her eyelids; she was asphyxiated no doubt about that.'

'Manner of death homicide, cause of death asphyxiation?'

'Absolutely, Ben, I wanted to be sure but yes, it is.'

'That's what I suspected.'

Declan continued, and Morgan struggled to concentrate. She wanted this to be over so she could get back to the station to check out Neil Barnard, then she was going to speak to his wife and find out if he was as perfect as he liked to make out. Everyone had secrets and she suspected that Neil Barnard had his fair share of them too.

FOURTEEN

When everyone had left to go and get changed, Morgan hung back a little, waiting to speak to Declan on his own. Susie took the hint and disappeared.

'What's troubling you, Ms Brooks?' Declan asked.

'I wanted to see how you were. Susie mentioned that you'd broken up with Stefan.'

A dark cloud passed across Declan's eyes, and he looked furious for a split-second, then it passed, and he was himself again.

'Did she now, what else is she gossiping about to everyone who walks through the door?'

'She only told me and Ben in confidence that you were a little bit down. We're your friends, Declan, we want to make sure that you're okay.'

He tugged off the gloves he'd been wearing, and the plastic apron, then crossed the room to where she was and gave her the briefest of hugs.

'You're the sweetest for sure, Morgan. I'm okay, just a little fed up with it all you know. You think you're madly in love and it turns out that they're not quite as madly in love as you. I'll get over it, don't you go worrying that pretty little face over me.'

'Why don't you come to ours for supper tonight? It's the pub quiz. If Ben gets home in time you could go with him, have a couple of beers, sleep at ours, God knows there are plenty of bedrooms.'

'Do you think he's going to be finished work in time to go to a pub quiz?'

'Probably not, but we have to eat at some point and go home. If anything crops up I can hang back and deal with it. It would probably do the pair of you good to get out for a couple of hours.'

'I'll think about it, thank you, Morgan, that's very kind of you.'

'Text me if you're coming so I can make sure Ben goes home. God knows they could do with someone intelligent to help them with the quiz. It's embarrassing how shit they are at it, and he could do with a break, too, he looks so worn out. I worry about him working too hard.'

'Me too, especially now he's on that medication for his heart, but some people thrive off stress and he's managed up to now to keep on going. Let's face it, you have brought your fair share of heart-attack-inducing stress into his life, and he's survived.' Declan began to laugh, and Morgan slapped his arm.

'Not on purpose though, Declan.'

He pulled her close, squeezing her; he was so much taller than both her and Ben that he towered over her.

'Put her down.'

Ben's voice echoed towards them.

'Ah, just having a bit of a friendly cuddle. Are you jealous, Ben? Would you like one?'

He laughed. 'I'm good thanks. Morgan, we need to get going when you can let him go.'

Morgan realised she still had her arms wrapped around Declan and released him.

'Got to take it when you can; Declan, text me.'

He smiled at her and gave her a thumbs up then disappeared into the office.

She waited until they were in the car before telling Ben.

'I just wanted to check he was okay, and I've invited him for supper tonight, told him you could do with help at the pub quiz because your team was the worst one in the history of pub quiz teams.'

Ben laughed. 'We're not that bad, and that's a good idea. How is he?'

'Fed up, I think he really liked Stefan.'

'I really liked Stefan; he sorted my heart out.'

'He hasn't dumped you though, has he? You're still his patient.'

'Poor Declan. I don't know if we'll make the pub quiz though.'

'It doesn't matter, him spending time with you is better than nothing for you both.' A thought popped into Morgan's head. 'We could invite Theo; I told him we would, and he might be a nice distraction for Declan.'

'Theo as in the priest you keep trying to pin every crime in the area on?'

'That's the one.' She started to laugh. 'C'mon, he is a bit odd at times, and he gave us both cause for concern it wasn't just me. He's okay though. I think we got off to a bad start. He's kind of Declan's type, don't you think?'

'I have absolutely no idea what his type is.'

'Tall, good-looking, intelligent, can we swing by the church on the way home?'

'Are you serious?'

She shrugged. 'No, don't be daft, it was just a thought.' She didn't tell him she was serious; she would phone Theo when she could or text him and drop a casual invite to the quiz. She could invite him to come for supper, but that might just tip Ben over the edge. He wasn't looking too impressed with her idea up to now.

'What are we thinking regarding Jasmine? She didn't have a phone on her, did she?'

'No, unless Amy found it at her home. We need to check in with those two and gather our thoughts, to come up with a solid plan of action.'

As if by speaking her name it flashed up on Morgan's phone screen. She pushed the hands-free button.

'*Where are you both?*'

'On the way back from the post-mortem, what's up?'

'*Her mum has gone off and left a suicide note. Smithy is on FLO duties and went to the shop to grab some milk and bread. He came back and found her gone and a note on the table.*'

Ben was shaking his head. 'Bollocks, get units to that lay-by now. Is anyone still there? I haven't released the scene. Can you get hold of whoever is guarding it and tell them to stop her?'

'*We're on our way now and there is a PCSO on scene guard, they've been told to look out for her.*'

'Does she drive?'

'*She drives an old red Fiat Punto.*'

'We'll head there too; unless you can think of anywhere else she might have gone?'

'*I don't know, it kind of makes sense she'd go to where they found her husband's and daughter's bodies.*'

Ben was nodding; he took out his radio that had been shoved in the glove compartment.

'Control from 1613.'

'*Go ahead 1613.*'

'I need all available patrols to the lay-by on the A591 over-looking Thirlmere, to search for a suicidal misper.'

'Judith Armer? Yes, we're aware and they're travelling.'

'Can you also get ambulance travelling, please. Is there a dog handler on duty?'

'Ambulance are on standby, the dog is out west, but should I put in a request for them to travel too?'

'Yes please, thank you.'

He turned to Morgan. 'We have to find her.'

'We will, everyone is looking for her. She can't be too far away.'

Morgan didn't tell him that the last place she would go to take her own life if she was in Judy's shoes was a place that was already guarded by the cops. She would go to her own little favourite place so no one could stop her.

At the thought of this her stomach dropped like a lead weight. She hoped that she was wrong, and Judy was found before she could do anything.

FIFTEEN

The area by the lake was crawling with police vans and two unmarked cars, and there were officers out on foot calling Judy's name. They hadn't located Judy's car, but she could have left it somewhere and be walking. Morgan sped past the lay-by.

'What are you doing?'

'Where would you park if you didn't want to stand out like a beacon, when there was a chance people were looking for you?'

Ben shrugged. 'I don't know.'

'I'm going to check the car parks for The Kings Head and The Lodge; there are enough officers at the lay-by.'

'This is why I like working with you so much, you think outside of the box.'

'Yeah, it's not very hard to though, it's common sense.'

'Something a lot of people are sadly lacking these days.'

She turned into the car park which had three cars parked outside. No lights were on in the pub and none of them were a Fiat Punto. 'Damn it.'

As she turned around, she noticed what looked like the

beam from headlights coming from around the side of the pub. Stopping the car, she jumped out and ran in the direction of the lights, praying she wasn't about to give the landlord a heart attack. She rounded the corner and saw the red car; the lights made it hard to tell if anyone was inside it. As she got closer, she saw that there was a woman slumped over the wheel, and she pulled the door open. The petrol fumes filled the air making her eyes water.

'Ben,' Morgan screamed for him but heard his footsteps on the tarmac as he ran towards her. She grabbed hold of Judy under the arms and dragged her out of the car, but she was a lot heavier than Morgan and she tripped backwards, managing to fall onto the floor with a semi-conscious Judy on top of her, landing with a loud thud.

'1613 ambulance to The Kings Head pub now, unconscious female, carbon monoxide poisoning.'

He lifted his hand across his nose and leaned into the car, turning the engine off and pulling the key from the ignition, then he slammed the door shut so they didn't have to inhale the toxic fumes. Judy let out a groan and Morgan thanked God that they had made it in time. She hadn't been able to help Jasmine, but she wouldn't let her mum die all alone, no matter how much she wanted to.

Ben pulled Judy off Morgan. Rolling her onto her side, he took off his coat and covered her as best as he could. Morgan took off hers and rolled it up to put under her head, both of them shivering in the frosty air.

A car screeched into the car park. Amy and Cain both got out and came running over to help.

'Good call, Morgan.'

She nodded at Cain, but was bent over Judy who was coughing and spluttering, rubbing and patting her back. It seemed to take forever for the sirens of the ambulance to get close enough that she could stop panicking and let them take over. The blue flashing lights illuminated the murky sky that looked as if it might either pour down or start snowing. She wasn't sure which but either way a storm was brewing.

They all stood back to let the paramedics take over and within seconds there was an oxygen mask on Judy's face.

Ben took out his phone and called Smithy.

'We found her; you need to get yourself to... Hang on.' He turned to the paramedics. 'Where are you taking her?'

'Westmorland General, West Cumberland has no beds.'

'Thanks, guys. Smithy get travelling to Kendal hospital and meet her there. You get the pleasure of sitting with her while she's assessed, seeing as how you're currently sat twiddling your thumbs. We're flat out with enquiries, and section staff are all busy.'

'An officer will be waiting for you when you get there.' Ben lowered his voice as he addressed the paramedics. 'Judy has had a terrible shock; her daughter was found dead yesterday and her husband took his own life six months ago.'

The paramedics looked horrified, both of them nodded.

One of them turned back to Judy. 'Come on, darling, let's get you to the hospital. The food might not be so good but it's warm and there's plenty of people to talk to.'

Morgan smiled at the older of the two men. He was kind and despite how busy and short-staffed they were, she knew they would take care of Judy as best as they could, which made her feel a little better about not travelling with her. She would go and visit her as soon as she could, but right now they needed to concentrate on finding Jasmine's killer. They couldn't afford to lose momentum on the investigation now they knew it was murder.

They all watched as Judy was put in the back of the ambulance and driven away.

It was Amy who spoke first. 'That was a close call, poor woman.'

Morgan agreed. 'It was too close. We need to find Jasmine's killer; it might give Judy the peace she needs to carry on.'

Amy turned to Ben. 'What now, boss, what do you want us to do?'

All of them turned to Ben who was still staring in the direction of the ambulance. He turned to them and for the first time Morgan thought she saw a hint of confusion cross his eyes; it was only there for a split-second, but it was enough to make her reach out for his arm.

'Good question, did you manage to search Jasmine's house for anything that might be of use?'

'We sure did, we found nothing of interest. Not even a diary. She has an iPad that she shares with her mum, and Judith let me look at it. There was just the usual social media stuff, and they shared an email address, but her mum said there was nothing she came across that would cause her concern.'

'What about her phone? She didn't have one with her, she must have one?' Morgan asked.

'She has an iPhone 11 with a cracked screen that she doesn't use for anything other than calling or texting, according to Judy.'

Morgan scrunched up her face. 'I find that hard to believe. She's not going to tell her mum everything, is she? She must have some secrets she doesn't share with her.'

Amy shrugged. 'Can we go back to the station? It's too cold to be discussing this here.'

'Yes, of course. Let's go back and regroup, try and work out where we go from here.'

Both Ben and Morgan were shivering. She bent down to retrieve their jackets, passing Ben's to him. He took it from her but didn't put it on, and she whispered, 'She wasn't bleeding.

She only had it on her for a few minutes, she had nothing catching.'

He smiled at her but still didn't put it back on. They got inside the car that Morgan had left running as she'd jumped out to help Judy, and for that they were both grateful. It was suffocatingly hot and utterly wonderful.

SIXTEEN

Morgan drove back to Rydal Falls. She stopped outside her second favourite café, The Coffee Pot. She needed a decent hit of caffeine, if she was to keep her brain working when she was half frozen and feeling desperately sad about this whole case. She needed food too; her stomach was rumbling, and she felt sick. Her absolute favourite café was in Bowness, it was called Practical Magic and run by her friend Annie, but it would be shut by the time she could drive there, and she didn't have the time to spare. She wanted Ben to go to the pub quiz with Declan, to cheer him up, and she also realised she needed to try and get hold of Theo, as he might make a pleasant distraction for Declan. Inside the coffee shop, while she waited for her lattes and tuna crunch sandwiches, she rang Theo, who picked up almost immediately.

'Is this thee Morgan Brookes?'

'Good afternoon, Theo, yes, it is.'

'Are you wanting to arrest me for something? Have you found a body that needs a suspect?'

She paused, telling herself he was just joking, he couldn't possibly know.

'Theo, are you psychic by any chance? Do you have a sixth sense that you seem to tap in to unknowingly?'

'*Oh Christ, you did find a body? Jesus I was just messing around, I'm not psychic and I didn't do anything.*'

There was a hint of pure panic in his voice, and she smiled. Morgan was getting used to Theo's language regarding God. She noticed that he didn't use it when dealing with the public but more so with his friends and she liked that he regarded her as a friend despite their rocky start.

'I never said that you did, and for a vicar you just took the Lord's name in vain to the extreme. You might want to work on that. It's going to upset your parishioners if they hear you blaspheming that way.' She laughed and heard him fumbling in the background.

'*Sorry, Morgan, if you have found a body, it's not a laughing matter.*'

'No, it isn't and stop panicking I didn't phone you because of that.'

'*You didn't?*'

'Not at all, are you busy tonight around eight?'

'*Hmm, let me see. It's the ladies' choir practice but they don't need me, and if they did, I would find an excuse not to be available because, well you've heard them, so no explanation needed.*'

She liked his easy way; they had got off to a bad start, but she realised that he had a very dry sense of humour which took a little getting used to.

'It's the pub quiz tonight.'

'*And what do you want me to do about that, come bless the teams?*'

'No, although they could do with a little help from high above because they are so crap. I wondered if you wanted to go along and help Ben out. His friend Declan is going to be there, and he's just split up with his partner, who Declan thought might be the one, but he apparently isn't because he dumped him. Long story short, Ben needs cheering up, so does Declan and I thought you might like to escape for a bit, and maybe help them win or at least not come last like they usually do.'

'*Gee, what a fun night that sounds like. It's a tough one, the ladies' choir or quiz night with two manic depressives.*'

Morgan giggled. 'Declan is hot.'

'*I'll be there, what time?*'

'About eight. To be totally honest it might be a bit of a push for Ben to make it on time. We have a lot going on at work.'

'*What about you, are you not coming along?*'

'I'll try, I might need to hold the fort at work.'

'*Last question, does Ben know that you've asked me? He might not be so keen on my company.*'

'He knows I'm asking you and trust me, he needs all the help he can get. He will be glad to have you on board as long as you don't talk about God all night.'

Theo laughed.

'*Black Dog at eight? Do I need anything?*'

'Just yourself, and Theo.'

'*What?*'

'Thank you.'

'*I'm not sure why I'm agreeing to this, but a hot guy is a good start.*'

He ended the call just as the barista passed over the hot drinks. Morgan pushed her phone into her pocket, grabbed the small brown handle of the paper bag containing their much-needed food, and balanced the drinks on top of each other.

Ben opened the car door and took the drinks from her. She smiled at him.

'I thought we better grab some food while we're at it.'

He waited until she was in the car then took the bag from

her and took out a sandwich. Taking a huge bite, he closed his eyes.

'Tuna never tasted so good,' he said through a mouthful of food.

'Did your mum never tell you it's rude to talk with your mouth full?'

He shook his head and carried on devouring his sandwich.

Morgan took a sip of her coffee then began the short drive to the station, wondering if she had been too optimistic phoning Theo, when she had no idea what was happening next.

Coffees sipped, sandwiches consumed, and hands warmed up on the radiators they all met in the office where Marc was ready to greet them all as they filed in. Cain kept pouting at Morgan, and she felt bad she hadn't brought him and Amy food, but she'd assumed they had already eaten.

She pulled open her drawer and searched around for something she could give him. There was a cereal bar that she was too scared to check the date on. Surely it wouldn't be bad. She waved it in his direction and his eyes lit up, so she launched it at him. She watched as he ripped the wrapper off and ate it in two bites. He didn't keel over or spit it out, so it must have been not too out of date.

They were waiting for Ben and Marc; Marc had disappeared into Ben's office with the door shut. A few minutes later they were back out, Ben standing in front of the knackered old whiteboard that had seen better days, with a dry wipe pen in his hand.

'I'll recap what we have so far. One victim, Jasmine Armer, who died of asphyxiation. There were rope marks around her wrists and ankles, so she was tied up while she was alive. She struggled against them. Whoever took her had someplace to take her and keep her where they wouldn't be disturbed. Once she was dead, she was then driven in her own car to the lay-by by Thirlmere and left there, where she was discovered by Amber. Based on the position of the body we're looking for someone who at least knows about Jasmine's father's suicide, and someone who wanted to flaunt her death. Someone with ego. A possible serial killer. Glue on her eyes may match an adhesive used at the dental practice where she works. She had no boyfriend, no known enemies. She may have had a crush on a colleague, but that's all we know about her so far.

'What else do we have and what do we need to find out?'

Morgan began to fire questions in his direction.

'Where is her phone? How did they get the car to the lay-by and get away? Did the killer know that Jasmine's dad killed himself in that exact same place?'

'Slow down, Morgan, I can't write that fast.'

She paused until he'd caught up. 'Who would want her dead? What is the motive? Why did her mum try and kill herself nearby?'

Morgan looked down at the sheet of paper she was also scribbling notes on. 'Oh.'

'What?'

'What if her mum killed her? They might have had an argument and then she drove her to the same spot as her dad killed himself. That might be why she tried to kill herself: she can't take the guilt.'

Everyone was staring at her, and Amy was nodding.

'You think Jasmine and Judy had an argument, and Judy killed her then tried to make it look like something else?'

Ben turned back to the board and wrote Judith's name on it.

'We can't rule that out. I can't say I'm a big fan of that theory, because for a start how did she leave the car and get home? She doesn't come across as the kind of person who is into hiking or long walks.'

'We've already discussed this; someone needs to go to the

bus station and see if they have any CCTV of buses that covered the route to and from that stop near the lay-by on Wednesday. There are also the car parks at the pub, hotel and campsite.'

Ben arched an eyebrow at her, and Morgan realised she was getting a little too fired up.

'Someone also needs to speak to the dental lab guy who dropped the parcel off. He may have been the last person to see her. I also think that Neil Barnard's alibi needs confirming because he's a bit strange, and someone needs to speak to his wife.'

Ben was writing it all down so the tasks could be ticked off as each one was completed. This would all be put into the system, but that would take time. This way they could all brainstorm together and it served as a reminder of the tasks that needed taking care of.

'Someone needs to go and speak to Judy and ask her some more questions about the phone and their relationship.'

'Anything else, Morgan?'

His tone was one of slight amusement, but Marc was reading each task on the list and nodding his head.

'I agree with Morgan.' He didn't elaborate over what it was he was agreeing with, and no one asked him to.

She held up her hand. 'I want to go speak to the dental lab guy.'

Ben lifted his wrist and checked his watch. 'In Kendal? It won't be open.'

'They might be open late, or there might be a phone number on the door for emergencies.'

'Right, well if you're happy to go sort that out, great. Amy, do you want to speak to Neil Barnard's wife? Cain, are you happy to go to the hospital and speak to Judy, if she's able to talk? I think we need to split up. We'll cover more ground that way. I'll phone the bus station and ask about the CCTV, and get

PCSOs to visit the pubs and anywhere else that may have CCTV in the area, to see if we can capture someone walking there. Surely, we're going to catch a break.'

'There are usually a lot of walkers about.' Amy stood up but stating the obvious.

'Not in bloody Baltic, cold December when the paths are all iced up and there's a good chance you'll get frostbite.'

Amy laughed. 'You'll be surprised, people walk, hike and climb mountains regardless of a bit of frostbite, boss.'

She left them.

Cain stood up next. 'Are you sure you want me out on my own?'

Ben nodded. 'Cain, you're going to speak to Judy in the hospital not conduct a prison interview with Jeffrey Dahmer. You've done it thousands of times; I think you'll be just fine.'

Morgan smiled at Cain, who leaned over and whispered, 'You're a bad influence on him, he's talking about serial killers now, that name just rolled off his tongue.'

'What was that?'

Cain straightened up. 'Nothing, boss, I'm happy if you are.' He turned and winked at Morgan, then walked out, leaving her, Ben and Marc.

'Anything you want me to do?'

Ben looked at Marc. 'Not right now, boss, but thanks I'll let you know if I need anything.'

He nodded, shuffled the stack of papers he'd picked up and left them alone.

Ben asked Morgan, 'Do you want me to come to the dental lab with you?'

'No thanks, I want you to do your enquiries then go home and meet Declan. You can pick up food on your way. I'll be home as soon as I've tracked down the lab guy.'

'I can't bail out on everyone; I'm supposed to be in charge.'

'I know that, but you also can't work twenty-four hour shifts straight without a break. I'm around if something crops up, I can handle it.'

Ben reached out a hand and gently traced a finger down Morgan's cheek.

'I know you can, that's what I'm afraid of.'

'Well, you don't need to be afraid or worry about me, I'm good. I haven't got into any trouble for at least six weeks, maybe even longer.'

He laughed. 'That is also another thing I'm afraid of.'

She stood up and shrugged her coat back on.

'Talk to the bus people, go home and get me food. I can salivate over thinking about it. Phone me with a list of what needs doing and I'll come back to talk to the others. You never know, we all might be super-efficient, and I'll make it in time.' She didn't want to be super-efficient because she couldn't think of anything worse than sitting through a torturous pub quiz. She would rather stay here and work.

Ben smiled at her. 'Thank you, what would I do without you?'

'Probably lead a stress-free life but hey-ho, in for a penny in for a pound.'

'You say the strangest things you know; you sound like an old fish wife not a twenty-four-year-old.'

'And you're full of compliments for an old guy.'

'Ouch.'

'Don't be so soft, get phoning or whatever it is you're doing and don't forget Declan, he's always there for you, now's your turn to be there for him.'

'Take Amber with you, or see if anyone else is available.'

'I'd rather not, thank you. I can manage, stop it.'

She left him staring after her. He was sweet, but he worried far too much about her, which was distracting at times and annoying. She knew what she was doing. This wasn't the first dangerous person she'd hunted down.

SEVENTEEN

Morgan typed the postcode for the dental laboratory into the satnav. She couldn't be bothered wasting time trying to look for it, there was too much to do. The roads weren't too busy, and it only took her twenty minutes to reach Kendal. Six minutes later she was turning onto the quiet street where satnav put the address. It was strange to think that in amongst the houses was a random dental laboratory, but there it was, almost at the opposite end of the street: a corner house with a big sign above it that read *Fix It*. It was a pretty apt name, she supposed. The front of the shop, which looked more like a house, was in darkness but there was a light on upstairs. Hopefully the guy she was looking for was still working away up there and would answer the door.

She debated on using her official police knock or whether a normal knock would do and decided to go with the first. The light was on upstairs, and she wanted them to hear her. She drew back her fist and hammered on the door four times. Peering through the glass she was rewarded with a light turning on, and the sound of footsteps running downstairs. The door opened a little and a woman's voice said, 'Can I help you?'

'Yes, I hope so. I'm Detective Constable Morgan Brookes, can I have a word with you?'

The door opened fully, and Morgan saw a woman dressed in a pair of navy scrubs, wearing a plastic pinny, and rubber gloves on her hands.

'Come in, I'm just in the middle of cleaning up. Can you follow me upstairs to the lab so we can talk?'

Before Morgan could answer she ran upstairs. Morgan closed the door behind her and followed. The smell of the dentists filled the air, making her stomach churn a little. Why had she suggested this? Twice now today she'd put herself through it when she could have let someone else who wasn't quite as scared of the dentist as she was come instead of her.

'Are you here on your own?'

The woman was rinsing down the sink area, and she nodded. 'I am, were you expecting anyone else to be here? My nephew helps out in the shop with the customers and deliveries, but he finishes at four thirty.'

'Can I ask your name?'

She turned to her. 'Of course. Melanie Price, my date of birth is the third of January 1970. I live next door; my favourite food is pizza and I love a glass of white wine in front of the TV each evening.'

Morgan smiled.

'Sorry, that was a bit rude of me. It's all true though. What did you want to know? I'm pretty sure it wasn't that.'

'No, I'm partial to pizza but I prefer rosé wine, it doesn't give me a hangover like white does. What I'm here for is to speak to your nephew about a delivery he made to New Smile in Windermere on Wednesday.'

'Why on earth would you need to speak to him about that? He made the delivery, didn't he? Have they reported it to the police for some reason?'

Morgan realised she hadn't heard about Jasmine. If she was

the technician there was a good chance she wouldn't have met her. She pulled out her phone and showed her a photograph of Jasmine. 'Do you know her?'

She shook her head. 'No, why are you asking?'

'This is Jasmine Armer, and she works at New Smile. She waited for your nephew to deliver the parcel on Wednesday. We found her body the next day, and I wanted to speak to him, because he may have been the last person to see her before she died.'

The woman's face drained of all its colour, and she sat down opposite Morgan.

'Oh no, that's terrible the poor girl. What happened to her?'

'She was killed.'

'And you think that Joe had something to do with it?'

Morgan shook her head. 'No, not at all. I'm trying to trace her last hours and I wondered if she said anything to him, or if he noticed anything or anyone unusual hanging around when he left. We have CCTV footage of him handing the package to Jasmine and then he leaves. He's not a suspect at this point.'

Morgan tried to make it sound as if he wasn't, but every person who saw and came into contact with Jasmine on that last day was a suspect in her mind. Especially one with access to the material they found on Jasmine's eyes.

'Oh, thank God for that. I'll ring him now and see if he can come back to speak to you.'

Melanie peeled off her rubber gloves, took out her phone and moments later was talking to who Morgan presumed was Joe.

'He's on his way. He's such a good lad, he wouldn't hurt anyone. I don't know what I'd do without him, he's always so helpful.'

Morgan smiled at her, hoping that he wasn't going to take forever to get here.

He didn't, a few minutes later she heard the front door

open, and slam shut, and heavy footsteps run up the stairs. He walked into the room, his cheeks flushed. He tugged off his beanie to reveal a shaved head.

Melanie stared at him.

'You didn't. Christ, Joe, you look like a thug. What made you do that?'

He started laughing. 'Thanks, Mel, it was getting on my nerves, I fancied a change.'

Mel shook her head. 'You idiot, that's the sort of thing you do in the summer not when it's freezing. Joe, this is Detective Morgan Brookes. She needs to ask you about the last delivery you dropped off at New Smile.'

His eyes widened and he looked a little scared, which immediately made the tiny hairs on the back of Morgan's neck bristle.

'Hi,' Joe replied, looking at Morgan in panic. 'But, I don't understand why they phoned the police because I dropped it off like I was supposed to, and gave it to one of the nurses.'

'No, they didn't phone about that, Joe. I'm afraid that nurse was found dead the next day, and I'm trying to piece together what might have happened to her.'

He sat down and put his head in his hands for a moment, then looked at her. His gaze searching out her eyes as he stared into them. 'I didn't do anything.'

'I know, I'm not here to accuse you of anything. I wanted to know how she was when you spoke to her, and if you noticed anyone or anything strange outside of the practice when you arrived or left?'

He let out a sigh of relief. 'Phew, I got scared then. What happened to her? She was fine when I saw her, we had a little laugh and a joke like I always do, then she took the package and shut the door.'

'She was murdered.'

He shook his head. 'How, I mean why, why would someone

do that to her? That's terrible, oh God I feel sick, look at my hands they're trembling.' He held up his hands and they were visibly shaking.

Mel stood up, opened the fridge and took a can of cola out of it. She passed it to him. 'Have a drink of that. It's shock, a bit of sugar will help.'

He looked gutted, and Morgan got the feeling that his aunt Mel mothered him a lot. He didn't look as if he had ever done something bad in his life.

'I'm sorry to break this to you, Joe, but it's really important to me that you think carefully about what happened when you left. Did you notice anyone loitering in the area, anyone watching the surgery?'

'No, I didn't. I'm sorry, should I have? Was the killer there waiting for her to come outside? I feel awful, I could have walked her to her car and made sure she was okay. I had nowhere else to go, I was only meeting my friend Travis for a game of pool; he would have waited.'

'It's not your fault, you weren't to know what was going to happen. Hindsight is a wonderful thing after the fact. We all think of the things we could have done to change fate that we didn't. How was Jasmine, did she appear to be worried about anything, nervous?'

'She was funny, she is always funny whenever I go there. We have a bit of a joke. I can't believe she's not going to see another birthday, she's always going to be the age she is now forever.' He stopped talking at the realisation that he would never smile and joke with Jasmine again, and looked across to his aunt, a look of genuine distress was etched across his face.

Morgan stood up, she fished a card out of her pocket and placed it on the worktop.

'Where did you meet Travis for a game of pool? Would he be able to confirm this?'

'We always play at The Sun. You can ask the landlord, we were there all night.'

'Thank you for speaking to me. I'm sorry to be the bearer of such sad news. If there's anything you remember or think about you can ring me any time on that number. If I don't answer leave me a message, I will get back to you.'

He nodded, then took a sip from the can.

Mel stood up. 'I'll see you out.'

'It's fine, I can manage, thanks for your time.'

Morgan left them to it, feeling sad once again for Jasmine who hadn't asked for any of this. She didn't get any bad vibes from Joe at all, which was normally a warning sign that something was off with a person. She did need to confirm his alibi though; as genuine as he seemed she still had to rule him out.

She got in the car and googled the phone number for the pub. Ringing it she heard a rough voice bark at her.

'Yeah.'

'Is this The Sun?'

'It is, can I help?'

'I'm Detective Morgan Brookes. I was wondering if you could confirm if Joe James was there on Wednesday evening.'

There was laughter on the other end of the line.

'What's he done? Him and that Travis are a pair of goons at times. Did they get caught stealing the lead off the church roof or something?'

'No, I'm investigating a murder.'

'Oh, well, the pair of them were here all night. Tight arses they are, buying a half of lager and making it last an hour so they could hog the pool table.'

'Do you know what time they arrived?'

'Joe was here just after six; Travis had been here since five, moping around waiting for him. Look I don't know much, but I

know that Joe is a decent lad apart from his lack of money. He really was here all night; I wouldn't lie for any of my customers in something this serious. I'm sorry I can't be much help, but if I thought they were involved I wouldn't hide it.'

'Thank you, I really appreciate your honesty.'

She ended the call. There was no way he could have taken Jasmine, killed her and then been at the pub for six, it would take him ten minutes maybe fifteen depending on traffic to get to Kendal from Windermere.

She was back at square one. Maybe Amy was onto something, had Judy killed her daughter then not been able to take the guilt? For the time being she could cross Joe off her hit list, but could Cain cross Judy off his?

EIGHTEEN

Amy drove along the secluded country road and missed the turning for the address she had for Neil Barnard. Turning around she drove much slower this time and saw a concealed driveway with a sign on the gatepost that said Pine Hall. She turned in and hoped that it was the right address; if not whoever lives here might be able to point her in the right direction. There was a sweeping gravel drive with pine trees along both sides. They had a sprinkling of frost on them and looked so wintery, glistening in the fading daylight. As the driveway opened out, she felt her jaw drop at the house that greeted her, well it wasn't just a house it was more like a mansion. There was even a huge water fountain in front of it that was frozen solid, the water hanging down in silvery icicles.

'I'm in the wrong job,' she whispered to herself.

There was a huge black Range Rover parked outside the front with blacked-out windows. She parked the small white Corsa next to it and got out, grabbing her notebook off the seat and her phone. She had her small tablet but the signal was rubbish in remote places, so she preferred to use good old pen and paper; it didn't matter how crap the Wi-Fi was when you could write stuff down.

Des would have loved this place, he was a sucker for big posh houses, and she felt a sadness inside of her that he wasn't here to see it for himself. Yes, he'd driven her mad at times, but they got on well and she missed not having anyone to be fully sarcastic with. Cain was the best replacement she could have wished for, but she still had to watch what she said because underneath his huge, tough guy exterior he was really quite soft. Her fingers were starting to go numb, and she realised she was stalling, so she strode up to the front door and rang the video doorbell, surprised that whoever lived here hadn't set their dogs on her while she'd been loitering outside the front.

The sound of footsteps running towards the door threw her at the same time the door was tugged open, and the face of a teenage boy was staring at her in what she could only call a look of total disappointment.

'Hi, are your parents home?'

'You're not the pizza guy then?' the boy replied.

'Sorry, definitely not.'

'Who are you then?'

She thought about her answer and decided to state the facts.

'Detective Constable Amy Smith from Cumbria Constabulary, and you are?'

This threw him and he looked at her puzzled. 'Tobias Barnard, why are you here?'

'Look it's freezing out here, are your parents in? I need to speak to them.'

A woman's voice called from down the hall. 'Who's at the door?'

Tobias rolled his eyes. 'My dad is at work; my stepmum is home,' he told Amy. 'Police,' he said, turning his head towards the woman behind him.

'Really, oh dear, let them in,' she said.

He opened the door wide and stood to one side to let Amy in, who could currently no longer feel her fingers it was so cold outside. She smiled, and both she and the woman glared at him at the same time. Amy hated teenagers with attitude, especially when they were as smug as he was. Standing at the foot of the stairs was another surly teenager who looked a little older than Tobias. She glared at him, too, for good measure.

Amy wasn't sure what she was expecting their stepmum to look like, but it wasn't someone who could have passed for Morticia Addams. She was the most strikingly beautiful woman Amy had ever seen, dressed from head to toe in black, with the longest, shiny black hair that made her want to reach out and stroke it. If she had to guess she would say she was in her early thirties.

'Forgive my son's rudeness, he's hangry and the pizza is late, and he didn't want to eat my chicken chasseur. Please come in, I'm Esmerelda Barnard but call me Esme, it's not so much of a mouthful.'

She smiled at Amy who smiled back. 'Detective Constable Amy Smith. Is it possible to speak to you about Wednesday.'

Esme began to laugh. 'My, word gets around fast; I would have played a much better Morticia Addams than Catherine Zeta-Jones, but unfortunately, they didn't have my phone number. You enjoyed the show then? Surely you didn't come here to talk about that?'

Amy decided that Esme was nuts, maybe slightly delusional but definitely borderline crazy.

'I'm sorry, I'm talking about this Wednesday just gone, the day after Tuesday.'

'I'm teasing you, darling, forgive me for being so rude. Let's go to the kitchen and I'll make you a drink while we chat, you look frozen to the core.'

Amy wasn't going to disagree with her there because she was, although, the heat inside of Pine Hall was already thawing her out nicely. The hallway was painted matt black with cream touches, and a huge cut-glass chandelier gave it Gothic vibes that Amy knew Morgan would die for. It was such a shame she hadn't come here instead. Morgan would have loved Esme; she was not her cup of tea though. She followed her past the striking black-and-white prints from old horror movies that looked pretty cool even to her, and she much preferred washed-out whites, beige and pale greens for her colour palette. The kitchen was amazing, though everything was black, the wall, the cupboards, the huge island. Esme pointed to a stool at the island and Amy perched on it.

Esme watched Amy glancing around. 'I know my taste is not everyone's but what can I say, I was born wearing black and shall die so too. Now tea, coffee, wine maybe something stronger to warm your bones? Although I guess not if you're on duty, but I won't tell if you don't.'

'Tea would be lovely, thanks. My colleague would die to see this house. She's very much like you; I think you'd get on.'

'Well then bring her around next time you're passing, I'm always happy to give a tour of my little homage to all things Addams Family. Of course, Neil hates it, well he doesn't hate it so much as he prefers a little more lightness to my darkness, but there is no way I'm having a house full of chalky white walls, with two teenage boys who make more mess than you could ever imagine. Filthy, smelly things who survive off pizza and energy drinks. No one warned me about that when I agreed to marry Neil and take them on.'

Amy was quite lost for words and that didn't happen very often, but she smiled at Esme who was in the middle of steeping the tea. She added milk and passed the black mug to Amy, who was glad to wrap her fingers around it for some extra warmth. Esme carried her own mug and sat next to her.

'Now, what about Wednesday?'

'Did your husband tell you about Jasmine Armer?'

Esme scrunched up her face, yet no wrinkles appeared; she seemed a little young to be having Botox injections.

'Who is Jasmine Armer?'

'A nurse at the surgery where Neil works. She was found dead in her car on Thursday, and we're just trying to find out what happened.'

'Oh, dear me, that's dreadful, the poor girl. Which one is Jasmine? Is she the pretty thing with the long black hair?'

Amy thought that for someone who claimed not to know Jasmine she was able to describe her to a tee.

'Yes, she is. I was wondering what time Neil came home on Wednesday?'

Amy had her notebook open on the counter and a pen in one hand, the other still touching the hot mug.

'Let me see, why do you need to know this exactly, is he a suspect?'

'It's just formality, we have to speak to everyone she knew. He's not a suspect, it's more a case of checking everyone was where they claimed to be, so we can rule them out and take them off the list.'

'So, he is a suspect. Have you spoken to him and asked him?'

'I haven't but my colleague did.'

'And he knows that the police were coming to speak to me about it?'

Amy wasn't a liar; she wouldn't deceive Esme to get her answers.

'No, he doesn't know.'

'I thought not, well what can I say? He arrived home around five maybe five fifteen, he always does on a Wednesday. Then he had a quick tea and took the boys to the leisure centre. Tobias plays football and Hugo spends hours in the gym, then he came home and spent time in his office. Don't ask me what he was doing in there because I don't ask, and I don't care as long as he's not under my feet. Around nine he went to pick the boys up and brought them home.'

'Right, thanks that's great.'

The front door slammed, and a man's voice called out. 'Esme, whose is that bloody car in my parking space.'

Esme rolled her eyes. 'There are acres of grounds, and he still moans about where he parks his damn car. I wish I could tell you something incriminating, but unfortunately, I can't.'

'It belongs to the detective, darling,' she called out in a singsong voice.

His footsteps hurried down the hallway and he strode into the kitchen and stared at Amy, who lifted the mug to her lips and sipped the tea. She noticed that his cheeks were flushed red and there was a spark of something in his eyes, anger maybe.

'Oh, I thought you were the girl I spoke to earlier.'

'No, that was my colleague. I'm Amy Smith.'

'What are you doing here?'

'Darling, don't be so obtrusive, she came to check your alibi was correct.'

His eyes widened and he stared at his wife. A look between them told Amy everything she needed to know. Neil Barnard was not used to anyone disbelieving him, and Esme wasn't quite as in love with her husband as she probably should be.

'I'm sorry, we're doing the same with everyone at the practice not just you. Esme has confirmed it so there's no need to worry.'

She took another sip of tea and watched his face as it seemed to contort before her eyes.

'I, erm, right, that's good then because I didn't have anything to do with it. I told your colleague I liked Jasmine, she is, was, a good dental nurse and a nice girl.'

Esme turned to stare at her husband. 'She was?'

'Yes, you know that she was. I told you that at the Christmas party, and introduced you to her.'

'You did, sorry, darling, I can't really remember. I was a little bit tipsy that night.'

She turned to Amy and winked. 'I had to be to survive four hours of dentists talking about rotten teeth and root canals.'

Amy stood up and smiled at them both. It was interesting how Neil referred to both Morgan and Jasmine as girls when they were clearly women. 'Well, I should get going. Thanks for the tea. If we need anything else someone will be in touch.'

'Neil, be a darling and see Amy to the door. I have a headache I need to lie down. I didn't get much beauty sleep last night and I don't want to risk bringing on any wrinkles. You have to take good care of your skin if you want to look beautiful forever.' She smiled at Amy.

He looked as if he'd like to drop kick Amy out of the door, but nodded his head and led the way down the hallway to the front door, where Tobias was standing with the door wide open, taking boxes of pizza off the delivery guy. It smelled amazing, and Amy felt her stomach rumble at the thought of hot pizza.

She smiled at Neil.

'That smells good, enjoy your pizza.'

Then turned and walked towards the car, not looking back.

Neil never said a word, he stood staring at her until she reversed and began to drive away, then she saw the front door close in her rear-view mirror.

Instinctively, she didn't trust him.

NINETEEN

Morgan headed back to the station, there was nothing else for her to do, and also she wanted to see what the others had found out and if Ben had made it home in time to meet Declan. She could drive past their street and see if either of their cars were parked outside. She knew that realistically he would have rung and cancelled Declan the minute she left, as he was dedicated to his work more than anything, but he still needed to take a break.

She made a detour past their street and was shocked to see Ben's BMW parked outside the house and the downstairs lights on. She didn't stop; she drove straight to the station – at least she could keep him updated if he messaged, it was the least she could do. From where she parked Morgan could see there were no lights on inside the office, so the others either hadn't made it back or had and gone home. The station was deserted, and she liked it best this way when there were less people around. Less chance of having to make polite conversation with people who she wasn't remotely interested in talking to. As she walked up the stairs to the first floor office she wondered if everyone thought she was bad luck; a lot of people gave her a wide berth, though it didn't bother her in the least.

'Morgan.'

She looked up to see Marc standing at the top of the stairs, his coat on.

'Boss.'

'How did you get on?'

'Nothing really, he didn't see anyone hanging around or get the idea that there was something wrong. Seems like a nice enough guy.'

'Damn, I was hoping he might crumble and confess at your feet then we can put this to bed.'

Morgan nodded, weren't they all. She wanted to find Jasmine's killer more than anyone.

'Have you heard from the others yet?'

'No, I have to go home, Morgan, family stuff but my phone's on if you need anything.'

'Thanks.'

He ran down the stairs with a lot more energy than she'd used to walk up them.

Turning on the office lights her eyes fell straight to the place where the awful mask was propped on top of the filing cabinet.

'Christ.'

She jumped, completely forgetting all about it, and decided she was going to bin it, she had no use for it whatsoever, and whoever thought they were funny sending it could go and get lost.

Cain's deep voice echoed up the stairs as he walked up behind her.

'Amy is on her way back, how did you get on?'

'He seems okay, didn't see anything suspicious.'

'Yeah, but what was he like? Did he have weird staring, black eyes or admit to having a fetish for anything?'

'No, he was normal. He was shocked when I told him about

Jasmine, in fact he was quite upset about it. There was one thing that was interesting: he'd been and had his hair shaved off, which his aunt was surprised about, but I suppose we can't lock him up for getting a haircut. He also has an alibi: he was with a friend called Travis, playing pool at The Sun, in Kendal. I phoned and the landlord confirmed it.'

'No weird serial killer vibes then?'

'God, I hope not or none that I could detect. Did you speak to Judy, how is she?'

'Furious with you.'

'Why?'

'She said she wanted to die, she has nothing left to live for and she was absolutely mortified when I began to question her about her relationship with her daughter. She hasn't seen Jasmine's phone and said she never went anywhere without it. Then she told me to get out of her sight.'

Morgan couldn't stop the smile that broke out on her face.

'You can laugh but she's scary, and I felt bad anyway. The poor woman is going through hell and, come on, what would she gain from killing her daughter? It seems like they got on okay.'

'So, what did you do?'

'Got out of her sight like she told me to.'

Morgan let out a full-on belly laugh, so loud it echoed around the empty office, and Cain joined in. She flopped down onto her chair and composed herself.

'Sorry, it's not funny, is it?'

'No, but I forgive you.'

Amy walked in, took in the sight of the pair of them looking so joyously happy and asked, 'Who tickled your fancy?'

This set Morgan off into a fit of even more laughter, so loud that even Amy cracked a smile. When she finally stopped herself, she whispered, 'Sorry.' Then coughed for a bit. 'Ben was commenting on my turns of phrase earlier and you just came out with that classic, it must be a CID thing.

'How did you get on with Mrs Barnard?'

Amy sat down at her desk. 'Where is Ben?'

'He's gone home a bit early.'

'Is he okay?'

'He's fine, he's taking Declan to the pub quiz, as he's a bit down, and we're still waiting on forensics to come back so there's not much to do at the moment.'

'Oh, that's good that he's helping a mate out. Do him good as well to not be here all hours.

'Morgan, you would love their house, it's a small mansion; but the wife is the double of Morticia Addams and just as strange. The entire downstairs is painted black with huge, cut-glass chandeliers; it's just your thing.'

'Really, I wish I'd seen it. Did you find out anything that gives us a reason to go back so I can have a nosy?'

'No, although she said you were welcome to pop in for a tour.'

'Haha, she was nice then?'

'I suppose she was. She claimed she didn't know Jasmine then changed her mind, so I couldn't figure out if she was lying or not. She vouched for him, said he was home by 5.15 then took his sons to the leisure centre and picked them up again. She actually said she wished she had something more incriminating to tell us, but she didn't.'

'She obviously thinks Neil is as much of a dick as I do then.'

Amy nodded. 'He's a bit strange. He called you and Jasmine "a girl".'

'He is weird and full of himself too, but if his alibi is confirmed we can't do much else. What about her though, could she have motive to kill Jasmine?'

'I don't think so, not unless she knew about Jasmine's crush on him. I didn't really get the impression she was a killer though, but I suppose we should maybe bear it in mind.'

Morgan stood up and ticked off that his wife had been spoken to and his alibi confirmed. Then she scrawled *Esme Barnard* underneath and *Intel checks to be carried out.*

'How did you get on, Cain?'

Morgan turned to Amy, grinning. 'That's what we were laughing at, he got scared of Judy and left because she told him to get out of her sight.'

Amy's mouth dropped open and then she began to laugh. 'Seriously, Cain, you were scared of her?'

'She was really mad, and I felt bad for her.'

'You're such a softie, I guess she still needs talking to, but it can wait until tomorrow. How did Ben get on with the CCTV enquiries?'

Morgan realised that he hadn't updated her or the board, which wasn't like him.

'I'm assuming he's waiting on them getting back to him.'

'So, what are we doing then, sitting and twiddling our thumbs or can we go home too?'

'I suppose we can go home, there's nothing we can do at this very moment, until we get the CCTV footage from the bus company or the shops surrounding the dental practice, and we have no viable suspect at the moment.'

Amy turned to Cain and high-fived him. The pair of them walked to the door and turned back.

'You should go home too, Morgan. What are you going to do, stare at the creepy mask all night?'

Morgan smiled. 'I am going home, not staring at the mask. I'll go soon as I've updated the case file on here and put all our actions on it, ready for Ben to read first thing.' She pointed to the computer.

Cain smiled at her. 'You're going to make a great boss one day, night, Morgan.'

Then they were gone and once more it was just her and that creepy mask that was really starting to freak her out. She scoured the intelligence systems for Esme Barnard, and nothing came up, not even a fixed penalty notice, so she was clean; still, she thought it might be worth checking out her alibi even if it was a dead end.

She stood up and grabbed hold of the mask, carrying it to the bin and dropping it inside. Whoever sent it had had their fun, enough was enough.

TWENTY

He knew this was going to be hard, and he'd prepped for it and done his homework like a good man should, but she was still going to cause him problems. She was so feisty there was no way she would go without a fight, though he wasn't so bothered about that part, it was making sure she didn't make a noise.

His fingers slipped into his pocket, and he felt the bottle containing the crushed up Rohypnol scored from a lad a friend had mentioned sold all the drugs money could buy. He'd rather not resort to this, but at least he was prepared if he had to. He knew where Ms Emily Wearing lived because she liked to talk about the time she helped a policewoman apprehend a killer in her own flat. All he'd had to do was google it and pages of newspaper reports had appeared with all the details from the incident a couple of years ago. Not to mention a whole ream of photographs of the house they both lived in, the grounds, street and even inside the building. That was when he'd seen the policewoman's face, and he'd known straight away what he was going to do. The pair of them had cheated death and defeated a killer once, and now he was going to show them that in reality they hadn't avoided it at all: they had just deferred it a little longer, exactly like that film *Final Destination*; he was the grim reaper, and it was going to be so much fun.

He loved the college; they had security but absolutely anyone could walk through the doors with a lanyard on and they didn't look twice. They didn't even look when a person didn't have one, and would wave them through or point them in the direction of the office.

There was a huge car park where he could wait around for hours doing nothing except people watch. He came here whenever he wanted, and no one batted an eye. His favourite was the art block, it reminded him of school, where he always liked messing around in art more than listening to lessons. He had an endless supply of art materials at his disposal, as long as he timed it right when the tutors were on a break.

He had visited earlier this morning and walked past the large art room where Ms Wearing was teaching, and a tiny jolt of electricity had run down his spine. She'd turned to look at him, giving him a small smile before turning around. He'd put his head down and left. He had to find a way to get to her a little more discreetly than here. It was too open, too many witnesses.

He left the building after only a short walk around it. How was he going to get to her? This was a problem; his only option was to visit her at home, but that had its fair share of problems too.

The killing was the easy part; it was the planning that went into it beforehand, to make sure it went smoothly, that was the difficult bit. He had done so much research before he even began because he wanted to be good at this, not just good but brilliant. He had borrowed all the books from the library, which weren't many on serial killers, then when he had finished reading what they had, he had started using the public computers, trawling the internet and reading so much stuff about them until it blew his brains.

Out of them all he found Ed Gein, the quiet man who had

inspired a legacy of horror books and films, including *The Texas Chain Saw Massacre* and *Silence of the Lambs*, the most inspirational. The thought of skinning his victims and using their skin to make masks made him feel physically sick, but he did love making masks and had no qualms about making masks of his victims' faces when they were close to death or even dead. He could capture the essence of their souls, the energy inside of the masks would immortalise them forever.

This interest in masks all stemmed from the history lesson in school where the substitute teacher had told them about the death mask made of Mary, Queen of Scots, and his interest in the subject had taken over everything including his morality and ability to see right from wrong.

All he cared about was making his own death masks, and he hadn't missed the connection between that detective, Morgan Brookes; her similarity to the death mask he'd been so consumed by as a ten-year-old child of Mary, Queen of Scots was uncanny. They both had red hair, small, pretty faces and he thought that Morgan was simply too beautiful not to make a mask from.

First though, he had to work out a viable way to gain access to Emily Wearing.

He had a lot of work to do, and he wasn't going to rush it for anyone.

TWENTY-ONE

Morgan drove from the station and felt all the pent-up stress and frustration begin to slide away. She could go to The Black Dog and see how the guys were getting on with the quiz, see if Declan made it and Ben kept his word, but instead she decided to go home. She rarely had the house to herself because she and Ben mainly worked similar shifts, and it would be nice to have a quick shower, put her pyjamas on, eat some leftover takeaway and lie reading on the sofa. Her current read was a Riley Sager book, *Home Before Dark*, about a haunted house. She was a sucker for a haunted house story. There was something so terrifyingly creepy about abandoned houses. She often wondered if Cindy was still stuck somewhere in Ben's house, because that was where she ended her life. She hoped not, it would be torturous having to watch Ben get on with his life with a new partner while she suffered in silence. She was almost tempted to go to the pub after cheering herself up with that thought about Ben's house being haunted, but she didn't; she drove home to a house that was brightly lit against the cold, winter sky.

Ben's car wasn't there, but Declan's was which made her feel all warm inside. She parked behind Declan's white Audi and got out, hoping Ben had ordered enough food to feed them all twice. Inside she reset the intruder alarm, a promise she'd made to Ben and kept when he had them installed that she must under no circumstances not arm it if she was home alone. The pair of them had witnessed and been through too much not to take precautions with their safety; and Ben had left the hall and kitchen lights on for her. She followed the aroma of food down to the kitchen and smiled to see the assortment of Chinese take-away containers that filled the worktop. Nodding in apprecia-tion she ran upstairs to have a shower.

Fresh pyjamas, make-up free and her hair wrapped in a towel, she began to pile her plate full of food. She sat at the table to eat, her book in one hand and her fork in the other, and she lost herself into a world of horror that had nothing to do with her.

Stuffed, she pushed her plate away and took herself into the lounge to continue reading, but now that she'd eaten and was full, she couldn't concentrate and her mind kept flicking to the image of Jasmine Armer sitting behind the wheel of her car, her eyes staring at something or someone she could never tell them about.

Why had she been left there by the lake? The killer must have known about her dad dying there six months earlier. It struck Morgan then, had her dad killed himself or had he been murdered? She wished Ben and Declan would hurry up so she could ask Declan if he remembered; then again, he was so bril-liant there was no way he would have missed it if there was anything remotely suspicious about Craig Armer's death. She picked up her laptop off the pine chest and opened it straight onto Google, so she could search what she could about him.

There wasn't much about his death: a few headlines about his body being found, then the inquest but nothing more. The *Cumbrian News* had surprisingly little to say about it, which made a change but wasn't very helpful for her, and the mention of Declan's name reassured her that there couldn't have been anything suspicious about it.

She logged into Instagram to search for Jasmine's account. It wasn't set to private which was great for Morgan, not so great for Jasmine. She scrolled through her posts and realised she must share them with Facebook, as they were the same, but there wasn't much on here. There were a few photos from what looked like the works' Christmas party, where everyone looked a little bit glassy eyed, their cheeks rosy. There was a photograph of Neil Barnard with his arm draped around Jasmine's shoulder, and she couldn't help but wonder if they had been much closer than he had revealed. What man wasn't going to be flattered by the attention of a much younger woman?

Morgan heard the key turn in the front door and slammed the laptop shut, not that she'd been doing anything Ben wouldn't have been doing, but she didn't want him to think about work if he'd had a nice couple of hours. She heard voices, Ben's, Declan's and was that, Theo's? She looked down at herself and suddenly felt self-conscious, wishing she'd got dressed again after her shower, instead of tugging on a pair of Hocus Pocus pyjamas. The men were loud, laughing and she wondered if she could slip upstairs before they noticed her. She stood up and grabbed her book off the sofa.

Ben stuck his head in the door. 'Any news?' She shook her head, and he smiled at her. 'I brought the guys back.'

'That's great, I think I'll go upstairs and read. Let you get on with it. I don't want to interrupt.' She was desperate to ask him about Craig Armer, but it didn't seem right. Especially after they'd been drinking. It would have to wait until the morning, even if it kept her awake all night.

'The hell you won't, you little minx.' Declan's head was leaning on Ben's shoulder.

'You arrange this and think you can slope off? Get in the kitchen for a glass of wine. Theo has promised to bless the bottle, and you don't want to miss this. Your own private holy communion might do you some good.'

Theo also peeked through the door and waved at her. 'Nice pyjamas, have you watched the new film? Best sequel I've ever seen; I can't stop singing the songs.'

Morgan gritted her teeth and smiled. She knew her cheeks were burning; she could feel the heat as it had rushed up her neck and face.

'It's amazing, I've watched it twice.'

He nodded in appreciation. 'Bette Midler though, isn't she just the best? I love her. I wish I could go and see her sometime.'

Declan began to laugh. 'Give her a ring, I'm sure she'll let you.'

All three of them ducked out of the living room, leaving her standing there wishing she could let them get on with it. Instead, she followed them down to Ben's large kitchen, where Declan was handing out plates and Ben was taking the lids off the containers of food.

'How was the quiz?'

Ben grinned at her; his eyes had a sparkle in them that meant he'd had a couple of drinks.

'Don't ask.'

'For the love of God, sorry Theo.' Theo waved his hand in her direction as he heaped beef chow mein onto his plate. 'Please tell me you didn't come last again.'

'Not last, we came a respectable seventh place,' said Declan.

'Out of how many teams?'

Ben shrugged, and Theo answered, 'Eight.'

Morgan began to laugh. 'Hopeless, all of you.'

They nodded in agreement, not turning around to face her because they were too busy filling up their plates. Morgan picked her phone up off the table and snapped a quick photo of them all with their backs to her, memories were precious. At the end of the day, you could have millions of pounds in the bank, but it meant nothing if you had no special memories in your heart. She realised that Declan must have taken a liking to Theo, or he wouldn't be here, sharing the food.

She sat down at the table and plucked a couple of prawn crackers out of the paper bag to nibble on while they took it in turns microwaving the food. When all of them were sitting around the table with a bottle of Ben's favourite red wine uncorked and poured into four glasses, Theo looked at them.

'Should we say grace?' And then burst into laughter. He pointed at Declan. 'Your face, honestly you look terrified. I'm joking. I'm not a priest twenty-four hours a day unless I have to be.'

Declan screwed up his face as he pushed a fork full of noodles into his mouth.

'I don't get it, aren't you always doing God's work? The priests back home in Ireland sleep in their dog collars.'

'Well, I don't. I'm not a Catholic though, so we are a little more relaxed. Anyway, enough talk about God. Thank you, Morgan, for inviting me to the quiz, even though you bailed out on us, and we still didn't win. I had a good time; I'm still having a good time and it's nice to have proper company for a change.'

Ben picked up his glass and raised it in the air. 'To Morgan, the absolute queen of my heart.'

Declan raised his and pretended to wipe a tear from the corner of his eye. 'Christ, will you listen to him the soppy sod. Can you not just get it over with and marry her, Ben? Theo could do the honours; I'll wear my best suit and we can all live happily ever after.'

Morgan downed her wine then stood up, leaned over and kissed Ben's cheek. 'You lot are getting on my nerves; I'm going to bed. Behave yourselves, if that's at all possible.'

She left them to it, closing the kitchen door behind her so it muffled the sound of their loud voices. Her cheeks were burning, did Ben want to marry her? She hadn't really thought about that, marriage had never been on her list of life goals if she was honest. Then again, she hadn't expected to fall head over heels in love with her boss either. She was going to struggle to switch off tonight, unlike Ben and Declan. If she could she'd bring in Neil Barnard for questioning right now, and ask him if he knew Craig Armer, and if he had a reason to kill him and his daughter.

TWENTY-TWO

Emily Wearing had promised her friend, Tara, she'd go to the gym with her and had complained about it ever since. She loved the gym and was fitter than most of her friends, but tonight she had wanted to go to the pub and get drunk with Esme, who didn't like the gym quite as much, she preferred yoga and running much to Tara's distaste.

So, Emily'd ducked out of the spin class after ten minutes and ditched Tara for the pub, but as she walked in and saw it was the pub quiz, she wished she'd stayed at the gym. Life was full of complications, especially when she recognised Ben Matthews sitting at a table with two friends. Her heart had done that double beat thing when you see someone you really like. It made her sad that their relationship hadn't gone any further than it had. He had been fighting his attraction to her neighbour, Morgan, who he worked with. She could see they had both been fighting it and hadn't been surprised when he'd called it off with her, but she had never really got over him. He was the one that had got away. He was older, funny, kind, handsome in that rugged way that comes with age.

Before she could turn and walk out of the pub, her friend,

Esme, had spotted her and waved her over, raising an empty wine glass in one hand and a wine bottle in the other. Emily smiled at Esme and waved back, skirting around the edge of the pub, to avoid having to speak to Ben, but he'd stood up just as she was walking past and smiled at her, which had made her heart hurt a lot more than it should have.

'Emily, how are you?'

She smiled back, trying to mask the look of sadness on her face. 'I'm good, how are you?'

'Failing miserably at this quiz.' He laughed, and she realised how much she'd missed his deep, throaty laugh. 'You're looking really well; do you want to join us?'

'I can't, my friend is over there with a bottle of wine, and I don't want to let her drink it all herself. You look great, Ben, how's Morgan?'

'She's doing okay, busy as always but you know Morgan.'

Emily nodded, she did and if she hadn't liked her so much, she would have done her damn best to flirt with Ben and drag him back to her apartment for old times' sake.

'That's good, tell her I said hi and we need a catch up, coffee or something, it's been too long.'

'I'll tell her, take care, Emily.'

She nodded and walked to the table, where Esme was rolling her eyes at her.

'Is that the copper you were head over heels with? He's lost weight and looks decent.'

She tried not to look his way. 'Yep, and yes, he does.'

'Are you losing your touch, Emily? I thought you had men throwing themselves at your feet?'

'Not lately I haven't, and stop staring at him, he'll know we're talking about him.'

'Well don't you want him to know you still have the hots for him?'

'Absolutely not, he's in a relationship and very happy. I'm a lot of things, but I'm not that. I won't get in the way of his happiness.'

Esme laughed. 'We'll see how you feel after a couple of glasses of wine. I bet you won't give a stuff about his girlfriend.' She winked at her, and Emily shook her head.

'Pour the wine and shut up.'

Esme laughed even louder, filling her glass to the top.

Emily took a huge mouthful and waited for it to warm her insides and loosen her up.

* * *

After two bottles of wine, the quiz finished to a lot of cheering and jeering. Out of the corner of her eye she saw Ben and his two friends stand up, and she turned to look at him and he waved at her then walked out of her life again.

'Why are all the nice men taken?'

'Not all of them are, you just have to look a bit deeper than Facebook dating.'

This set them both laughing.

Emily stood up. 'I have to go home; I have a lot to do tomorrow.'

Esme arched an eyebrow at her. 'Are you going to follow the handsome copper out and make a move after all?'

'No, I just need to go home and feel sorry for myself.'

'Your loss, I've just ordered another bottle and Jane is on her way.'

'Definitely time to go. You know I don't care for Jane, she's always bragging about everything.'

'Yeah, but she's sober so she can buy the next few bottles.'

Emily blew her a kiss. 'See you next week.' Then she walked out of the pub into the freezing cold air and realised she should have phoned a taxi first.

Ben must have already had a lift because he was nowhere to

be seen and, yes, she had come outside to see if he was still there. A couple of glasses of wine and her morals were not quite as intact as they were an hour ago.

She stumbled down the steps and pulled her phone out of her pocket, looking for a taxi number, when a voice spoke.

'Hiya, did you need a lift home?'

Emily looked up and saw a face she recognised. He sometimes walked past the art room where she taught.

'Hi, what are you doing here?'

He shrugged. 'Meeting some friends but I can give you a lift home if you want first. It's too cold to hang around waiting for a taxi.'

She shivered and her teeth began to chatter, as if to confirm his statement. 'That would be amazing, thank you.'

He pointed across the car park. 'Your chariot awaits.'

She laughed. 'Thanks, this is so kind of you.'

'Always ready to help a damsel in distress.'

Emily followed him to the car, wondering if she was a damsel in distress or just a desperate woman, trying to take her mind off a man who would never love her the way she loved him.

TWENTY-THREE

Morgan's phone began to vibrate under her pillow, and she let out a low groan because no one ever phoned her this early in the morning unless it was work. Ben was out for the count next to her, not snoring but his breathing was heavy and on the verge of it. She turned on her side and felt under the pillow for her phone, and she saw Marc's number flashing across the screen which made her groan again.

'Hello,' she whispered so as not to wake Ben.

'Need you and Ben now. Where is he? Why isn't he answering his phone?'

'Asleep, and where do you need us?'

There was a slight pause and then she realised that his voice sounded panicked.

'Are you okay, boss?'

'No, I mean I'm okay but what I'm looking at is not okay. I'm at my place, your old apartment, and there's a dead woman staring back at me.'

She jumped out of bed, no longer whispering. 'Who is it?'

'The girl from upstairs, Christ, this is a mess. I got up to go for a run and found her like this.'

Morgan's heart was racing as she began to get dressed. She put him on speaker and shook Ben's shoulder to wake him up. He lay there staring into space and blinking as Morgan began to pull on her Docs and lace them up.

'I'm on my way, boss.'

'Morgan, drive careful the roads will be icy.'

She hung up and stared at Ben. 'Have to go, they found a body at my old apartment.'

Ben sat up too quick and his face went white. 'The boss?'

'No, that was the boss. He found it, I'm going now. You might as well get dressed and bring Declan with you.'

She couldn't hang around for Ben to brush his teeth. She ran into the en suite, uncapped the mouthwash and chugged a capful of it, then spit it out. She didn't even brush her hair. As she ran down the stairs she grabbed her coat, car keys and pulled a black beanie onto her head. She never went to work with unbrushed hair and it not in a bun or ponytail, but her heart was racing so fast, and she felt sick.

She had to see for herself who the dead woman was, and as she defrosted the windscreen all she kept repeating was *please don't be Emily, please God not her*, over and over to herself.

Once she could see out of the windscreen she set off. The roads were coated in thick sheets of white ice and she couldn't drive fast if she wanted to. As she drove the familiar road to her old apartment her stomach was churning and there were so many questions spinning around inside of her head. She turned onto the quiet, semi-rural, treelined drive of Singleton Park Road, and heard sirens in the distance. That's good, he'd phoned it in. She had been worrying he hadn't and was waiting for her to get there, which wouldn't be good. In fact, it would have looked terrible, as if he was trying to hide something, and for a second she wondered if he had done something to Emily. She shook her head, there was no guarantee it was her friend and Marc wasn't a killer; he was a bit odd at times, but he was okay, wasn't he? She was convincing herself that he was when she turned into the drive and saw him standing at the entrance of the beautiful Georgian house which had been turned into three apartments that held nothing but terrible memories for her.

Emily's Mini Cooper was facing the house, and he was pointing at it then telling her to stop where she was. She did, stopping the car at the entrance, right bang in the middle of the driveway. She jumped out and walked as fast as she could towards the car. Her breath was caught in the back of her throat, and her heart was beating so fast she thought it might explode out of her chest like one of those aliens in the film with Sigourney Weaver.

She looked through the window and saw Emily in the driver's seat, her eyes open as she stared at the entrance to the flats. Not thinking about gloves or anything else, she yanked open the passenger door.

'Emily, Emily.'

She leaned in to gently shake her by the shoulder, but as her fingers touched her friend Morgan snatched them back, recoiling at how cold and solid her body was.

Then Marc was there, pulling her away.

'She's dead, Morgan, there's nothing you can do for her.'

She felt herself being dragged away from the car. Her legs had turned to jelly, and it was impossible to keep herself upright. As she reached the steps that led up to the front door, she felt them give way and she slowly sank to the floor. It was wet and cold, but she didn't care. She couldn't tear her eyes away from the car and Emily's dead eyes that were staring straight at her.

She knew she was crying, could feel the wetness of the tears as they rolled down her cheeks, and for once she didn't try to stop herself. How many times had Emily texted her to meet for coffee, to come see her for lunch, and how many times had Morgan made some kind of excuse because she couldn't face coming back here again and again, but Emily had never given up on her, had never stopped asking. Yet here she was, only there would be no more messages from Emily, and no more reasons to come visit the place where most of her nightmares stemmed from.

The police van screeched to a halt. Hitting the brakes the van skidded on a patch of black ice and almost rear-ended her knackered VW Golf, stopping millimetres away from it. Amber jumped out with Mads, who had been driving.

'Christ, Morgan, what a place to park your rust bucket. I nearly wiped it off the face of the earth.'

He realised she was on the floor in a heap and didn't say another word.

He turned to Marc. 'What's happening?'

Declan's Audi came into view, and he parked behind the van. Ben clambered out of the passenger seat and came running towards Morgan. She didn't want him to see this, to see Emily this way. The pair of them had dated for a little while and he would be devastated to see her body. He ran straight past the Mini, not giving it a second glance, until he was crouched down next to her.

'Morgan, talk to me.'

She couldn't find her voice. Her throat felt as if it was parched dry like she'd been in the desert for days with no water. She sucked in a deep breath, and he gently helped her up off the floor. She noticed he was avoiding looking at Emily's car, and she wondered if he knew, deep down inside of him, he knew that was where she was and that was why he wouldn't look at it.

It was Marc who began to talk. 'I came out to go for a run

and saw her sitting there like that, just staring at the house. I thought she might be ill or something, so I knocked on the window and could tell straight away when I was close up that she was dead. I rang 999 then I rang you, then Morgan.'

Ben looked at him. 'Tell who was dead?'

Marc pointed to the Mini. 'The woman from upstairs, Emily. I only know her to say hi to but it's definitely her.'

Ben slowly turned to face the car as the full force of the situation hit him.

Morgan wanted to say something, do something but the truth was she couldn't, she was in shock because it was so unexpected, so unfair.

Emily was larger than life, vibrant, fun, beautiful, she loved to read romantic comedies, watch romcoms, had been obsessed with Hugh Grant; her favourite film was *Notting Hill*. She was everything that Morgan wasn't, they were polar opposites of each other, but they had been friends because Emily had made Morgan be her friend. She hadn't taken no for an answer, and then she had made Ben be her boyfriend, even though at the time it had broken Morgan's heart. Emily lived for the moment and didn't believe in wasting time, if she wanted something she went for it and usually got it too. Morgan wished she could be more like Emily.

'No, no, this can't be right. She was there last night, at the pub with her friend, they shared a bottle or two of wine. She looked so happy, so—' Ben stopped, and she wondered if he was going to say *so beautiful* or *so alive*. He didn't finish his sentence as he stared at the body of the woman who had been forceful enough to make him have a relationship after Cindy's death, had helped him to move on and to start living again, and for that Morgan would always be grateful to her, because although at the time she had been devastated about them getting together, Emily had taught him it was okay to live again. If they had never had that brief relationship Morgan wouldn't be with him now.

Morgan was shocked that Emily had been alive mere hours ago.

Declan appeared, looking a little bit worse for wear. He was the only one of them suited and booted. He clapped his hands so loud the noise echoed around the drive like a gun shot.

'Everyone, I need you all to focus and get a grip. This is sad, this is terrible and I'm sorry for your loss, but we need to focus. If this turns out to be suspicious you are jeopardising the crime scene and we can't have that. Everyone step back, take a moment, go inside and have a cup of tea. I'm sure the boss or whoever lives here will brew up for you and let me do my job. Let the CSI come and do theirs, okay, I need you all to focus.'

Morgan nodded, and Ben stopped in his tracks, realising he wasn't wearing any overalls or gloves, and he turned around.

Marc spoke. 'Ben, Morgan, let's go into one of the other apartments and talk this through. Mads you can handle it for a while, can't you? Until Dr Donnelly is finished. Amber, you're on scene guard, no one else except CSI through this entrance gate.'

Both Amber and Mads nodded. Marc ushered her and Ben inside the entrance of the house and into Morgan's old apartment.

It was furnished a lot better than when she'd lived here, all she'd had was an oversized chair and her bookcase, stuffed full of books on serial killers. Marc had lots of tasteful art on the walls, a huge TV, corner sofa, and what looked like expensive antiques dotted around.

She was cold and shivering, Marc pointed to the sofa then ran ahead of her and threw a towel on the beige seat, so she didn't get it dirty. Once she was sitting down, he grabbed the throw off the other chair and wrapped it around her shoulders.

Seeing Des's body all that time ago had been awful, brutal and horrifying, but as much as she worked with Des most days, he hadn't been her friend. Emily was and this was far more shocking. Morgan had thought that the pair of them were inde-structible, especially after they fought and overcame a cold-blooded killer in Emily's apartment years ago. Now there was only Morgan left, and the reality was there once more, reminding her that death could come knocking at any time and take you away from this lifetime in the blink of an eye.

TWENTY-FOUR

Ben couldn't tear himself away from the huge picture window that looked directly onto the gardens and driveway to the house. Morgan couldn't tear her gaze away from him. A cold fear had lodged itself inside her heart that seeing Emily like this would set him back, and bring back all those memories of his wife's death.

Marc handed them both a large mug each. The aroma of fresh coffee smelled good, and Morgan sipped hers even though it was far too strong for her liking. Ben took his but didn't take a drink, he cupped it in his hands and kept on staring at the car and Emily's body.

'Can I get you guys anything?'

Morgan shook her head, and Ben carried on staring.

'I'm sorry, I know this is a shock to you both, but I'm not sure you're going to be able to work this.'

Ben turned to face him so fast Morgan worried he'd spray filter coffee all over the beige sofa and off-white carpet.

'I'm shocked and I'm sad, but I am working this, Marc, and you can't stop me. I spoke to Emily last night in the pub and she was happy. When I left, she was still there with her friend.'

'Ben, this is precisely why. Did anyone see you leave?'

Morgan wondered if Marc had a death wish, he was pushing Ben too far.

'Yes, as a matter of fact they did. I left with Declan and Father Theo, and they came back to my house and Declan stayed over. So, plenty of people saw me leave before Emily. Have you been and checked her apartment? Did anyone see her come home last night? Did you?'

'No, to all of those questions. I hardly know the girl. Why would I see her when she came home? I never heard her; I was probably in bed. I don't tend to keep an eye on what my neighbours get up to.'

'What about the video doorbell, did that capture anything?'

'That thing is a waste of time; it only works once a week when the Wi-Fi decides to work. It hasn't been on for days along with my broadband.'

Morgan stood up. 'Well, if neither me nor Ben can work this case then neither should you. If you're going down that route, we all have connections to Emily that could be misread. If that happens then you're going to have to wait for headquarters to send a couple of detectives to take over from us, because from what I heard South and West are even more short-staffed than us. You're going to waste precious time on the investigation, and we're going to be sitting around doing nothing when you know fine well that no one can work this case like we can.'

Marc's mouth was open. 'Are you trying to blackmail me into letting you work this case, Morgan?'

'Blackmail is a strong word, boss; I'm just pointing out the facts, and it doesn't look good that the DI let his neighbour get murdered right outside his front door.'

Ben was watching the exchange between Marc and Morgan with a look of shock on his already ashen face.

'We are sad, but we are professional, and you know that if anything. The fact that we both know Emily is going to make us work even harder, if that's possible, because we don't slack around anyway.'

'We don't know that this isn't a suicide.'

Morgan carefully placed the mug down on a side table and strode across to the window. She forced herself to stare at the car with her friend inside.

'Look at her. Jasmine Armer was found in her car staring out onto Thirlmere, the place where her father took his own life. Emily is staring at this apartment block, the place where she had to fight for her own life, to survive a serial killer almost two years ago. I don't think finding two women in the space of two days left like this is a coincidence, as much as I'd like it to be. I'd rather Emily decided she'd had enough and took enough pills to end it all, because the alternative is too awful to think about; but I know Emily and out of all the people I have ever met, she is the most unlikely to get so down that she would do this.'

A knock on the door and Declan's voice filled the hallway. 'Are we okay in here people?'

'Come in.'

He walked in and looked at the three of them, all of them standing there with their shoulders tensed, hands clenched and looks of desperation on their faces.

'Homicide, well I'm pretty sure it is. There are similar rope marks around her wrists and there are petechial haemorrhages inside her eyelids. It looks like the same manner of death as Jasmine Armer, but it's not a hundred per cent confirmed until the PM. You, my friends, have a much bigger problem than your egos.'

Morgan shook her head. 'I knew it. This is not about egos, it's about whether we are morally and ethically the right detectives to be investigating this case. We are just discussing it.'

Declan nodded. 'Not my judgement call to make, but if I was you, Marc, I'd be letting them get on with this and not wasting time, unless it becomes too difficult for them both emotionally.

'And by the way, I don't want either of you at the post-mortem. Amy and Cain will suffice, you are free to carry on with your investigations. I think you should be working this case because of the similarities, but I also don't want you watching the trauma of your friend on my table. I wouldn't wish that on anyone. I remember her from last night; she kept glancing over to our table and smiling.' He turned to walk away then stopped. 'By the way, remind me next time you invite me for a sleepover to politely decline. This is the worst wakeup call I've had in quite some time.'

He smiled at Morgan, and she smiled, but it didn't reach her eyes. She was in shock, denial and grieving for Emily. She wanted to catch the person who had done this more than she had wanted to find any other criminal. This felt personal, it felt as if whoever had done this had known that Morgan and Ben would be first on scene because of the small team that worked Rydal Falls, the small towns and villages surrounding it.

She turned to stare at Marc. 'Are we on the case or not?'

His face was a mask of misery, but he nodded. 'Yes, if you want to be or at least until someone gets wind of this and removes you both. Ben, I understand if you don't want to work it.'

Morgan felt as if she'd been sucker punched in the gut. She hadn't considered that he wouldn't want to work it while she'd been arguing with Marc, and she felt awful.

Ben was staring out of the window at Emily's car. He didn't turn around, but he whispered, 'Yes, boss. I'm good. I want to work it.'

She released the pent-up breath she'd been holding and walked towards the front door.

'I'll go check her apartment.'

.   .   .

Morgan went outside first, to get suited and booted, before going upstairs. She couldn't afford to jeopardise any possible evidence. She was back in the game. As she passed by the car, she blew a silent kiss and made a promise to Emily: *I'll find the bastard who did this, I promise.*

Declan was at the rear of his 4x4, removing his overalls, and he waved her over.

'For what it's worth I'm sorry.'

She smiled at him. 'Thank you, she was my friend, but I was a crap friend in return. I suppose I'm going to have to live with that now. Every time she invited me for coffee, I'd make an excuse, all because she'd slept with Ben a few times before we got together, and I struggled with it.'

'Did she know how you felt about him?'

'Probably not, I don't know; I might have mentioned it in passing.'

'Then she wasn't a very good friend, was she? If she knew how much you liked him and still swooped in to steal him from underneath your feet. If I was you, I wouldn't be feeling too bad about not meeting her for coffee, Morgan. You are a very busy woman, you risk your life, several lives to be exact, saving victims from dangerous killers. You hunt the sick bastards down and make the world a safer place. You have no guilt here, just sadness at a life so young taken away in its prime. I want you to remember that you're not a bad person; in fact if the Church still celebrated living saints I'd nominate you right now.'

He stepped towards her and wrapped his arms around her, and she melted into them glad of the warmth and the comfort, plus he always smelled so good. He let her be the one to pull away first.

'Thank you, Declan.'

'For what, the advice or the hug? which I apologise for. If I'm a bit whiffy I only had time to clean my teeth before rushing out.'

'Both, and you smell divine, you always do.'

'I mean it, Morgan, no guilt or shame, grief yes, sadness, yes, but do not try and blame yourself for any of this, and tell Ben the same from me. I'll tell him myself anyway, but the pair of you have nothing to be guilty about. Out of all of the seven sins, guilt is the one that I would say ruins more lives than anything. Now get yourself suited and booted and treat this like another day in the office. It's the most fitting thing you can do for Emily now. Turn on those bad-guy-seeking-out super powers and put a stop to this bastard before he kills anyone else. This is what you do, and no one does it better.'

He smiled at her, and she managed a half smile back, feeling a whole lot better about herself.

'Yes, boss.'

'Ahh, imagine if I were your boss. I'd be as bald as Benno, the stress you cause and don't tell me he isn't losing his hair, because why else would he shave his head in winter?'

'Declan, you have a shaved head too, the pair of you are like unidentical twins.'

'Ha, but mine is a fashion statement. I'm pretty sure his is because you're making him go bald.'

She stared at him then began to laugh. 'He'll kill you if he hears you talking about him like that.'

'I know, got to keep the man on his toes now, haven't I? Don't forget to make sure it's Cain and Amy who come to the post-mortem, because if you two turn up, as much as I love you both, I can promise you that I won't let either of you in. I have to draw the line somewhere and that's as good a place as any.'

'I will, take care, Declan. You can have my key if you want to go back for breakfast and a hot shower.'

'No thank you, I have a breakfast date with a hot priest thanks to you.'

He got in his car, leaving her standing open-mouthed as it sank in: he was going to meet Theo for breakfast. She smiled at him as he waved, and this time it did reach her eyes, because she loved Declan as if he was an older brother and she wanted him to be happy, and the thought of it made her happy. Then he was reversing, and she finished slipping the blue plastic bootees onto her feet, and she wondered if she would make it to the house and up the front steps without breaking her neck on the ice and adding to the body count.

TWENTY-FIVE

Ben walked towards Morgan, and she pulled out a plastic packet with a crime-scene suit in, then handed it to him.

'We can do this.'

'We can, I'm sorry, Ben, I know how hard this must be.'

He held his hand up. 'No, Morgan, let's not do this bit. If we want to focus, we need to push the fact that we both knew her to one side and treat this like we would if it were anyone else that we didn't know.'

She nodded. 'Okay.' Then walked off towards the house, head down, making sure she didn't slip on the frozen ground and fall over. She left Ben getting dressed. She knew he wasn't being horrible on purpose, but it still stung.

Tugging on a second pair of purple nitrile gloves, she began the walk upstairs, a little bit scared and nervous of what she was about to find up in Emily's apartment. She tried not to think about the time a killer had hung her from these railings; she tried not to think about her brother Taylor, who had also been a killer and had chased her here, into Emily's apartment, to try and kill her. She stood for a moment, inhaled a deep breath and pushed all of her bad memories to one side to clear her mind.

This isn't about you, it's about Emily. Focus. It was difficult to do that though, when this place brought them all flooding back. Thank God Ben had begged her to move out of here and move in with him. Living here would probably have tipped her over the edge with this, and she wondered if not for the first time if this house or the grounds had bad energy attached to it like in all those horror movies she'd watched as a teenager. Her aunt Ettie believed that ground could be tainted, so maybe this house was built where it shouldn't have been. Emily lived in the top floor apartment, and she wondered who occupied the middle. She knocked on the door, wondering what sort of person was able to block out all of the police activity happening on their own doorstep, there weren't many. There was no answer, and no sound of life inside. Maybe it was empty, she'd have to ask Marc, although he knew very little about anyone except himself.

When she reached the top step and could see the little hallway that led to Emily's front door she paused and looked around. The door was ajar, there was nothing else out here, no shoes or a discarded umbrella. There were no signs of blood, scuff marks, nothing that screamed a body was dragged out of here. She wondered if she should be letting Claire photograph this first, but she was busy enough with the crime scene, and she knew the score, just a quick look. She wouldn't touch anything, she just needed to take a peek inside and check it out.

She heard Marc's voice below her; he was on the phone but she could only hear his side of the conversation.

'No, don't travel down today something bad has happened and you won't be able to get into the apartment.'

A slight pause. 'I'm not lying, for God's sake if I didn't want you to come, I'd say don't come. I'd have no reason to make something so awful up to keep you away.'

Morgan zoned out his smooth if not angry voice, then stepped onto the landing area and kept to the left not touching any of the banisters in case the killer had leaned on it at some point and left them some nice juicy prints. She studied the front door, no smears of anything, no obvious prints. Emily was on top of her cleaning; she was a little more obsessive about it than Morgan could ever be. She kept Ben's house hoovered, they both did, but they didn't dust religiously or bleach everything in sight, because they were too busy working to care about such matters. When she'd first moved in Ben had said the dust gave the place character and she knew then he wasn't a cleaning freak, which had suited her fine. Morgan would rather curl up with a book on her precious days off than spend hours scrubbing.

Using the tip of her finger she pushed the door open and sniffed. It didn't smell of anything bad; the scent of cinnamon, orange and mulled wine lingered in the air, and she noticed the plug-in air freshener near to the front door. One of those Christmassy ones to put you in the mood for winter nights and sparkling fairy lights. The hallway looked like it always did: the small table with a vase of flowers and a miniature Christmas tree was the only thing in it. Emily kept all of her workout stuff, outside coats and shoes, tucked neatly away in the cupboard by the door.

Morgan carried on walking until the narrow hallway opened into the open-plan lounge, kitchen area which showed no signs of a struggle. There was an open bottle of wine and a glass on the coffee table, and there was another glass that had been rinsed out and turned upside down to drain next to the sink. Proof someone was here and that someone had the thought to wash the glass they'd drunk out of; hopefully, there was still something left behind on it. Some traces of DNA would be like hitting all six numbers on the lottery jackpot, but you never knew, it did happen occasionally. She would make sure Claire bagged it up for forensics.

This room was so Emily: bright, very pink with lots of silk

flowers, there was a yoga mat on the floor in front of the same huge picture window that was in her old flat downstairs. She could see Emily in her yoga pants and crop top, standing there doing her sun salutations. It hurt, the sudden pain inside of her chest, but she kept on going. For a moment she imagined Emily carrying on with her routine, going about her daily life, and as Morgan walked towards the bedroom, Emily nodded and gave her a huge smile.

Then she blinked and Emily disappeared, but it left Morgan wondering if this was what actually happened when you died; your body stopped breathing, but your soul carried on doing what it loved. A hot tear fell down her cheek and she brushed it away with the sleeve of her white suit, which was as much use as trying to dry yourself with a brand-new towel that hadn't been through the washing machine yet.

As she pushed the bedroom door handle and opened the door to step through, her mind came back into focus at the mess. She didn't go any further inside; she knew that ordinarily the bedroom was as clean if not tidier than the rest of the apartment. This was chaos, the bed covers were strewn all over in a big mound, a lamp had been knocked to the floor, the bulb smashed, and pieces of glass were strewn around it. There was a broken vase too, and Emily would not leave such a mess unless she'd had a breakdown and then gone on to take her own life. That wasn't what had happened though, Declan had said homicide. Why had someone wanted to kill Emily? Why did anyone ever want to kill another living, breathing soul just for pleasure? She would never understand that as much as she might try, and she did try. She backed away from the open bedroom door straight into Ben and screeched.

'Jesus, Ben, why did you creep up on me?'

He had caught her shoulders with his hands. 'Sorry, I thought you heard me come in.'

'Lost in my thoughts. It looks like the bedroom is the primary crime scene.'

She watched his face, he was the one who had probably spent more time in there than anyone. He had a stony expression and nodded as he walked closer. She knew he was trying to look impassive, and she wanted to shout *It's okay you can cry and scream, I get it and I know that was before us. I'm okay with that*. She didn't, instead she whispered, 'I'll let Claire know, she's going to have to get the crime-scene manager anyway, to come and deal with this.'

She left him standing where she had been moments ago, staring into Emily's muted pink and cream bedroom, wondering what horrors she had suffered in there.

TWENTY-SIX

They went back to the station for a briefing, leaving a miffed Amber on scene guard until the PCSOs could take over. Inside the office Amy and Cain were waiting for them, both of them subdued which made a change.

As they walked in Cain stood up. 'Coffee?'

Morgan smiled at him. 'Yes, please.'

Ben nodded then walked into his office, closing the door behind him.

Amy looked his way then turned to Morgan. 'Is he okay?'

'As okay as anyone can be, I suppose, in this kind of situation, it's a difficult one.'

'Are you?'

Morgan thought about it. 'Not really, I was a crap friend to her and avoided her invites for coffee, and now I feel terrible.'

Cain left them to it.

'Is that the one who Ben was seeing for a while?'

'Yes.'

'Did she know how you felt about him?'

'Maybe, she didn't deserve this.'

'Nobody deserves this, I'm saying don't go beating yourself

up feeling guilty about not meeting her. You are busy and this is not your fault, okay?' Amy was the second person to tell her this and yet she still felt bad.

'Thanks, I'm worried about Ben.'

'He's had a shock, but he'll be okay. Should I go tell him he has nothing to feel bad about too? What are you two like, we live in a small town, and everybody knows everyone's business, it drives me insane. You can't have a decent argument with your boyfriend without everyone hearing about it.'

Morgan stared into his office; he was on the phone.

'No, you better not go in.'

'Well, you can give it to him straight later when you're alone. He still wears the guilt he feels about Cindy like some kind of battle scar, he doesn't need this as well.'

She hadn't realised Amy was so perceptive. 'I will.'

'Good.'

Cain came back in with two mugs and handed one to her.

'Have you watched *Happy Valley*?'

Morgan shook her head.

'Well, you should, gives us a run for our money. Sarah Lancashire is brilliant, reminds me of you, Amy, all straight-talking and doesn't suffer fools.'

'Really, I suffer you lot. It's on my list of things to watch when I get the time.'

Morgan sipped at the coffee, it was bitter and hot but exactly what she needed to clear her head.

Cain knocked on Ben's door and handed the other one to him and came back out.

'So, what's the crack? Is it the same killer? I read the incident log and it said the boss found her dead in her car outside their apartments. I bet he had a heart attack, I mean his neighbour was killed on his watch and he didn't know a thing about it.'

None of them heard the door open or saw Marc standing there until he spoke.

'I did, you are right, Cain, and yes I feel dreadful, wouldn't you, if it happened to you?'

Cain's cheeks turned an angry red, and Amy had to hide the smile that was threatening to erupt.

'Sorry, boss, I didn't mean to offend you.'

'None taken, everything you said is true.'

Marc walked towards Ben's office, knocked and walked inside, leaving all three of them staring at each other.

Amy whispered, 'Cain, you're an idiot.'

'I am.'

Morgan smiled. 'But we love you anyway, even if you do put those size 14s in it more often than not.'

'Should I make him a brew, do you think, a bit of a peace offering?'

'You better do something if you don't want him on the war path all day.'

Cain hurried out to the kitchen area, and Amy whispered, 'Never a dull moment with him, he's so funny.'

Marc walked out of the office followed by Ben, who had a thick file under one arm.

'Blue room in five, please, folks.'

They both nodded, Cain met them at the door, and he passed the mug of coffee to Marc.

'There you go, boss.'

'Thanks, just to give you advance warning, I'm going to need you and Amy to attend the post-mortem later on, once the body has been moved.'

Then Ben and Marc were gone, leaving them alone, Cain's mouth open.

'I thought that was your job, Morgan, you and Ben are the dead people liaison officers?'

Amy stood up. 'Cain, for Christ's sake how can they go? They both had relationships with her. It would be awful.'

'Sorry, sorry, Morgan. I'm being an insensitive pig and very selfish. I'm just not good at the old bone saw thing when it starts to whir.' His face paled just talking about it.

'Honestly, Cain, you can scrap with the best of them and don't mind cuts and bruises, but you can't hack a post-mortem?'

'It's different when the person is dead.'

'What, could you handle it if the person was alive when they started to saw off their skull cap?'

'No, don't be stupid, Amy. I mean it's okay fighting a living breathing person, dead people are too dead.'

'Somebody help me, the man is an idiot.'

Morgan smiled at him.

'Hey, Morgan, we also have another missing person case that I think you can help with.'

'No.'

'Oh yes, at approximately 07.54 hours this morning I reported Barb as a MISPER and I'm worried about her, what did you do with her?'

'Cain, you are an arse, I thought you meant an actual person. That creepy mask is in the bin where it belongs, and whoever sent it can go suck eggs.'

He stood up. 'Noo, you can't throw her away like a piece of rubbish, she's cool.' He rushed towards the bin and looked into the empty container. Then disappeared out of the door in search of the cleaner, to go get Barb back.

Amy was shaking her head. 'Come back, Des, all is forgiven.'

A sharp pain shot through Morgan's chest at the mention of Des's name. She would forever associate his death with her guilty conscience. Maybe she needed to see her aunt Ettie as well as Ben, and get something to help her with this guilt complex she seemed to have.

'I'm going to the blue room.'

She left the office, better to go get a seat for the briefing than have to face Barb all over again, if Cain managed to get it back. She hated the creepy face. It looked as if they were dead. Who made a mask of someone asleep? There were no eye slits in it. Which made her think that if Cain was so attached to it, he was the one who sent it to her. She would get him back and find something equally weird to send to him when she got a moment to herself.

TWENTY-SEVEN

The briefing was long, and Morgan was glad when it was over. She couldn't tear her gaze away from the picture of Emily's face that Marc had enlarged onto the Smart Board. She was staring out of the front of her car straight at the front door to the shared house. She hadn't realised how hard she was gripping the sides of the chair she was on, until she tried to unclench her fingers. Ben had stated that the enquiries up to now regarding Jasmine's case were not very successful. There were no CCTV hits from the pub or hotel near to the lay-by, to show the killer walking away. There was nothing from the area of the dental surgery either; there had been nothing of forensic value found on the hiking trails down to the water and around it. Her phone was still missing and hadn't been located, despite a request to the phone company to ping it and see if they could triangulate the area it could be in and where it had last been used. Craig Armer's suicide report had been checked again, and there was nothing to suggest it was anything but that. It was a complete dead end.

Why leave Emily there? It had to have some significance to the killer or to Emily, just like Thirlmere was significant to

Jasmine. If that was the case then the killer knew both places meant something to his victims, how? And how cruel to make them endure that final horror.

Ben had tasked her to go to The Black Dog and speak to the landlord, Mike, get any CCTV if there was some. She could do that on her own; Amy and Cain were off to the mortuary; Ben was going back to the scene with Marc, to see how task force were getting on with the search of the grounds.

She was okay if she was busy, but when she wasn't that image of Emily's face filled her mind. It wouldn't be so bad if it was Emily full of life, but it wasn't, it was as if she was wearing a death mask like the one she had been sent.

She shuddered and pushed that thought to the back of her mind. She needed to concentrate on one job at a time, the pub, and then she wondered who was passing the death message. Had it been done already or was Ben going to do it with Marc? Had Ben even met Emily's parents? She didn't know a thing about them, where they lived or their relationship with their daughter. There was one thing she was glad of: she didn't have to do that awful task or attend the post-mortem.

The car park of The Black Dog only had one black pickup in it. She parked next to it and walked to the door, pushing it, expecting it to be open, but it wasn't. Morgan knocked loud and heard footsteps, then it opened, and she saw the landlord, Mike, smiling at her. She didn't know him very well, but she knew him, which counted for something.

'Afternoon, can I help you?'

She pulled her lanyard from around her neck. 'DC Morgan Brookes.'

'I'm joking, come in, I know who you are. You come here sometimes with that awful excuse of a quiz team.'

Morgan laughed. 'They're terrible, aren't they?'

He nodded. 'I actually thought they might have a chance last night. Ben had two new guys with him that looked intelligent.'

'They are very intelligent.'

He shrugged as he went back behind the bar. 'I suppose Ben didn't come last for a change. What's up anyway, can I get you a drink?'

Morgan stared at the wine fridge longingly.

'I take it you're not having a good day.'

'Lemonade would be great, please and no, it's been shocking up to now.'

'I'm sorry to hear that.' He poured her a lemonade and passed it to her.

'Do you know this woman?' She showed him the picture of Emily which she had. It was zoomed in to cut Morgan out. It was the only picture she had on her phone of them both. 'She's called Emily Wearing and she was here last night.'

He pulled the glasses down off the top of his head and squinted at it, then nodded.

'Yep, I know Emily, and she was here last night with, oh God what's she called? Esme, I think it was. They shared a couple of bottles of wine. Emily left first, and Esme was joined by another friend.'

'Did she speak to anyone apart from Esme?'

'Ben, she looked as if she was trying to avoid him, but it's not a big pub so it's pretty hard to do.'

'Why do you think she was trying to avoid him?'

'Oh, you know that look when you see someone and you're debating on whether to speak or not, she had that kind of look on her face.'

Morgan smiled. It would have been because of their complicated history, but it was interesting that Mike had picked up on that. 'Wow, you're good.'

'Been doing this far too long not to be able to read people.

They said a quick hello then she joined her friend, but she kept glancing back at him the whole time he was there, only he didn't notice because he was too busy being crap at the quiz and concentrating.'

He started to laugh. 'Anyway, I thought you and Ben were in a relationship. What's this about? Do you think he might be seeing her behind your back?'

Morgan realised that Mike was quite the gossip. She hoped they hadn't been seeing each other behind her back, although God knows when Ben would have time for that. She shook her head. 'No, they had a couple of dates a while back, before we got together. Emily was found dead this morning.'

Mike dropped the glass he was polishing onto the slate floor, and it exploded everywhere. She felt a sharp prick on her cheek and lifted a finger to prod it. As she held it up, she saw there was a fine film of blood on it.

'Oh shit, I'm sorry, your face is bleeding. Are you okay?'

She nodded.

He passed her a tissue and leaned in to take a closer look.

'There's a tiny piece of glass sticking out of your cheek, you might want to go to the hospital.'

She shook her head. 'I'm good.' Turning the camera on her phone so she could see her face, she turned her cheek to the side and carefully plucked out the slither of glass then dropped it in the ashtray.

He passed her some kitchen roll, and she held it to the cut for a few seconds.

'I'm so sorry, Morgan, I never in a million years expected that, it's such a shock.'

'I know, it's so sad, bless her. I can't believe it either.' She stopped for a moment to compose herself. 'And don't worry about my cheek, it was an accident. Do you know where Esme lives, so I can go and speak to her?'

'Fancy old house called Pine Trees or Pine Lodge something with Pine in it. I can't believe it; I mean she was here laughing and joking with Esme and now she's dead. What happened?'

Morgan scribbled down *Esme, Pine Trees, Lodge*.

'We think it's suspicious. Do you know of anyone who might have been hanging around who seemed a bit out of place? Did anyone pay Emily extra attention that kind of thing?'

'I was doing the quiz, hosting it; I wasn't really paying that much attention to be honest, apart from when she walked in because she interrupted my flow a bit.'

'Do you have any CCTV?' Morgan had her fingers crossed.

'Absolutely, do you want to watch it now? I can't download it for you – I'll have to get my son Mattie to do it – but I can replay it.'

She followed him to a small office next to the kitchen area, where there were a couple of monitors.

'I'll get you to the bit where the quiz starts, but I'm waiting on a delivery from the brewery so I might have to leave you.'

'That's great, thank you.'

He nodded and began to input the date and time into the computer.

'Just use the mouse; if you want to rewind, pause or anything else the buttons are on the screen. I can't believe Emily is dead, it's not right.'

'I know, she was my friend too. I can't believe it either.'

A loud bang on the front door jolted them both.

'Delivery, can you manage?'

She nodded. 'Yes, thanks.'

He left her to it, and she felt glad, because she wasn't sure how it would feel watching Emily and Ben's interaction knowing she was dead now. Talk about surreal. She sipped the lemonade that Mike had brought in for her. There was a mirror on the wall, and she took a quick peek at the cut on her cheek. It was only a thin sliver of dried blood now, nothing compared to some of the injuries she'd sustained over the last couple of years, but it didn't half sting. How did the tiniest things hurt so much, like paper cuts?

Sucking in a deep breath she pressed play and watched in silence as the quiz commenced. Ben, Theo and Declan were on the table furthest away, but they were all leaning over the piece of paper with a look of pure concentration on their faces. What a handsome trio they made. The pub was filled with mainly men.

There were a couple of teams with women on them, but the majority of customers were male. She spied a woman on her own in the corner with a bottle of wine, sitting on her phone, and decided that she was Esme waiting for Emily. With a heavy heart she sped the recording up a little until she saw another woman walk through the door, when she paused it and whispered. *Oh, Emily.* Then she watched as she faltered when she looked in the direction of Ben's table. It only took moments, but it felt like forever as she watched Ben greet her. They exchanged a few words then she was next to Esme downing the wine her friend had poured her, as if it was a shot of tequila. Morgan sped the video up so everything was happening super-fast. She watched as the pub quiz concluded then Ben, Theo and Declan left. When they left Emily was still there with Esme, but she did get up herself a few minutes later and walk out the door. She rewound that bit, this time scanning the pub carefully to see if anyone followed her out, but no one did. Morgan sat back and let out the longest sigh then rewound it and watched it all again in case she missed something.

'Anything?'

Mike's voice startled her; she was hunched up staring at the screen.

'Unfortunately, not, what about outside cameras?'

'Some little arsehole smashed it; we only have the one on the door.'

'When did you notice it was broken?'

'When I came to work today, but it could have been like that awhile. I don't really have much reason to look at the CCTV, I only have it because of the licence conditions. I was checking the roof this morning on my way in and noticed it was smashed.'

'Can you check when it was last working for me?'

He came back inside the room and switched to the other camera that showed a view of outside. 'Oh, actually it happened last night; look, it was working until about nine and then it went offline.'

They watched the screen; it was dark outside and very blurry anyway with lots of shadows. Then it switched from a picture of the entrance to the pub to black-and-white snow. She looked down at her notepad, Emily left at just after ten. Ben and the others at 21.57 so the camera was already broken. Someone knew Emily was inside and that person must have followed her here, broke the camera and waited for her to come outside, then somehow lured her into their car or followed her home. Which meant that Ben, Theo and Declan could have walked straight past whoever it was.

She took out her phone, and Ben answered straight away.

'The killer was waiting at the pub for her to come outside; in fact you all probably walked past him. Did you see anyone?' Morgan asked, walking out of the pub and away from Mike.

'No, I didn't, definitely not. It was really cold; I'd have noticed someone hanging around in the car park. I've been thinking about it all morning.'

'What about someone sitting in a car then or a van?'

'No, Morgan,' Ben replied, getting annoyed.

'Come on, think, Ben, this could be the killer and you all probably walked right past him.'

'Morgan, don't you think I would have told you if I saw something suspicious when I left the pub?'

She let out a sigh. 'Sorry, it's just you were probably so close to whoever it was, and you know we could have nailed them if you could remember.'

'I know that. I feel bad enough as it is. Why don't you speak to Declan and Theo, they were with me too.'

'I will, where are you?'

'I've just watched Emily's body get bagged up and put in the back of a private ambulance.'

Morgan felt the enthusiasm drain away from her as if the plug had been pulled out. She had begun to get hopeful that they might have a lead and now they were back to square one.

'I'm sorry.'

'Got to go, speak soon.'

He hung up on her, and she stared at her phone, both of them were feeling this so hard it was making them grouchy with each other and she didn't like it.

She needed to find Esme, and also it might be worth speaking to Theo, as Declan clearly didn't remember much because he didn't say anything. They were probably going to have to track down everyone who was in the pub, too, but before she did that, she would check with Ben in case something more pressing came up.

TWENTY-EIGHT

Once Morgan was back inside her car, she rang Amy.

'Hey, can you look up Pine Trees or Pine Lodge for me on Quick Address, please.'

'Who lives there?'

'The woman who Emily was in the pub with last night. Esme.'

'I visited an Esmerelda Barnard at Pine Hall yesterday; she told me to call her Esme.'

Morgan felt the tiny hairs on the back of her neck prickle. 'Neil Barnard's wife?'

'That's the one; I told you about the house, it's the sort of place you'd love, all the Addams Family vibes.'

'Where is it?'

'You know the road between Ambleside and Rydal Falls, where you can turn off? I think it's called Under Loughrigg. It's about a mile along there on the right-hand side. Should you be going there on your own? She's married to the dentist who worked with Jasmine Armer.'

'I'll be fine, he should be at work anyway. What are the chances that Neil Barnard is connected to both victims?'

'Yeah, it's slim but so is his wife. She told me she didn't really know who Jasmine was, then changed her story when Neil said that he'd introduced them, so, you know, it could be her. Jealous wife killing his crushes sort of thing.'

'There's only one problem with that: she was in the pub until closing time. Emily left and ten minutes later another friend arrived who Esme continued drinking with. I do think we need to check where she was the night Jasmine was killed though, you just never know.'

'Maybe they're working as a team, the gruesome twosome.'

Morgan smiled. 'I hope not, but if you don't hear from me in an hour come looking for me.'

Amy laughed. 'Does Ben not want to go with you?'

'He's busy and I'm quite capable.'

'Your funeral, kid.'

Morgan frowned at the phone and ended the call; Amy's sense of humour was a little too dark at times.

She knew where Under Loughrigg was and began to drive in that direction. The church was the other way; Theo was her next stop after the Barnards' house.

She almost missed the turn off for Pine Hall, but saw it at the last moment. As she wove the car along the drive up to the house she wondered if the Barnards strung Christmas lights from all the pine trees. It would look so pretty. She found herself staring up at the house that had come into view in front of her and sighed; she was definitely in the wrong job, although she couldn't be a dentist for a million pounds a year, but did they really make enough to live in houses like this? It was huge, there was a Land Rover parked outside, and she hoped it belonged to Esme Barnard and not Neil. Getting out of the car she wondered if they had dogs; with this much land she'd have a couple.

The door opened before she could even get up the steps to knock, and the woman from the pub CCTV stood there. She looked as if she was ready to go out.

'Can I help you?'

'Detective Morgan Brookes, have you got a minute?'

Esme Barnard rolled her eyes at Morgan, which instantly annoyed her.

'Your friend was here yesterday. Have you come for a guided tour of the house? She said you would love it.'

She shook her head. 'No, I've come to speak to you about Emily Wearing.'

Esme had turned to walk back inside, and she snapped her head back towards Morgan.

'Why, is she in some kind of trouble?'

'You could say that.'

Morgan followed her inside; it was dark until Esme hit the light switches and the cut-glass chandeliers came to life, illuminating the hallway and stairs. Amy was right, Morgan did love it, but she wasn't going to tell Esme that; she had a right attitude – how had Amy thought she was okay?

Esme led her down to the kitchen, which was all black cabinets and walls with touches of gold, and Morgan did indeed find herself falling in love with the house. It wasn't as nice as the one on the TV that she had a mild obsession with. She'd caught *We Bought a Funeral Home* on the Discovery Plus Channel while searching for a serial killer documentary back in October, on her week off, and had been captivated by the wonderful Blumberg family, their amazing funeral home and Heather Blumberg's passion for design and all things Gothic. As she followed Esme into the kitchen, Morgan thought about how many death messages she had passed in people's kitchens, how many interviews; most people she dealt with instinctively led her to the kitchen, the heart of the home, where they could make you a drink or one for themselves, if they needed to.

'So, what has the silly bugger done now? Did she drive home after the pub and get done for drunk driving?'

'I'm afraid it's much worse than that.'

'Oh, okay what could be worse? Is she hurt?' She pointed to a black velvet bar stool at the huge kitchen island. 'Take a seat.'

Morgan did and wished she wasn't here doing this, but lately this was all her job seemed to consist of: dead bodies and death messages.

'Emily was found dead in her car early this morning.' She watched Esme; her face went through a whole range of emotions then settled on grief stricken as her eyes filled with tears and her lips parted slightly into the perfect O shape. 'I'm sorry for your loss,' she continued.

'Oh my, no way, absolutely not, she can't be dead.' Esme was standing next to the sink, the fingers gripping the handle of the kettle so tight the blood had left them.

'I wish that she wasn't, but she is.'

'But how? How is she dead when we were together last night?'

'It is suspicious, and we are currently investigating it.'

'Suspicious as in she was murdered?'

'Yes.'

'Oh fuck, oh no, you can't come here and tell me that when I already have a raging hangover. I mean come on, I was with her last night. We shared two bottles of wine before she left to chase after that copper who is twice her age and apparently shacked up with some bit of fluff young enough to be his daughter. I mean he's fit in a rugged way, so I can see the attraction, but I don't know why she didn't just let him go and move on with her life after he dumped her. I suppose he must have been the one. We all have them, don't we? That one partner who we fall head over heels in love with, but they don't love us back the same way.'

Esme slammed the kettle down onto the worktop.

Morgan had never felt so small or mortified in all her life. She wanted the ground to open up and swallow her whole. Was this how people saw her and Ben's relationship? She was his bit of fluff? She was horrified and found it hard to speak.

'Are you sure you have the right Emily?' Esme rooted in her Louis Vuitton handbag for her phone and pulled it out. Scrolling for Emily's number she pressed it, and they both heard Emily's bubbly voice say:

'Hi this is Emily, I'm a bit busy, I'll ring back, bye for now.'

Esme stared at Morgan. 'Emily ring me back right now, it's urgent.' She hung up, then dialled again, torturing them both with the same voicemail, listening to an Emily full of life on the other end.

'I am one hundred per cent sure it was Emily Wearing. I know her, have known her for a couple of years.' Morgan wasn't about to divulge that she was the bit of fluff that Ben was seeing, no matter what.

'Oh, what do I do now then? I've never been in this situation before. What does one do when their friend has been murdered?'

'I don't know. Can I ask you some questions?'

Esme nodded. 'I need a drink; do you want one? And don't tell me you're on duty because it must have been a terrible shock for you too, if you saw her and, you know...' She couldn't complete her sentence; Morgan shook her head.

'I'm okay, thank you.'

She watched as Esme took a bottle from the fridge and poured herself a large glass of gin, not bothering with the tonic. She raised her glass in Morgan's direction.

'Emily and my hair of the dog.'

She watched as the woman began to cough and splutter

from the neat gin, her face going from white to puce in seconds. When she finally managed to stop coughing, she laughed.

'Bleugh, I don't recommend that, tastes awful without an elderflower mixer.'

They stared at each other, Morgan trying to remember what the hell she was doing here, and suddenly she felt the crippling sensation of not being good enough wash over her, like it used to in the early days, when she started doing this job, or she should say when she was thrown in at the deep end. Hearing Esme describe her as a bit of fluff who was too young for Ben had knocked all her confidence and she wanted to get up and walk out. She didn't though; she forced herself to stay where she was and try to concentrate despite the pain in her head and her heart.

'Did you know you have a cut on your cheek, it's bleeding?'

'Yes, I do.'

'Okay, just checking, should I get you a plaster for it? I have a first aid box under the sink.'

Morgan shook her head. 'No, thanks, it will stop soon.'

'So, what happens next? Are you going to tell me how Emily died? Do I need to come and identify her body, or is that just what they make people do on the TV?'

'Myself and my sergeant, Ben Matthews, were able to positively identify Emily, so there is no need to put you through that.'

'Ben, the copper who she's been pining for saw her dead body?'

'Yes.'

'Poor guy, I wonder if he knew she was madly in love with him. Did she get to speak to him outside of the pub last night? Did he say anything? Is he a suspect? Maybe they had a disagreement and he strangled her.'

'I, erm, not that I know of. He'd left by the time Emily went outside, and his two friends can confirm this, so we are not looking at him in any way, shape or form as connected to this.'

Esme was staring at the glass of neat gin. 'Yeah, but you lot would say that, wouldn't you? Corrupt coppers and all that, look at all that terrible stuff going on in the Met. How did she die? She wasn't...'

The words *sexually assaulted* hung in the air between them.

'Not that we know of. The post-mortem is scheduled for later this afternoon, so we'll know more then. How did you and Emily become friends?'

'I've known her since college, she always wanted to be an art teacher. I hadn't seen her for a few years but then Hugo went to the sixth form, and she taught him. I saw her one day coming out when I was waiting to pick him up. We got talking and forgot about the years we hadn't spoken to each other; it was as if we'd never stopped. We made a conscious effort to have a weekly meet up after that, much to Hugo's embarrassment. I told him we never once discussed him; he wasn't interesting enough for a start.'

'Did he like Emily?'

'He thought she was okay, but he dropped out of college anyway, so it didn't matter. Teenage boys are hard work, especially when they don't know what they want to do with their lives, but he's a good boy. He's always been very kind to me, and step kids can be brutal. Tobias is a lot harder work; his attitude can be horrid at times.'

Morgan nodded sympathetically.

'How did the boys get on with Emily?'

'They adore her, once Hugo got over his embarrassment that was, and to stop you right there they had no desire to kill her, or any reason to either, so you can drop this line of questioning right now.'

'That's good, I wasn't suggesting anything. How about Neil, did he know Emily?'

'Of course, he did, she's my friend. She comes to the house.'

'How did they get on?'

'Like a house on fire. They both love red wine, which I think is just horrid, but they would sit and talk about the merits of whatever crap bottle Neil would uncork; it used to bore me stupid. Emily was good though, she would humour him when I wouldn't but that's the sort of person she is, or was, always putting others first, always taking care of their needs before her own.'

Morgan didn't recognise the woman Esme was describing. She had always thought that Emily was forward, didn't mince her words and always went after what she wanted instead of humouring people to be nice.

'Did Neil and Emily ever have any disagreements? Was he home last night?'

Esme stood up. 'For crying out loud, this is the second time one of you lot have come here to ask questions about my husband, and practically accuse him of murder. He is a lot of things, but he isn't violent. He doesn't beat me up; he doesn't like to kill women for thrills. He is a decent bloke who works his hardest to provide for his family.'

'I'm sorry, I didn't mean to upset you. I just have to ask these questions. This is a beautiful home; I'm seriously reconsidering my choice of career if it means I can live somewhere like this.' Morgan tried to defuse the situation.

Esme threw back her head and laughed. 'Ha! You think he earns enough to pay for this, not bloody likely. This is my home, has been in my family for generations. Neil doesn't support me or my lifestyle, he pays for himself and his sons. I support myself; now, are there any more insults you'd like to throw my way?'

Morgan tried to rephrase the question. 'Did Neil not want to go to the pub with you?'

'He doesn't like the pub; he prefers the golf club not that

he's any good at golf, but he thinks it's a better class of customer.'

'Was he there last night, at the golf club?'

'You are persistent, aren't you? No, he was home with the boys, as far as I know. He never left. He had no reason to go out until he picked me up just after eleven.'

Morgan stood up, pushed her notebook into her pocket and shook her head.

'I'm sorry, I didn't mean to upset you.'

Esme was chugging back the rest of the neat gin; she waved her hand at her.

'It's okay, not your fault, darling, I'm a bit of an emotional wreck. It's me who should apologise for shouting at you, but I'm not because I'm all sorts of angry and sad. Is there anything else you need? Because I'd like to be left alone to try and digest this terribly sad news.'

'No, thanks. I'll see myself out.'

She nodded at her and was unscrewing the cap on the gin bottle to refill her glass.

Morgan wanted to tell her not to drive but thought that she might actually drag her out of the house by her hair, so she didn't and hoped that the woman had the sense not to be so reckless.

TWENTY-NINE

Ettie Jackson knew that company was coming. She had known when she had woken before the crack of dawn. Whoever had said that nighttime was for sleep had never been a witch. People scoffed at her way of life, but they couldn't get enough of her teas and potions, or advice which she was happy to give. The teas were a splendid way of keeping up the life of luxury that she'd become accustomed to; in particular, the never-ending supply of M&S cakes and biscuits. She smiled to herself as she looked around her quaint cottage in the middle of the wood. People had always called her a witch, and this morning it had seemed true: she had dropped her butter knife when she was spreading the jam onto her toast earlier and muttered, *a man is calling, now who are you and what do you want?* Then she had set about making her latest batch of teas for the farmers' market in Kendal. When she saw movement out of the corner of her eye late in the afternoon, she stopped what she was doing and put the old, cast-iron kettle on to boil. A knock on the door signalled the arrival of her visitor, and she made her way to her lilac painted front door to open it.

'Well, this is a surprise. Is my niece here with you?' Ettie said.

Ben shook his head. He knew she was talking about Morgan. 'Can I come in?'

'That depends on whether you are going to arrest me again.' She winked at him, and he had the grace to look embarrassed.

'No, absolutely not. In fact, I'm here with an overdue apology, a long overdue apology and a request for some help.' She heard a loud caw and looked up to see her pet raven land on the windowsill outside the living room, a little too close to Ben who jumped. 'That bird is huge; does it peck or bite?' he asked.

'I know, he's got an impressive wingspan but he's a real softie. Come on inside and have a cup of tea. You can tell me how sorry you are, then tell me what I can do to help you.'

He smiled at her; she was grinning back.

'You look just like Morgan when you smile.'

'I do? That's a lovely compliment; you can have extra biscuits for that. I like the thought of my niece and I sharing the same beautiful features.'

She grinned at him, and he followed her into the cottage.

'Take a seat, I've already put the kettle on to boil.'

She busied herself in the kitchen with her back to him. When she brought the tray over with a plate of shortbread biscuits, pot of tea, jug of milk and two mugs, his eyes lit up.

'Hungry?'

'I didn't realise I was until I looked at those biscuits.'

'Help yourself, there are plenty more where they came from.' She didn't tell him they were from Marks & Spencer's, and she had another four packets in the cupboard.

'Ettie, about the arrest last year.'

She waved her hand at him. 'I'm jesting with you; I know you were only doing your job and besides it was Tom who came and got me the second time. It's done, all in the past and forgotten about. Tell me why you are here, does Morgan know?'

He shook his head.

'I thought not, otherwise she would be here with you.'

'I don't know what's wrong with me. I just feel so hopeless. There have been so many awful murders recently, and each one seems to take a piece of me with it. Today a friend was found dead in suspicious circumstances. I just wondered if you could help, give me something to perk me up a bit; and I wanted someone to talk to...'

'Have you told Morgan how you feel?' Ettie asked.

'No, I don't want to worry her, but I'm scared that it will get to her the same way. I feel so tired all the time and unless I have a stiff drink, I struggle to sleep all night. I lie there and see all the faces of the victims I couldn't save. It's like a slideshow of the dead running through my mind and, well, it's affecting me a lot more than I'd like it to. I don't want it to get in the way of my job because I love what I do, even if it means it tears my heart with each new case.'

'Well then, we don't want that getting out of control. Ben, have you talked to your doctor?' She moved to sit next to him and took hold of his hand.

'No, I haven't told anyone. Morgan swears by your Sleep Well tea, but I'm too scared to try it in case...'

'In case what? I poison you?' She laughed, patting his hand, and then stopped herself at the sight of his reaction.

'Sorry, that was very bad taste. I didn't mean that. Look, you sound to me like your job is getting too much for you. How is your heart after that scare? Morgan told me you collapsed outside of work, but that was a terrible business, losing a colleague that way.'

'It's good, I take tablets so it's all under control and, yes, there is the guilt about Des too, the memories are always there on the fringes ready to overpower me when I least expect it.'

'You're not at risk of a heart attack?'

'I hope not.'

'Well then I can mix you some tea but not for bedtime. I want you to take a cup first thing in the morning, to give you a kick-start to your day.'

She poured out two mugs of tea and passed him one, then held the plate of biscuits out towards him. 'You'll be doing me a favour if you eat these. I can't stop nibbling at them, I'm like some greedy field mouse.' He laughed at her, and she carried on. 'You are a good man, Ben; you work too hard, but you already know that. The world is lucky to have you in it, you're one of the good guys, and Morgan is happy with you. I love that you make her so happy because that girl deserves to be loved the way you love her.'

He smiled.

'So, if you can come back tomorrow, I'll have your tea ready. I haven't got any of that particular blend mixed, and I will need to dry out some herbs in the oven. If you can't come back, I would be more than happy to drop it off for you on my way to the farmers' market in Kendal tomorrow.'

'Ettie, that would be wonderful. I'd say I'll come back but it's kind of hard to slip away unnoticed, especially now there are two unsolved murders in as many days.'

'This place is cursed, I've been saying it for years. They built Rydal Falls on tainted ground.'

She stood up and went over to the old pine dresser that had rows of jars stacked on it. After rifling in the drawer, she came back with a black rock the size of matchbox, which looked like a chunk of glass, and passed it to him.

'Hold that in your right hand for a few minutes, now close your eyes.' He did as she told him, which surprised her. Lowering her voice, she whispered, 'Think of nothing but that stone, how good it feels wrapped in your fingers, how its warmth is protecting you. This piece of tourmaline belongs to you, it is your protector against all things that want to drain your energy, it will shield you from any psychic attacks and it will protect your aura so that it can re-energise itself. How does it feel?'

'My hand is tingling and getting really warm.'

'Good, that means we have programmed it correctly. Give it a few more squeezes then open your eyes.'

He did as she told him then looked at her in amazement. 'Wow, I felt that whatever it was, it was weird but in a good way. I feel a bit less stressed. What do I do with this?'

Ettie grinned at him. She loved it when someone opened their mind a little: spiritual enlightenment was good for the mind and the soul.

'Try to carry it with you, especially when you're at work. It will help to dispel negative energy. Anytime you feel over-whelmed with your job I want you to take a few minutes to hold it in your hand. Don't ask me how but it works, but if you trust the process, you will feel better in a couple of days. Especially once you start drinking the tea.'

She smiled to herself, watching him squeeze the stone and look down at the palm of his hand in wonder.

'Wow, you're good,' he said, already feeling better.

'I know, thank you. Is there anything that you're particu-larly allergic to? I don't want to give you my tea and kill you off in the process, the irony would be too much to bear.'

He laughed. 'Nothing, I'm good with most things. Will it taste horrid?'

'Not if you steep it in a pot with some honey and lemon; make sure you put it through a tea strainer though, or you'll be picking dried herbs out of your teeth all day.' She winked at him, and he finished his tea after eating most of the biscuits on the plate.

'I feel better already.'

'A problem shared is a problem halved. You really should think about telling Morgan how you feel though. She will understand, and she will know you've been here once she sees the jar of tea and the chunk of tourmaline.'

'I will, when I get the chance. We're so up to our neck in it we've hardly seen each other all day.'

She nodded. 'Please give her my love and tell her to come visit soon.'

Ben stood up and she escorted him to the door; Max was still sitting on the windowsill outside.

'Thank you, Ettie. I'm sorry, I didn't ask you how much this is and the tea?'

'Pft, go on with you, I don't want any payment of the sort, you are practically family. One day in the not too distant future I'm hoping to have an excuse to wear my best frock and Sunday hat.' She winked at him.

He smiled back.

'I don't think Morgan is the marrying kind, I don't want to tie her down.'

'Have you two ever discussed it?'

'No.'

'Well then how would you know what she wants? Unless you've developed a sixth sense and somehow, Ben Matthews, you don't strike me as that kind of man.'

He laughed and turned to walk away.

She went back inside and stared into the cup he'd been drinking out of, to check if there were any tealeaves that had escaped. She had a bad feeling that Ben might be in some kind of trouble, but she hadn't wanted to scare him to death. Maybe it was time for her to pay Morgan a visit and check on her. There was something dark looming on the horizon and she couldn't discern whether it was Morgan or Ben who was going to be on the receiving end of it.

THIRTY

Morgan drove away from Pine Hall more depressed than she knew she could feel. She hated the way that Esme had talked about her and Ben – she didn't like being referred to as his bit of fluff. Emily had to have told her friend about them, and it made her feel sad all over again. She had no idea that Emily had loved him so much. But it wasn't Morgan's fault that Ben hadn't felt the same way about her – he'd found her too overpowering. At the time, Ben had said he'd agreed to go out with Emily as a distraction. He was already madly in love with Morgan at the time.

Morgan found herself outside St Martha's. She hadn't even realised she was driving in that direction, which jolted her out of the funk she was in. She knocked on the vicarage door, desperately hoping that Theo was in.

The door opened and a grinning Theo greeted Morgan. He was dressed in black jeans, a black shirt and crisp white dog collar. He opened his arms and hugged her. Morgan fell into them and hugged him back. When she finally pulled away, he laughed.

'You look a little troubled, Morgan, what can I do for you?'

'Do I not look perpetually troubled to you, Theo?'

'Now you come to mention it.' He laughed again. 'No, you don't. You work too hard and are under what I can only imagine is immense pressure. What's up? Come inside for a coffee and tell your uncle Theo what's troubling you. Did you know that my listening skills are one of my better qualities? Just ask the many sinners that turn up to confession.'

'Are there many?' Morgan asked, lifting an eyebrow.

'No,' Theo replied.

'I thought not.'

She followed him inside; he led her straight to the kitchen, and she smiled to herself at the gaudy paper still covering the walls.

'Make yourself comfy, if you can.'

'Blimey, Theo, that wallpaper gets more offensive each time I look at it.'

'I know, it's proper vile, isn't it? I think I might make a start on getting it stripped this week.'

'Really? Has something made you change your mind about staying?'

'You know fine well; my, you are a crafty little minx, Detective Brookes.'

'Did you like Declan?'

'He is what I would call ideal man material. If I'm honest, if he asked me to marry him tomorrow, I'd probably say yes, just because he's so damn good-looking.'

Morgan laughed. 'You are so shallow; it's not about looks.'

'No, it's not and, yes, I am but boy does it help! Imagine waking up next to him each day. He's like some male model and just utter perfection.' He sighed, a long drawn-out sigh.

'When are you seeing him again?'

'We had breakfast this morning, and he hated the wallpaper as much as you by the way. We are going to go for supper this evening, if he gets finished in time. He told me that you rudely called him out to a crime scene early this morning.'

'I did, the whole investigation is a mess, Theo. Did you see the woman who Ben was talking to last night in the pub?'

'I did, they only had a brief exchange of words though, nothing more than pleasantries.'

'Did Declan tell you she was found dead this morning?'

He nodded. 'Terrible shame.'

'I wanted to ask you if you saw anyone suspicious last night in the pub, either paying her attention or just generally hanging around? I'm asking everyone who was in the pub that night. It's likely the last place she went before she died. And I've got reason to believe she may have been taken from the car park.'

'I didn't, we were focused on that quiz. It was so bloody hard. I didn't pay her much attention after she'd sat down, and I didn't see anyone odd.'

'How was Ben after he'd talked to her? Did he seem down, look wistful, sad?'

Theo arched an eyebrow. 'Is this official police questions, or are you asking for my opinion on Ben's demeanour for personal reasons?'

She shrugged.

'Morgan, if you ask me, he was relieved that she went and sat with her friend. He was friendly and polite towards her, but I got the impression he didn't want to be stuck with her, if you get my drift. Now, do you want to tell me what's going on because something is. You can't fool Theo, I have a direct hotline to the big man in the sky.'

Morgan smiled. She was relieved. 'You're funny, I never realised this before.'

'Why are you worried about Ben anyway?'

'It's been a long day...' Morgan sighed. Why did she ask? She wasn't even sure herself. 'I just talked to someone who referred to me as Ben's bit of fluff,' she admitted. 'Emily went out with him a few times and that's what she thought of me, apparently. I guess I'm feeling a bit sensitive about everything.'

He nodded. 'I get that. She is, or was, a very attractive woman. But by the way he let out a sigh of relief when she walked away – a really big one – I'd say she was not his cup of tea at all. In fact, I would go so far as to say that he much prefers tattooed, ginger Goth girls with a penchant for Doc Martens and an attitude. She wasn't his type and never would be.

'Any fool can see how he adores you, so I don't know why you're fretting. And as for being referred to as his bit of fluff, well there are a lot worse things to be called than that, trust me. I've been called far worse over the years, and it doesn't define who you are or your relationship.'

She laughed and felt a load lift off her shoulders. 'You're good, you should be a priest, has anyone ever told you that?'

'Funnily enough.' He winked at her and pointed to the dog collar. 'Thank you though.'

'What for?'

'Inviting me to the quiz. I do really think Declan is a nice guy and so is Ben when he's not stressed out with work.'

'You're welcome. We both love Declan; he's kind, funny and the most caring man I've ever known. He's so wonderful with his patients even though they can't hear him. Nobody makes me cry like he does when he talks to them. You know he always chooses a radio station to play in the background for a post-mortem, one that he thinks the patient would have liked to listen to while they were alive; he really is one of a kind.'

Theo swallowed. 'You're making me cry, Morgan, stop it.'

She laughed. 'He's also got a wicked sense of humour, much like yourself. Thank you for making me feel better.'

'That's my job, but you got the special treatment that I reserve for friends. I never mentioned the Lord has his reasons.'

Morgan's radio blared to life in her pocket, and she took it out. There hadn't been much chatter on it since the discovery of

Emily's body, and the initial flurry of the crime-scene investigation early this morning.

Theo's eyes opened wide.

'Ooh turn it up, please. I've always wanted to listen to a police radio, and you owe me big time.'

She shook her head but turned the volume up anyway, because it sounded as if there was a riot going on in the background, and someone had hit their red button which meant everything that was being said was transmitted over every single police radio on that channel, plus it kept vibrating. She caught the words *Windermere, New Smile urgent assistance, officer injured* and stood up.

'Got to go, sorry, Theo.'

Then she ran out to her car, wondering what the hell was happening at that dental surgery now. She wished she'd never heard of the place.

THIRTY-ONE

By the time Morgan arrived at New Smile there were two vans and a car with flashing lights strewn across the road in all directions. She parked the small white car a little more appropriately and jumped out. A call for urgent assistance meant that every available officer had to attend, and she had been available, plus she needed to know if this had any bearing on the investigation. She could hear lots of shouting and crashing noises from inside and wondered what on earth was going on. She noticed the Land Rover from Pine Hall had mounted the pavement and had been abandoned with the engine running.

Oh crap, Esme, she thought.

Two coppers were standing inside the entrance, and she squeezed past them.

'What's happening?'

'One of the dentists' wives has gone nuts apparently. She's locked herself in a room with her husband and one of his patients, and is making threats to kill him. She threw a chair out of the window, and it hit Phil on the side of the head. He's in the van bleeding. The nurse rang us.'

'Where are they?'

'In the staff room.'

'Who is upstairs?'

'Amber and Mads.'

She rolled her eyes, and the taller of the two, who she thought might be called Evan, smirked.

'Yeah, that's what we thought. By the time Amber has finished talking to them they'll both want to throw themselves out of the window.'

She ran up the stairs to the sound of Michael Bublé crooning 'It's Beginning to Look a Lot Like Christmas' through the speakers that were dotted around, looking for the room which might belong to Neil Barnard. It was easy to find because Mads was standing outside of it on his phone to Control, and Amber was trying to talk to Esme through the door. She glanced at Morgan and shrugged. Morgan, who had nothing to lose, knocked on the door.

'Esme, it's me, Morgan. I spoke to you earlier.'

'So, this is your fucking fault then, is it?' Neil's voice hissed through the door.

Mads cupped a hand over his phone. 'What did you say to her, Brookes?'

She glared at him. 'Esme, can I come in?'

Mads was shaking his head at her, but she knew she needed to see her face to face in order to calm her down.

'I'm coming in, I'm not armed or anything. It's just me okay.'

She pushed the door open and stepped inside the room. It looked as if it had been ransacked; the sterile instruments and the tray were strewn all over the floor and there was a cold breeze blowing through the broken window. Neil was cowering in the corner, and Esme was standing in front of him holding a lump hammer big enough to do serious damage.

The patient, who had been sitting in the chair too afraid to move, jumped up and ran towards Morgan as soon as she entered. Esme was distracted by Morgan's presence. The woman ran out of the door to where Mads and Amber were shut out on the other side.

'You don't want to hurt him, Esme, give me the hammer,' Morgan said, putting her hand out towards her.

Esme turned to stare at Morgan. 'Yes, I do. After you left my house I checked our CCTV footage. And do you know what?' Morgan shook her head. 'That sneaky, creepy little bastard left the house thirty minutes after I did, and guess what time he came back? Forty minutes after you said Emily left the pub.' She turned to Neil and raised the hammer in the air. 'Did you kill my friend, you pig?'

Neil ducked at the same time Morgan launched herself towards Esme. She hit the woman from behind, pushing her forwards towards Neil, and grabbed at her arm to get her to drop the hammer. The door burst open and Mads rushed in, followed by Amber who had her taser drawn.

Esme was a lot stronger than Morgan had anticipated. In their struggle over the hammer she managed to lash out with it. She aimed for Neil's cowering head, but swung too hard and it whooshed past him and connected with Morgan's instead. In one loud crunch, Morgan heard the crack as it hit her temple and the room lost focus. She lurched to one side and fell to her knees.

Mads ran at Esme while Morgan felt herself sliding to the floor. She heard Amber's voice in the distance warning Esme that she was red dotted and was about to be tasered, but it was fuzzy. It sounded like it was a long way, a really long way off.

She was vaguely aware of the metallic sound of the taser being deployed, and saw Esme jerking to the floor as she collapsed in a heap next to her and she passed out.

THIRTY-TWO

It was utter chaos inside the room by the time Ben arrived with Marc. When Ben had heard Morgan's voice on the radio, he'd known then that she was in trouble and had driven at speeds no Vauxhall Corsa should ever be driven at, to reach the surgery in Windermere. He ran straight in, taking the stairs two at a time, and looked through the open doorway, where Mads was bent over someone laid on the floor.

When he arrived, Amber was on her radio asking for an ambulance, the suspect had been tasered and there was an officer down. He saw the tip of a Doc Marten and felt bile rise up in his throat, afraid to see what state Morgan was in, but not able to walk away. He ran to where she was out cold on the floor. There was a bright red stream of blood running down the side of her face.

'Is she breathing?'

Mads nodded. 'Yes. I told her not to go in by the way, but she never bloody listens.'

Ben pressed two fingers to Morgan's neck to make sure she was breathing and felt her steady pulse.

'What's the ETA for the ambulance?' he asked.

Amber, who had Esme cuffed, but couldn't take her eyes off Morgan, whispered, 'Four minutes.'

Ben sat on the floor next to Morgan and softly cradled her head in his hands. He'd been short with her today, all because of his own messed-up feelings around Emily, and now she was hurt, and he hadn't been there to protect her.

Morgan let out a groan and he wanted to whoop with joy.

'Hey, how are you doing? Can you talk to me, Morgan?'

She blinked a couple of times and opened one eye.

'Headache.'

He smiled at her. 'Yes, I imagine it hurts a lot.'

'Sorry.'

He didn't care who was looking, he bent down and brushed his lips against her forehead.

'It's okay, I love the smell of blood on my clean suits.'

She smirked at him then tried to push herself up, not getting very far before she fell back into his arms.

'Bad idea.'

'Just lie there and wait a little while, I've got you. There's no rush to go anywhere.'

'There isn't?'

'No.'

Mads knelt next to Ben.

'The wife, even though she was going nuts, thinks her husband had something to do with the murder this morning. She checked their cameras, and he snuck out of the house after she went out and came back forty minutes after the victim left the pub last night.'

Ben turned to look at the dentist who was pale-faced staring down at his twitching wife on the floor, then turned back to Mads and said, 'Cuff him and bring him in.'

'Good stuff, I was going to anyway, just giving you the heads-up.'

Pounding footsteps as they ran up the stairs made Ben

breathe a sigh of relief, as the paramedics looked at the two casualties on the floor. He recognised one, a guy called Nick who had treated Morgan's injuries at various crime scenes. He dashed towards her and shook his head.

'Morgan Brookes, we have to stop meeting like this. I thought you were behaving yourself lately.'

She smiled at him, opening one eye. 'Nick.'

'The one and only. Wow that's a nasty head wound you have there. I bet you feel like you've been hit by a train. It's bleeding a lot too, but hopefully it looks a lot worse than it is. We'll get you patched up and taken to hospital. Did you lose consciousness?'

'I'm good, no hospital.'

Mads butted in. 'Yes, she did, she went down like a sack of shit and passed out.'

She glanced his way. 'Grass.'

Nick laughed. 'You, my friend, are busted. We're going to have to put the woman in the ambulance to get her checked out, but I'll get another travelling for you. How many fingers am I holding up?'

She clenched hold of his wrist. 'No ambulance, I'm fine.'

Ben shook his head. 'I'll bring her.'

'You sure?'

'Absolutely, she needs a scan or something, to check there's no permanent brain damage.'

'Let's get you sat up first and see how you are.'

They helped her to a sitting position, and she cupped a hand to her mouth. Neil, who was still looking on in horror, reached up for a cardboard bowl and passed it to Ben, who held it underneath her chin. She took it off him, holding it herself but wasn't sick.

Mads turned to Neil. 'We can do this two ways, it's up to you, but either way I need you to come to the station with me to answer some questions.'

He nodded. 'Don't cuff me, I haven't done anything, of course I'll come. What's going to happen to my wife?'

'She'll get checked over and then she'll also be brought to custody, where she will be charged with at the least grievous bodily harm on a police officer and criminal damage.'

'Christ, Esme, all you had to do was ask me where I was, and I could have bloody told you without resorting to all of this violence.'

Nick pressed a thick pad of gauze against Morgan's head, then began to wrap a bandage around it to keep it in place.

'Are you sure you don't want to ride in the ambulance, Morgan?'

'I'm sure, I feel okay now apart from the headache.'

'You still need to get examined. You were unconscious. That head of yours is rock hard, we know that after our previous run-ins, but you know it can only take so much, and you don't want to risk getting a blood clot or something then dropping dead because you don't like hospitals.'

She smiled at him. 'You should have been a night club comic.'

'So, I've been told.'

He turned to Ben. 'Make her go, please, just to be safe.'

'As her boss I am going to say that it's a done deal; you are in work's time, Brookes, and I can't have you bleeding all over my office. It's messy enough as it is without your bodily fluids all over the place.'

Ben grabbed one arm, Amber the other and they hauled her to her feet. She was fully conscious now. Her legs were a little unsteady, but she was able to walk with Ben's aid. He helped her along to where there was a tiny lift and helped her inside. When the doors closed, and it was just the two of them he wrapped his arms around her, holding her close.

'You scared the shit out of me.'

She held him, too, and the doors opened and Cain, who was standing outside with Amy, groaned.

'Put her down, Benno.'

Ben shook his head, but slowly released her. 'We're going to A&E, are you two going to the mortuary for the post-mortem? Mads is bringing in Neil Barnard for questioning.'

Amy looked at Morgan's head. 'Are you okay, Morgan?'

'Headache.'

'I bet. Yes, boss, we're on our way to the mortuary. Who's going to interview Barnard?'

'I will once I've got Morgan booked in at the hospital, and made sure she doesn't leave.'

Cain smiled at him. 'Good luck with that one, rather you than me, boss.'

Ben ushered Morgan out past the staff who were all watching, wide-eyed, from the staff room doorway. This respectable dental practice had now just been thrown into chaos. Ben helped Morgan into the passenger side of the car, and leaned over to strap her seat belt on.

'What happened to your cheek? How did you cut that?'

'Smashed glass in the pub, a piece hit my cheek.'

'You're not having a good day, are you?'

She didn't answer him, and he closed the door and stared up at the sky, thanking God or whoever had been watching over her, then he got in and drove her to the hospital before she could make too much fuss about it.

Once Ben had checked her in at the desk, they had taken her straight through into the cubicles and let him go with her for a few minutes. He watched as the nurse took her observations.

'They're pretty good considering, I'll go get you something for the headache. The doctor will be here soon and then he'll send you down for a CT scan just to be sure. You won't be here too long; you picked a good time to arrive. It's not been too hectic today.'

She walked out and tugged the curtain across, leaving Ben and Morgan looking at each other.

'I told you I was fine.'

'I don't care what you told me, promise me you'll stay here until they've checked you over and then I'll get someone to come pick you up when you're done.'

She hadn't told Ben or the others she felt a lot worse than she was letting on, not wanting to worry him, but she wouldn't be getting up and walking out anytime soon. The pain inside of her head was a deep throbbing that hurt and resonated throughout her entire body.

'I will, thank you.'

'You will?'

'Yes, you better go and speak to Barnard. I went to the pub, then I went to the Barnards' house because that's who Emily had been drinking with last night. She mentioned that Emily would drink red wine with Neil and was always so nice to him. Then I left. Esme was drinking neat gin, she must have been thinking about it then checked the CCTV. For her to have done that she must have had some suspicions about him and his behaviour. It might be worth getting the hard drive and seeing what he was doing the day Jasmine was killed, in case she was covering for him the first time.'

He kissed her cheek, the one that wasn't covered in dried sticky blood.

'You are a genius, a complete liability, but an absolute genius, Morgan, and this is why I love working with you.'

She laughed. 'I'm glad that you do, I'm also glad my brain is still working. I'll phone you later when they say I'm good to go. I love you, Ben Matthews.'

'I love you more, Brookes.'

She smiled at him, and he lifted a hand to wave before he

also disappeared through the royal blue curtains, leaving her alone with her headache and her thoughts. The room tipped and swayed if she moved her head much in any direction, so she closed her eyes and hoped the nurse wouldn't be long with her tablets. She needed something to numb the pain of the whole day and not just her headache.

It would be the answer to her prayers if they could link Neil Barnard to both murders and stop him killing again.

THIRTY-THREE

By the time Ben arrived at the custody suite, Esme had recovered from being tasered, had the barbs from the taser removed, and had been booked in. According to the detention officer, Michelle, who used to be a PCSO, she was in a cell crying. Michelle buzzed open the door for him.

'How's Morgan?' Michelle asked.

He smiled at her. 'She's okay, bad headache but could have been a lot worse.'

She smiled back. 'Phew. They told me what happened when they brought Esme in. I suppose it's been a while since Morgan got herself in trouble.'

'It certainly has, Michelle, where are my two detainees?'

'The woman, who hasn't stopped crying, is in four; her husband is in interview room B, waiting on a solicitor. Mads didn't arrest him and said he's here on a voluntary.'

Ben thought about that for a moment. He wondered what Mads was playing at, then nodded. They had no proof of his connection to the murders, except for Esme's accusations. They needed to secure the CCTV evidence for themselves and take it from there.

'Who do you want to see first?'

'Neither really but I'll take the husband.'

'Actually, can you stick your head in and tell Esme that Morgan is alive? She thinks she killed her and is beside herself.'

'Let her stew, she could have killed her.' Ben watched Michelle shrug. 'Stop looking at me like that.'

'Like what?'

'Those big brown eyes trying to guilt trip me.'

She smiled.

'I'll speak to Esme.'

'Thank you. I don't think she's a bad person, I think she was in a bad place.'

'You should train to be a psychologist.'

'Nah, too much hard work, lad.'

He followed her down to cell four and peered through the small viewing pane. Esme was in a standard detainee uniform; grey sweater, joggers, slip-on shoes. Her hair was in a messy bun, and she was sitting up on the bed with her knees pulled up to her chest and her head buried in her arms. Her entire body was shaking.

'Oh God, she's a mess,' Ben muttered to Michelle.

'She has never so much as had a parking ticket and now she's in here charged with GBH, but she thinks it's a murder charge.'

'Have you not told her Morgan's okay?'

'She didn't believe me,' Michelle claimed.

Michelle waved at Jo, the duty sergeant, who buzzed the door so she could step through.

'Esme, this is DS Matthews; he took Morgan to the hospital.'

Esme looked up, her eyes swollen and red, black mascara trails down her cheeks.

'DC Brookes has a head injury, which you already know about,' Ben said. He arched an eyebrow at her. 'But she is alive and currently in A&E at Westmorland General Hospital, being treated for that. She hopefully has no lasting damage and should be released later today.'

The relief was clear on Esme's face. 'I'm so sorry, I didn't mean to hit her. I wanted to hit Neil.'

Ben held up his hands. 'Save it for our interview, for now just know that Morgan is okay so calm yourself down a little. Michelle will get you a nice cup of tea and some biscuits. I'm sorry about your friend. I knew Emily too.'

Esme stared at him and nodded. 'Oh God, I'm sorry for you too, she really liked you, did you know that she still really liked you? Last night you were in the pub, and she couldn't take her eyes off you.'

He blinked. 'No, I didn't.' Now he felt even worse than he had. He slipped his fingers into his pocket and wrapped them around the black chunk of stone Ettie had given him.

'You must be having a rubbish day, with Emily and now one of your officers.'

Ben didn't know why he did it, he wouldn't normally discuss their relationship with a suspect, but he felt as if he had to let her know he was committed. 'Morgan is my partner not just my colleague, so yes it's been a hell of a day up to now.'

Esme nodded. 'Sorry.'

'Have that drink and calm down a little bit, then we'll get you interviewed and out of here.'

'What? Can I go home? Not prison?'

He smiled. 'Yes, you'll be going home. On bail with some conditions, but no, you're not going to prison today.'

She let out a sob. 'Thank you, the boys will need one of us to sort them out and explain stuff to them.'

Ben got a sinking feeling inside of his chest. He had no idea there were kids involved. 'How old are they and where are they?'

'Sixteen and almost nineteen, college or with their mates probably. I can't remember what days they do what.'

He breathed out a sigh of relief; he'd imagined that with all the drama they'd left a couple of eight-year-old kids home alone with no one to care for them.

'I'll speak to you later okay, Esme.'

'Thank you.'

She still looked miserable, but she'd stopped crying, the tears had dried up.

He stepped outside, and Michelle smiled at him.

'Thank you, I owe you.'

'You do?'

'Well, a brew or a cake or something, not a big IOU.'

Ben laughed. 'I'll take a coffee and some biscuits if you have any, I'm starving, and every time I think about food something goes disastrously wrong.'

He walked to the interview room and knocked on the door, then walked in to see the duty solicitor, Lucy O'Gara, mid-conversation with Neil Barnard.

'Sorry, let me know when you're ready.'

He left them to it; he needed someone to come in with him anyway. Amy and Cain were at the post-mortem.

Someone knocked on the heavy-duty steel door, and Jo released the catch. As if summoned by magic Marc appeared looking a lot calmer and cooler than Ben. He didn't miss the look Jo and Michelle gave each other at Marc's appearance, or the giggles. Marc stopped, turned and called out, 'Forgot my phone be right back.'

He slipped out of the door before it automatically locked itself again, and Ben leaned across the tall desk staring at the pair of them.

'What's that about? I saw the look you gave each other.'

Michelle laughed. 'She fancies him, thinks he's fit, don't you, Sarge?'

Jo's cheeks began to burn as she shook her head. 'I said he was nice-looking. He reminds me of Luther; they both have those rugged shaved heads and big brown eyes.'

Ben rolled his eyes. 'Oh God, please. I'll tell you one thing, he might look nice, not that I've noticed 'cause you know, he's not my thing, but he's definitely no Idris Elba – that guy oozes charm. Marc oozes confusion and irritation along with a good old dose of stress to top it off.'

Jo laughed. 'Are you jealous, Ben? Remember when everyone used to get all dreamy-eyed over you?'

Michelle passed him a mug of tea, and he managed to spit the mouthful he'd just taken all down the front of his white shirt.

'No one ever got dreamy-eyed over me, Jo.'

'Oh, yes, they did. The PCSOs used to gush about you. Why do you think they always bent over backwards to do your crap jobs that you gave them? Then all those new female coppers who were always trying to get attachments to CID because you worked up there.'

'Well, that's news to me, someone could have mentioned it before. No, you're taking the mickey.'

Michelle smiled. 'It's all true, boss, but since you've got with Morgan everyone has backed off, because they respect you both. Now the DI is getting the limelight.'

He was brushing his shirt with his sleeve, trying to blot up the big wet stain that he'd made.

'But he's an arse.'

'Doesn't matter when you look that good.'

The buzzer went again, and in walked Marc with his phone and a clipboard. Ben side-eyed Jo and Michelle who were grinning at him. He shook his head and didn't think he would ever understand how women's minds worked, as he studied Marc; he grudgingly had to accept that the guy was good-looking, and his suits were always well-cut, expensive. He also had no big tea stain on the front of his shirt. Ben began to faff with his tie, to move it to try and cover the mess he'd made.

'Shall we?' Marc asked.

Ben nodded. 'He's still in with Lucy. Have you got a strategy, boss?'

'No, just going to go with the flow really, unless you have one.'

'We need to seize the CCTV footage from the camera system at the house, to see what made his wife lose it in the first place. I think we focus on his work relationship with Jasmine Armer, and see how he reacts before casually dropping in what he was doing when he left the house last night. I've asked Mads to send an officer to seize it, if we can, or to get it downloaded. Sam has messaged to say that they've spoken to most of the people identified by the landlord at the pub, and no one saw Emily leave the pub; they were too focused on the quiz, which is a shame as it would have been great to be able to place him outside of it.'

'It really would, but that sounds like a great idea to me, happy to follow your lead.'

Ben couldn't smile at him; he was furious that he hadn't even asked after Morgan.

'Oh, how's Morgan?'

He wondered if the guy could read minds, then decided he probably couldn't, it was a coincidence. 'Waiting on a CT scan.'

'Glad she's okay though, she gave us quiet the fright.'

Ben thought to himself, *You don't know the half of it.*

Lucy walked out of the interview room and straight towards them.

'We're ready when you are.'

The two men followed her back in, and they all took a seat. Neil Barnard's skin was pale and clammy, his eyes wide as he took in

Ben and Marc sitting opposite him. He looked skittish, and Ben wasn't sure if it was because he was guilty of the murders or if it was because he'd never been in trouble with the police before.

'My client is happy to answer all of your questions, he has nothing to hide,' Lucy stated.

Ben had to stop himself from glancing at Marc.

'Good, that's great. The quicker we get through this, the faster you can go home. I'm going to caution you, Neil, but you're not under arrest, you can choose to end the interview at any time.'

Neil nodded.

'I'm Detective Sergeant Ben Matthews and this is Detective Inspector Marcell Howard. This interview is being recorded and the purpose of it is to speak to you about your actions, movement and possible involvement in the murders of Jasmine Armer and Emily Wearing. You do not have to say anything, but it may harm your defence if you do not mention when questioned something which you later rely on in court. Anything you do say may be given in evidence. Do you understand?'

Neil was staring at Lucy, who smiled at him and nodded. He turned back to look at Ben.

'Yes, I do.'

'That's good, so I'm going to ask you to cast your mind back to Wednesday. Can you tell me how your day went?'

'It was just another day, I got up, ate breakfast, made a coffee then drove to work. I spent all day at work, then I left before five to go home.'

'Did you see Jasmine Armer?'

'Yes, I saw her a couple of times through the day, and she was still there when I left. I already told your officer that, the one who got hurt. How is she?'

'She's waiting on a CT scan, but she's fine.'

'I'm glad she's okay, I'm sorry that happened. I've never known my wife to act like that.'

Ben studied him for a second. 'Thank you. Going back to Wednesday when you left work what did you do?'

'I went to get diesel at the Shell garage on Windermere Road, then drove straight home. I saw my old university friend, and we had a brief chat before I went home. You can ask him if he saw me, he's called Dave Paton, and he will confirm that.'

'That's good, we can do that. Did you leave the house again?'

'Well yes, I dropped the lads off at the Leisure Centre in Kendal, and then I picked them back up again. I didn't do anything to Jasmine, I liked her. I'm not some sick weirdo who goes around killing girls. While you're wasting time doing this, how do you not know the bastard isn't out there hurting someone else?'

'We don't, and we hope that he isn't, but we have to make sure we have covered everything and talked to everyone. Did Jasmine ever talk to you about her friends, her boyfriends, that kind of thing?'

'No, why would she? As far as I know she had no boyfriend and if she did, she never mentioned him.'

Ben nodded.

Marc leaned forwards and asked, 'How did you feel about Emily Wearing? She was good friends with your wife and came to your house a lot, from what I can gather. She was a very attractive woman, would you say she was your type, Neil?'

He looked at Lucy, who said, 'You don't have to answer that.'

'I'm going to because I didn't do it. I liked the woman, okay? She was funny, talkative, we shared the same taste in wine, we had a similar sense of humour, but I wasn't screwing her and neither did I want to. I also didn't want her dead, if that's your next question. She was my wife's friend. I spent a lot of time with her, and I'm grieving over her death as much as anyone, so why don't you take that list of questions and shove it up your arse.'

He was glaring at Marc, and Ben thought that he might actually stand up and punch him.

Marc smiled at him. 'I'm sorry for your loss, but you obviously liked Emily. Did she like you back? We know that she was a woman who would go after what she wanted and take it without a second thought. Did she go after you and your wife found out?'

Neil scrambled to his feet and launched himself across the table at Marc. Ben jumped up and hit the emergency red button on the wall, to summon officers to come and calm him down. Marc had managed to push himself away and was standing a good distance away from Neil, who was being held back by the arm by Lucy.

'This interview is over,' she hissed at Marc, who shrugged.

Three officers burst through the door, but Neil had managed to compose himself enough not to need dragging out and putting into a cell.

Ben, however, was furious with Marc. Who the hell had told him that information about Emily?

Ben looked into Neil's eyes. 'You are free to go, Mr Barnard, we might need to talk to you again. One of these officers will drive you home.'

He turned to Smithy, who was standing there all tall and imposing. 'Please can you seize the hard drive to Mr Barnard's CCTV system and bring it straight back.'

Neil's head dropped as he stared at his feet. 'What about my wife?'

'She will be interviewed and released on bail; she won't be able to come home, if that's what you're asking. She will have to go to a separate address because she tried to attack you.'

'I can't make her move out, it's her house, and she was just a little angry. She's half Italian, she has fire inside her veins. She didn't hurt me.'

'No, but she seriously hurt my colleague. Then I suggest you find somewhere to go, pack a bag and see if you can sofa surf for a couple of nights until we get this cleared up.'

Ben had to get out of here before he hurt someone, and if Marc didn't get out of his sight it might just be him. He left them all to it, to clean up the mess. Today was one big mess after another, all he wanted was some calm and time to think.

As he strode towards the stairs Marc chased after him.

'What's wrong with you? We rattled his cage.'

He turned to face him. 'Rattled his cage? Who told you about Emily not taking no for an answer and chasing whatever she wanted?'

'Well, she did, we only chatted a couple of times, but she told me she was very goal-oriented. I was just using what I knew about her to try and catch him out.'

Exhaustion washed over Ben as he realised he'd been too focused on his own feelings around Emily and her murder. Of course, she would have talked to Marc, she was the kind of woman who would take a plate of homemade biscuits around for a new neighbour, to try and get to know them.

'Oh, sorry it's been a rubbish day. How are you, boss? I haven't asked if you're coping with it all okay?'

Marc reached out a hand and gripped Ben's arm.

'Same as everyone, I suppose, tired, shocked, determined to find the bastard who could do something so horrible to someone so nice. I liked her, she was a nice woman.'

'She was.'

Ben turned and walked away towards the toilets. He put the lid down, locked the door and sat on it, trying to breathe deep in through his nose and out through his mouth, like Morgan had taught him so many times to help with his stress, but it wasn't working, and he could feel the tears that were on the verge of spilling down his cheeks, because he wasn't a machine that could deal with stuff like this and turn it off when he needed to. He was a human being with a heart and a conscience. He felt something sharp sticking into his thigh and pulled the stone out of his pocket. Gripping it in his right hand he held the curled-up fist to his forehead, no idea what he was doing but hoping something good might happen. His phone began to vibrate in his other pocket, and he pulled it out to see Morgan's name. He whispered, *'Wow, that was quick.'*

'Hey.'

'Hey back, I can come home. Are you busy?'

'I'm never busy for you, I'll be there soon.' His voice was a whisper, and he struggled to keep it from cracking.

'Are you okay, Ben?'

'Yeah, I am now, don't go anywhere until I get there.'

'I won't, thank you.'

He pulled a wad of toilet paper off the roll and blotted at his damp eyes. That was a close call, he'd almost lost it. He stood up and pushed the stone back into his pocket, lifted the lid took a pee then washed his hands and splashed cold water over his face. He didn't want anyone to think it was all too much for him and take him off the case.

THIRTY-FOUR

The carnage at the dental surgery was thrilling. He watched it on the news again and again; the cops arrived on scene with flashing lights and ran inside. Whoever had filmed this was good, they didn't miss a thing.

He'd watched as she ran from her car inside, then it was all quiet outside; the action was going on out of the person filming's view, which was a huge shame. After a few minutes, more coppers arrived, then along came an ambulance. Another period of time with a shaky camera view of the front of the surgery. Eventually a man who had raced in last helped her out; she was struggling to walk and had a huge bandage wrapped around her head. He zoomed in to see the side of her face covered in blood, and had been furious. The detective was helped into a white car and then they were speeding off to the hospital, he presumed. He'd continued to watch it; eventually, a woman was brought out on a wheelchair thing and put into the back of the ambulance. A big burly brute of a copper had gone inside it with her. It was all over. He bet Windermere had never seen such excitement.

He sat back. He was still raging about the detective getting hurt like that. He didn't want her mask to have a big dint in the side of the head. He could pad it out underneath the clear plastic film, he supposed that would work but it was totally unnecessary and a waste of his time. He knew that she wouldn't go without a fight, so he wouldn't have the time to mess around.

He didn't know where she lived but if he went to the hospital and waited around, maybe phoned up the reception on A&E, he could find out. He decided to phone before he set off, in case she'd been taken to a different hospital, FGH down in Barrow, or Lancaster Infirmary.

The woman at Westmorland had been very friendly, for a change, when he said he was concerned about his colleague. They told him that a policewoman had been brought in with a head injury and was being taken for a CT scan, but that she would hopefully be released later. Now here he was, parked up in a corner of the car park with a view of the entrance doors, ready to follow her home. He wanted to know for definite which house was hers. He didn't think he would be trying to get her from her home address, but he had to make sure he had a backup plan if anything went wrong.

He was more than a little impressed with the way things were going. He wasn't gloating yet, though he might be after he snatched Morgan Brookes.

She had such a pretty name. She wasn't very old for a detective, but she was very good. He knew this once he'd found out her name and searched for her; the number of articles about her had surprised him, and her family history left a lot to be desired. One day someone would write a book about her, he was sure of it, especially once he'd finished with her. She truly would stay young and live forever, what greater gift could you bestow upon anyone?

THIRTY-FIVE

Morgan felt like crap. Her head, despite taking two Co-codamol, was still throbbing. She could feel the pulse inside of it thrumming away as if someone was pounding on a drum. The doctor who had reviewed her scans had told her there was a small haematoma, but he was confident if she took a daily aspirin, it wouldn't give her any problems and would break up itself. They had glued the wound and put a dressing on it. She hadn't tried to look at herself in any of the reflective surfaces around. She didn't want to scare herself; the nurse had told her she was going to have a black eye to be proud of because it was already purple and blue.

She wanted to get back to work, had to, there was a killer out there who needed locking up before they killed again. She felt terrible that she was stuck in here leaving Ben a detective down. Her curtain was drawn, and she was glad no one could see the sorry state she was in. The next time it opened she saw Ben's handsome face smiling at her through the gap, and she wondered if she was dreaming.

'Hello, beautiful, am I glad to see you.'

She wasn't dreaming. She tried to sit up but was too fast and the room swayed a little bit. He rushed towards her.

'Whoa, take it easy, where are you rushing off to?'

He sat next to her on the trolley and picked up her hand.

'Work, need to get back, we have a lot to do.'

'You, my friend, are not going back to work. You are going home to rest, and if you're feeling okay tomorrow then we'll see about you doing a couple of hours, nothing more.'

'You are such a spoil sport.'

'Yes, that's what your boss is supposed to be. We're not supposed to be anything else really.'

He stuck his tongue out at her.

'Childish too.'

But she laughed and stuck hers out at him just as the nurse walked in.

'Your lift is here then, that's good. She must not do anything strenuous for the next twenty-four hours at least, any signs of dizziness, or if she blacks out even for a second, she's to come straight back.'

'Oh, she won't be doing anything, I'll make sure of that.'

Morgan declined to tell the pair of them she was still dizzy, but she was no use to anyone cooped up in here. At home she had access to the internet and coffee, she could help from behind the scenes, was determined to be of some help. She felt guilty that Esme had lost her shit, but that was her job: she'd had to inform her of Emily's death, someone had to.

She pushed herself up off the bed. 'I need to get changed. I hate the smell of dried blood, it makes me feel like throwing up.'

Ben looped his arm through hers and nodded. 'It's not my favourite perfume.'

They walked out arm in arm, him leading her towards the exit and his BMW. She smiled when she saw it. 'Where's the Corsa?'

'Probably needs a new engine the speed I had to drive to get to you. Which reminds me, as your boss I need to know why you felt the need to rush into a dangerous situation like that unarmed, no body armour.'

He opened the car door, and she got inside, sinking into the soft leather seat and closing her eyes. 'It was sort of my fault; I went to visit her and told her about Emily, then I was pressing her about Neil and well, she started drinking neat gin. I left and thought she was going to sit there and get drunk; I didn't know she was going to drive to his work and have a bit of a break down.'

'You didn't, that's true. You should have let Response officers handle it though, and you wouldn't have had your head smashed in. Lecture over, I know you were trying to help, but sometimes...'

'I won't be doing it again, if this is what I get as my thanks, so you don't need to worry about it. For what it's worth I'm sorry.'

He laughed. 'No, you're not, you will do the same thing again in a heartbeat if you have to. I just like pretending that, as your superior, I might be able to influence your split-second decisions. Morgan, do you know what it does to my insides? When I ran in there and you were out cold, I thought I was going to lose it and don't tell me you wouldn't feel the same.'

'I was reckless, and I really am sorry, Ben. I would be distraught if it was you, so you have every right to admonish me. I promise I will try and think before jumping in feet first in the future. I can't give you better than that.'

'I know, it's who you are, my fiery, crime-fighting super hero. Thank you though, I'll take it.'

Ben double-parked on the street outside of their house and put the hazard lights on, so Morgan didn't have to walk a long distance, and she realised he wasn't staying. She knew he couldn't, there was too much going on, but she'd have liked it if he could just for a little while.

Inside, he led her to the living room then paused.

'Would you rather go upstairs and lie down?'

'No, I'm good in here. I don't know what I'm going to do yet.'

She sat on the sofa, and he bent down to unlace her boots, tugging them off.

'Can you have a shower?'

'I will later. If you get me some clean stuff, I'll have a good scrub in the downstairs toilet.'

A loud burst of laughter erupted from him. 'I'd rather you used the sink, the toilet?'

'You know what I meant; I didn't mean the toilet bowl, you idiot.'

She stood up and began to strip off her coat, then her blood-soaked blouse, and trousers until she was standing in just her underwear and a pair of fluffy socks. She could hear him rummaging around upstairs and smiled; he would bring her something odd down, he always did.

She filled the tiny sink with hot water and a few pumps of the antibacterial handwash that smelled like lemon sherbet. Using a towel she scrubbed at the skin on her face and neck, removing the leftover bits of dried-up blood. Once she was red-faced but clean, she blotted it dry and stared at the bruising around her right eye. It spread from the wound on the side of her head across her cheekbone towards the eye socket. She let out a sigh as she prodded it. She supposed she should be grateful her cheekbone hadn't been fractured.

Ben knocked on the door then opened it.

'Just checking you weren't standing in the toilet.'

'You're funny.'

'I know, here's your pyjamas. I reckon you should lie around being comfy if you have to have a sick day.'

Morgan took them off him and smiled. 'You're a pretty decent boss you know.'

'Yeah, I think I'm all right too.'

She climbed into the pair of mismatched pyjamas. He had chosen the softest pair in the drawers and for that she was thankful. She felt sick with the painkillers on an empty stomach and her head was still throbbing; she wanted to lie down. By the time she walked back to the living room he had some soft pillows and a duvet on the sofa for her.

'Thank you.'

He shrugged. 'I want to stay with you, but I can't, you know that, don't you? I would be here in a heartbeat if it wasn't for the murders.'

'Of course, I do, I'm a big girl. I can look after myself until you get back.'

'Okay, I'll go make you a sandwich and bring you a couple of drinks in. I only have one request.'

'What's that?'

'You do not leave this house today.'

'I won't, I don't feel that good, so I'm going to lie here and watch *The Munsters* on Prime from episode one.'

'Promise?'

'I do.'

He narrowed his eyes at her but seemed to accept she was telling the truth, which was good because she was. She had no intention of doing anything other than sleeping and hoping that the bloody headache would subside by the time she woke up.

In fact, she lay back, pulled the duvet up and closed her eyes as if to prove a point. She felt his shadow as he leaned down over her and kissed her cheek that wasn't swollen and bruised.

'See you later, ring me and keep your phone on loud so I can get hold of you.'

'I will.'

He left the room, and she heard him moving around but couldn't keep her eyes open any longer. Sleep would take her into a darkness where hopefully there would be no replays of the last few days.

THIRTY-SIX

Amy and Cain left the post-mortem in silence; in fact neither of them had spoken much at all to each other or to anyone else. As they got back in the car to drive back to the station, she turned to Cain.

'Are you okay?'

He nodded slowly. 'Yeah, I guess I am. I'd forgot how awful they are. It's all fun and games when you're on probation and trying to look cool like nothing bothers you, 'cause you're a big, strong, tough cop, but...'

'But?'

'I'm getting older, and she was so pretty, so young, she had her whole life ahead of her and now she's dead, gone, wiped off the face of the earth because of some sick bastard and his fantasies.'

'We have to stop him. What do you think he meant about not finding any of the rubber stuff on her like he did with Jasmine?'

'I guess we should have asked, but I was too busy staring at the cracked tile in the corner of the room. I'm not as hard or as tough as I thought I was.'

She smiled at him. 'No, you're human, Cain, it's not a bad thing. Ben and Morgan will know, they attended Jasmine's PM. I can't imagine how they must be feeling, especially Ben; he went out with Emily a few times.'

'Poor Ben, first his wife then his girlfriend. No wonder he gets so protective with Morgan. He's going to be even worse now.'

'He's had a terrible time; I better ring him and give him an update.'

She took out her phone and waited for Ben to answer.

'Hi, Amy, how did you get on?'

'Rubbish, Declan said that the manner of death was the same as Jasmine's, death by asphyxiation. He said to tell you he did find a tiny sample of the latex stuff he found on Jasmine. He thinks it's the same killer, or he said it all points to the same guy. He's emailing you over his full report.'

'Thanks, I thought as much.'

'Where do you want us, boss?'

'Get yourselves back, have a breather. We need to regroup anyway, and you won't believe what's happened while you've been at the post-mortem.'

'You made an arrest?'

'We made several, not directly to do with the murders though. I'll explain when you get back, we're a bit short-staffed. Morgan had to go home.'

'Is she ill?'

'No, she got hit in the head with a hammer by Esme Barnard, and has just been released from hospital.'

'No shit.'

Ben hung up, and Amy stared at the phone.

Cain was driving and he glanced at her.

'What's wrong?'

'Esme Barnard attacked Morgan with a hammer.'

'Oh God, is she okay?'

'I think so, but why the hell did Esme do that? She seemed like she was okay. I liked her, she was a bit odd but in a nice way.'

'Is that the dentist who is a bit weird's wife?'

She nodded. 'She was lovely when I was at her house yesterday though.'

'Maybe she took a disliking to poor old Brookes! Do you think we should go and check on her before we go to the station?'

'Yes, it won't take long. We could just check she's okay, see if she needs anything.'

'And get the gossip. Benno won't give us much, will he?'

'Cain, you're terrible.'

'I know, but you know Morgan likes a gossip as well as the rest of us. Plus, she'd rather we heard it from her and not some watered-down version from section staff who didn't actually attend the incident.'

Amy laughed. 'I'm sure she really won't give a shit if she's got a head injury, but I'd rather go check on her just to be sure. I bet she's furious she's out of action.'

Cain drove straight to Ben's house.

As they walked up the small garden path, Cain stopped. 'Should we have got some flowers or chocolate?'

'We can do that later; I just want to see her and get the lowdown, make sure she's okay after Des. It's all a bit hard trying to keep a brave face on it when all you want to do is bloody cry about how unfair everything is.'

'You cry, like actual tears?'

'As a matter of fact, I do, not in front of people obviously, but sometimes when I'm on my own.'

She knocked on the door and rang the doorbell, and Cain lifted the flap on the letter box.

'Morgan, it's me, Cain, and Amy, let us in, we want the gossip.'

'You don't do subtle, do you?'

'You know how stubborn she is, if she thinks it's the boss or anyone else.'

The sound of the key being turned in the lock stopped their chatter as the door swung inwards. It was dark in the hall and Morgan didn't step into the light.

'What are you two up to?'

'Came to check on you. We can't leave you alone for five minutes, and I thought you might need a hug because Amy has an aversion to any form of human contact, and even if you don't need one, I do.'

Amy stuck her finger in her throat and made a puking sound. Morgan laughed, and they both stepped inside. She shut the door and locked it again then turned to face Cain, who flicked on the light switch, illuminating the entire hall.

'Bloody Nora, what a mess.'

He shook his head in wonder at the state of her bruises and patched-up head, then stepped forward and scooped her into his arms. Morgan didn't fight it; he gave the best hugs in the world, everyone knew that.

'Put her down, Cain, you're suffocating her.'

He let go. 'Did I hurt you?'

'No, you didn't. Thank you for that, it was very much needed. If you want a brew, you can make your own.'

Amy smirked. 'Your hospitality skills leave a bit to be desired.'

Morgan pointed to her head. 'I have a concussion, I can't remember how to boil a kettle.'

Cain was frowning, the concern etched across his face.

'No, she doesn't, you numpty; if she did, she wouldn't be standing here, she just can't be bothered to brew up, can you, Morgan?'

Morgan shrugged; Cain walked towards the kitchen.

'Well, you two ladies sit down, and I'll be mother.'

'Oh God, he's turning into Norman Bates.' Amy was smirking at Morgan.

'I heard that, I haven't started wearing your clothes yet, Amy, so don't worry.'

Amy followed Morgan into the big cosy living room with stripped pine floors and a huge rug. She noticed the duvet and pillows on the sofa and felt bad.

'Did we wake you up? Sorry.'

Morgan had sat back down; she tucked her legs underneath her and pulled the duvet over her. 'I was only dozing. How did the PM go?'

Amy lowered her voice. 'Not good, he really struggled with it. I felt bad for him.'

'I bet it was, thank you for going. I don't think I could have stood it, and as for Ben he would have been devastated to have to watch that. Did Declan say anything, are they connected?'

'He said they were the same cause of death, by asphyxiation; he mentioned there was a minute amount of the rubber stuff on her face though.'

'Alginate?'

Amy nodded. 'Yeah, that's it. I couldn't remember what it was called; all the way back I've been trying.'

'It's weird, isn't it?'

'What's weird?'

Cain walked in carrying three mugs and put one down in front of Morgan on the wooden packing crate Ben used for a coffee table.

'The alginate on Jasmine's face.'

'She worked in a dental surgery, they use it all the time to take impressions of your teeth and stuff. It's a nightmare, it feels as if they're going to suck your teeth out of the sockets when they try and remove it.'

'It was on her eyelashes though; it would have driven her

mad, and wouldn't someone have pointed it out to her so she could pick it off?'

'Did Declan find anything else?' Morgan asked.

'The same rope marks on her arms and feet, but no sexual assault.'

'Why did he need to tie her down then? You expect someone who does that to have some kind of sexual motive. Yet he tied her down and then asphyxiated her. Do you think they were scared they couldn't control her? If this is right, I think whoever is doing this is inexperienced, and don't ask me how, but maybe he's younger than we anticipated.'

Amy shrugged. 'Who knows, but it's a good point.'

Cain was looking around; Amy was sipping the coffee he'd made for her.

'Maybe no one looked at her that close. Anyway, what happened, spill it. I want the full, gory details. What did you do to make Esme Barnard lose her shit, Morgan?'

Morgan spat the mouthful of coffee she'd just swallowed back out.

'Nothing, it wasn't my fault. Well not really, I suppose it might have been though.'

'What's that, some kind of denial turned confession.'

Amy glared at Cain, who blatantly ignored her and carried on talking.

'Does your head hurt a lot? How many times did she hit you with the hammer, and did you know she was going to do it? Couldn't you have at least ducked, because that's pretty crap reflexes if you didn't see a big hammer coming your way. Have you learned nothing from all those self-defence classes at HQ?'

It was Morgan's turn to glare at him, but it didn't last long before it broke into a smile.

'You know who you remind me of, Cain?'

'Let me see, Tom Hardy, or that blond Australian actor that played Thor?'

'No, not Chris Hemsworth or Tom Hardy. I was thinking more that annoying kid in *Home Alone* 2 that asks the bus driver a million questions before they head to the airport.'

'Oh, thanks that's nice, I'm pretty sure you've said that before, so yeah, you must have concussion.'

Amy began to laugh. 'That serves you right.'

Morgan blew him a kiss. 'I found out she was the friend with Emily, drinking in the pub, so I went to break the bad news to her. I didn't know she was going to implode and do that, but don't you think she must have had a good reason to? There is something she's hiding from us; I'm telling you she knows something. I've told Ben the CCTV needs seizing and checking, to see if it shows Neil Barnard's coming and going the night of Jasmine Armer's murder.'

'We will check it's been done. How is your head?'

Morgan looked at Amy. 'Painful, it was one of those big square hammers.'

Cain grimaced. 'Still can't believe you didn't duck.'

'Well believe me, I wish I had because now I'm stuck here and can't do anything useful.'

'How long do you have to be out of action for?'

'I'll be back in tomorrow.'

Amy looked shocked. 'Erm, no you won't, Ben won't let you.'

'We'll see about that; he needs me, he needs all of us if he's going to make an arrest.'

They finished their drinks and stood up.

'Can we get you anything, food, alcohol?'

'I'm good thanks, we have plenty. Let me know if anything happens in between now and tomorrow.'

'We will, try and take it easy.'

Morgan smiled at Amy. 'Not much else I can do right now.'

THIRTY-SEVEN

Ben gave a curt nod at Amy and Cain as they walked in the door. He'd been worried they'd got caught up with something on the way back and not informed him. He had been getting himself all worked up. They were a team member down and these two were later back than he'd expected.

'Was there an accident?'

'No, boss, we called in to see Morgan and check she was okay.'

He smiled at Amy, not expecting that to be her answer.

'Thank you, was she?'

Cain spoke. 'Yeah, apart from the obvious she seemed to be.'

'Good, that's good. Let's see what we've got. I've spoken briefly to Declan about the post-mortem. Thank you both for attending. Have we got anything from that we can follow up on?'

'The rubber stuff, oh sorry I keep forgetting its name.'

'Alginate?'

'Yeah, that. It's a bit odd that Jasmine didn't wipe it off, and there was a tiny sample on Emily.'

'If she didn't wipe it off then it got transferred to her when she was already dead.'

'Why? And my question is who would have access to that kind of stuff apart from Jasmine?'

'She worked in a dental surgery, Amy, anyone else in that surgery.'

'Have we definitely cleared them all and confirmed their alibis?'

Ben was running his hand across his head. 'No, Morgan has spoken to them, but the only confirmation we had of an alibi up to now was for Neil Barnard. It's too late now, it will be closed, but tomorrow I need you both to go to the sixth form where Emily worked and speak to the staff, and even students who took her classes.'

'What did she teach?'

'Art.'

'No problem.' She looked up at the clock on the wall. 'We could go there now. Won't they have nighttime classes?'

'If you want, then that's great. Get alibis for everyone. Ask around if she was having problems with anyone, that kind of thing.'

'Oh, boss, Morgan said that because they were both tied up and not sexually assaulted why was that? She thinks it's because the killer is inexperienced or maybe even younger than we thought.'

Ben nodded. 'Something to consider that's for sure.'

She stood up. 'Come on, Cain.'

Cain groaned. 'What about tea?'

'We'll grab something on the way.'

He nodded and followed her back out.

Ben watched them go, wondering if he'd been a bit too harsh with them. They'd barely had time to sit down for a few minutes and he was expecting them to be out of the door doing follow-up interviews. He was about to go back into his office when the door was thrown open with a loud bang. He looked to see Brenda from the front desk standing there with a brown box in her hands, smiling at him.

'Parcel for Morgan. How is she, Ben?'

'As okay as she can be, under strict orders to take it easy.'

'Do you think she will?'

'I wouldn't like to bet on it. Thanks, stick it on the desk. I'll take it when I go home.'

She did. 'Not sure what's in it, feels very light.'

Ben shrugged. 'I have no idea what she buys.'

'Give her my love, tell her I'm thinking about her, won't you? I worry about her a lot; I was beginning to think we were over all that horrible stuff.'

'What horrible stuff?'

'The Morgan getting assaulted on every case she works.'

'Oh, yeah that, and I was hoping so too.'

She left him there staring at the box. He picked it up and shook it. Must be make-up or maybe tights, he thought to himself, possibly a book. Morgan had a pile of true crime books that almost filled the huge bookcase in the lounge, along with her collection of Stephen King and Joe Hill novels. He didn't quite understand how she could read that stuff and still sleep at night. She did though, and who was he to question her choice of reading materials? There had been one or two times it had come in handy solving cases.

Marc walked in. 'Neil Barnard, what are you thinking about him and his involvement?'

Ben smiled; the boss wasn't one for small talk.

'Hard to say, he's a link to both victims that's for sure, but so is his wife.'

'Yeah, but have you seen the state she's in? She hasn't stopped crying since she was brought in according to the detention officer.'

'Michelle.'

'No, she's called Esme short for Esmerelda Barnard.'

'Michelle is the detention officer.'

'Oh, right yeah.'

His people skills left a lot to be desired. Ben knew that he must be struggling coming from working in a busy force like Greater Manchester Police, but Rydal Falls was small and more intimate; it wouldn't hurt him to try to make an effort to get to know the staff.

'You don't think she has it in her to kill two women?'

'God no, do you?'

He shrugged. 'I don't judge a person by the number of tears they shed. It's very possible she is a good actress and can cry on tap.'

'No, she's genuinely beside herself, I can tell. I'd rather put my money on her husband, and anyway she was still in the pub when Emily left.'

'I know.'

'Oh, good. What's happening then, where are we going with this? Because it doesn't feel as if it's going anywhere. I have itchy feet; I want to be making a move on and finding the suspect before he strikes again. You know what happens when he has a third victim, don't you? All bloody hell will break loose and the whole world will be watching, saying we have a serial killer on the loose. MIT are already making plans to get down here and review everything.'

'That's okay, we could do with their help.'

'We could? I thought you were a close-knit team who liked to keep it in the family and solve cases yourselves, without external departments coming in and taking over.'

'We are, but I'm not going to turn down help at the risk of putting anyone in danger, especially now Morgan is out of action. We need all the officers they can spare. Their input is welcome, although to be fair we've always managed to find the killer before they did, but I'm not holding that against them.'

He smiled at Marc whose face was scrunched up as he considered all of this.

'Right. Well then, what are we doing exactly to try and find our person of interest, if you don't think it's Barnard?'

'I didn't say it wasn't either of them. I think we need to monitor the pair of them as much as we can. We have their DNA and prints on file now, but everything we have is circumstantial. We haven't ruled out Jasmine's mum, but I can see no reason for her killing Emily in the same way. It would only make sense if Jasmine was a one-off and they weren't connected. Morgan has confirmed the alibi for the guy from the dental lab, and the PCSOs have managed to speak to most of the people who were in the pub.'

Marc flopped down onto Morgan's chair and let out the longest of sighs.

'Has Morgan not got any wild theories?'

Ben stared at him. 'Not at the moment, oh actually there is one she mentioned to Amy: that she thinks we could be looking at a killer who is younger than we're anticipating.'

'That's a damn shame because I would consider anything she comes up with at this moment in time, if it meant we might be closer to making an arrest. What is her thinking behind the age thing?'

'She said why is he tying the victims up if there is no sexual assault. I guess she's thinking he's not strong enough or confident enough to be able to do what he does without having them fully under control.'

'That's worth bearing in mind when we find a suitable suspect. There's a press conference tomorrow at ten, we could do with something to throw them and get them off our backs.'

'Well, I'll ask her when I go home if she's managed to solve the case for you.'

Marc looked him right in the eyes. 'Is that sarcasm? 'Cause if it is there's no need.'

It was Ben's turn to sigh.

'You're right, sorry. I'm struggling with the killer's motivation though, what is driving him to kill women and leave them in their cars at places that mean a lot to them? They would surely have to know them on a personal level. Damn, we need to find out if Jasmine and Emily knew each other, see if they have any mutual friends.'

'Where's Amy, she's good for that kind of social media stuff.'

'Gone to the sixth form to speak to staff who knew Emily.'

'Should I tell her to come back?'

'No, I'll have a look, see what I can find.'

'Why don't you go home, do it there and see how Morgan is. If she'd be up to it she might help you.'

Ben didn't want to tell him there was no way he was making Morgan work after today's assault, but he did want to go and see her.

'That's a great idea, I'll do that. What about you? It's been a long day, are you okay? Should you not be going home for a glass of wine or whatever it is you drink?'

'I might, I'll be able to get in, won't I?'

'You can go home; Emily's flat is still a scene guard and the entrance to the house is a scene still, but you can park on the street. The PCSO will let you in. Who lives in the middle apartment? We couldn't get an answer?'

'Some guy who works offshore, he's never home. Comes back once a month for a week then he's gone again.'

Ben nodded. 'Okay, well give me a shout if you need anything. It will be hard going back there.'

Marc swallowed hard. 'Too bloody hard. Emily told me once about all the trouble Morgan had in her apartment. Do you think it's cursed or something?'

'Cursed, I don't know about that, boss, but it's definitely had its fair share of bad luck.'

A vision of Emily, staring out of the car windscreen at the

door to the apartments, sent a cold shiver down his spine and made a lump form in his throat. She didn't deserve this, she had so much to live for, and seeing her so alive in the pub last night made it all even harder to digest.

Marc stood up. He glanced at the box on the desk but didn't say anything. Ben waited for him to leave then he phoned Amy.

'Hey, unless you get some relevant information that we need to move on tonight, I'm going to suggest you two get yourselves home after the college.'

'*I was going to phone you, it's shut.*'

'Oh, well go home. You can go there tomorrow first thing, goodnight.'

'*Night, boss.*'

He put his phone away, grabbed his jacket and the box, turned off the lights and left the station, to go home and do what, he wasn't sure. He would really like a large glass of whisky to numb the pain, but it wasn't going to help anything. Morgan was still injured, Jasmine and Emily were both dead, and he needed to figure out if there were any connections between the two victims.

He needed to focus on his next move. They needed to be smarter than the killer and work out who he might go after next, because Ben knew that now he had started and was having so much fun, there was no way he would be able to stop himself. It just wouldn't happen.

THIRTY-EIGHT

Morgan woke before Ben. All night she'd tossed and turned unable to push Emily's dead gaze out of her mind. That and a headache from hell hadn't helped. She got up and went into the bathroom, scaring herself at the sight of the reflection staring back at her from the mirror.

To try to cover the mess of her face with make-up or not, was the question as she prodded at the bruising which spread from the side of her temple across her cheekbone to her eye. It was tender and swollen. She never went into work without her eyeliner on. Splashing cold water all over the bruises, she patted it dry and began to apply her foundation as best as she could. It didn't cover it completely, but by the time she'd finished, it didn't look quite as shocking.

Her eye wasn't swollen shut thankfully, just a mess, so she followed her usual routine and carefully drew her little black wings on. Then she brushed her long copper hair and tied it up into a messy bun, pulling strands down to try and cover the dressing on her temple. When she'd finished she took one final glance and burst out laughing. Dear God, what a fright. She hoped she didn't have to speak to any little kids today, she would terrify them and leave them scarred for life. She could pass for the Bride of Frankenstein, but there was nothing she could do about it so she might as well get on with it.

Downstairs she made herself a large travel mug of coffee, then Ben one, along with two bacon rolls. She had dressed for work, black trousers, black shirt, Doc Martens – her staple choice in footwear. Before Ben came down she searched through the drawers for the box of Co-codamol she'd been given for her fractured ankle, and swallowed two with some orange juice. Hopefully they would lift the fog inside of her head so she could at least think clearly enough to be useful today. She wasn't giving Ben or Marc the slightest excuse to send her home. What was the point? She would be here doing nothing but worry about what she should be doing. It wouldn't be counterproductive for the team in the least.

There was a knock at the front door, and she hurried to open it.

Standing on the other side was the most wonderful sight she'd ever seen.

'Ettie.'

'My God, Morgan, what happened to your face?' Her aunt reached up and tenderly touched the side of her cheek.

'Long story, come in, I've just made bacon rolls. Would you like some breakfast?'

Her aunt stepped in, her long velvet cloak flowing behind her. Morgan half expected her to prop a broomstick up against the hall wall.

'What brings you here so early?'

'I was on my way to the farmers' market and had this overwhelming urge to pay my favourite niece a visit.'

'Well, I'm glad that you did. It's so lovely to see you. How are you?'

'I'm good, much better than you I think, so what happened?

It wasn't...' She didn't say Ben, but she rolled her eyes upstairs, as if she knew that's where he was.

'Oh no, he wouldn't ever, he's not that kind of guy. I had a falling out with a hammer-wielding woman at work. It looks a lot worse than it is really.'

'It does, I bet it hurts like a bitch though. I have something in the van that will help with the bruising. My wonder balm, it treats everything but is especially good for bruising and swelling. I'll grab you one before I go.'

Morgan pointed to the kitchen table, and Ettie pulled out a chair. She looked across at the coffee machine. 'I'll not say no to one of those, Morgan, but I've already eaten thank you.'

Morgan took a coffee pod out of the jar and poured milk into the frother, pressing the button. Theo had a fancy bean to coffee machine; she had her trusty Nespresso which was so much quicker and easier to clean. She passed the latte to Ettie and sat opposite her.

'I also wanted to drop something off for Ben.'

'You did?'

She nodded. 'I think we got off on the wrong foot, and I've finally got over his arresting me, so we're all good now. It's a little thank you gift from me to him.'

'A thank you for what, not charging you with murder?' Morgan giggled. Ettie didn't, her face was straight.

'It's just a morning blend of tea to help him get going. I had this feeling he might be struggling with the pressure at work. You both work too hard, although thank God you do, because no one does your job like you two, but still with his heart scare and everything I think this might help to put a bit of a spring in his step.'

Out of nowhere a jar of tea appeared on the table in front of Morgan as if by magic. Her aunt if anything was very dramatic at times.

'Well, that's very kind of you. I'm not sure he'll drink it

though, he's a bit of a wuss when it comes to anything remotely herbal, especially if it smells funny.'

'He will drink this.'

Morgan nodded; she wasn't going to hurt Ettie's feelings.

'Thank you, I'll make sure he tries it.'

'Now, what is going on with you two? Has he tried to get you to marry him yet? Have you talked about children?'

Morgan's mouth dropped open, and she looked around mortified in case Ben could hear.

'No, we're quite happy as we are. I don't think either of us is ready for marriage or kids, especially not with our job. It's full-on day and night. It wouldn't be fair to a pet or a child.'

As if summoned, Kevin, who had been asleep on Ben's feet all night, strolled into the kitchen and let out a loud miaow.

Ettie turned to look at her. 'What were you saying about keeping a pet?'

'Kevin is different, he belonged to Des, and he is used to being on his own while Des was at work.'

'Kevin, you called a cat Kevin?'

'I didn't, Des did.'

Ettie was smiling. Kevin had taken a liking to her and was rubbing himself against her cloak.

'Animals love you.'

'Shame men don't, but you know I've been on my own that long now I wouldn't want a man to come in and mess up my routine. Yes, all animals and I have a great affinity for each other.'

Ettie sipped her latte as Kevin jumped up onto her lap. 'You're getting white hairs all over me, cat, but it's a good job I like you. Morgan, before I go, I need to know if there is anything troubling you. I couldn't sleep last night worrying about you and look at you, proof I was right to be worried. I just knew something was brewing.'

'Same old, I'm afraid, Ettie. I need to find a killer before he strikes again, and I had a thumping headache.'

'This is different, I feel as if I need to give you a warning, but I'll be damned if I don't know what about, so I'll say it anyway. I don't think you should be going anywhere alone at the moment. I don't want to know what you're working on. I'm not like you, I would never sleep again thinking about all the horrible people and terrible things you have to deal with, but I need you to be very careful. It looks as if you already lost one fight. I'm worried about you, so do you think you can bear it in mind?'

'Of course, I will. I don't go anywhere alone anyway. I usually have someone with me, but we're short-staffed at work, so I may have to do enquiries alone. Is that okay?'

Ettie thought about it. 'I suppose it should be as long as you tell people where you are going. I'm probably being silly, far too overprotective, and you can tell me to stop interfering anytime, but you're all I have left, and I love you far more than you could ever know.'

Morgan stood up and walked to where her aunt was sitting. She wrapped her arms around her, breathing in the smell of lavender, rosemary and lemon. Ettie stood up and the pair of them stood in Ben's kitchen, holding on to each other, rocking.

'I needed that, thank you, Morgan, I best be going, or I'll miss my spot at the market.'

'Me too, thank you for calling and bringing the tea.'

'There's a guy who sells eggs, he's annoying and always tries to pinch my space.'

'What a cheek, have you told him to back off? Would you like me to?'

Ettie laughed. 'Oh, I've told him, don't you worry about that. Make sure Ben tries the tea at least; if he adds lemon and honey, it won't taste as bad, and it might even make him feel a lot better in himself.'

She turned and swept out of the kitchen, down the hallway and out of the front door, where she turned to wave.

'Morgan, I love you. Please don't work yourself too hard.'

Then she shut the front door behind her, leaving Morgan staring at it.

Ben's voice asked, 'Was that Ettie?' as he was emerging from the bedroom.

'It was, she brought you a gift.' He let out a groan and she began to laugh. 'Come on, Ettie's orders, you have to drink this every morning to give you some of your umph back.'

'Did she actually say that?'

'Sort of, I've made breakfast, so after you've had your tea you can wash it down with a bacon roll.'

'You know how to treat a man.'

'I do.'

He stepped down and pulled her close. 'How's your head? And why are you fully dressed, are you going somewhere?'

She kissed him then pushed him away. 'You know why. I feel fine, I cannot stay home all day twiddling my thumbs, while you're working your socks off, trying to find the killer. You might as well let me come to work and be useful. If I feel ill or my head is too sore, I'll go home, but don't leave me here when I can help out.'

'You promise you'll tell me if you feel ill and need to have a rest?'

'I do solemnly swear.'

'I'm not going to argue with you, I haven't got the energy and there's a lot to do. I have one condition.'

'What's that?'

'You are office bound unless I need you.'

'Deal.'

He followed her into the kitchen and stared at the jar of tea. 'That looks absolutely terrifying.'

She began to laugh. 'It probably is but bless her heart she

was thinking about you. You at least must try it, especially after she went to all the effort of making it and hand delivering it to you. I think you're forgiven and deep down she likes you.'

He nodded, and she began to boil the kettle ready to steep him some of her aunt's magical tea blend that could cure almost anything.

THIRTY-NINE

All the way to work Morgan couldn't stop trying to work out the killer's motive. What was it, what was it about these two particular women that had stirred up something inside of him, to make him want to kill them? His modus operandi, his MO, was to tie his victims up then suffocate them... he had done this to both Jasmine and Emily. His signature, what he needed to do to serve his fantasy about his victims, was what? To leave them in places that had significant meaning to them.

By the time they got to work she was on fire and itching to do something to get things moving. When she walked into the office, she was relieved to see that Barb hadn't made an appearance again. Cain must have been unsuccessful in tracking her down, and hopefully, by now, she was at the landfill site covered in tons of rubbish.

Amy and Cain had both looked at her but decided not to say anything when she walked through the door followed by Ben.

They barely had time to remove their coats when Marc stuck his head in. 'Ben, meeting now.'

Ben dutifully followed his boss out of the door, and Cain whispered, 'Wonder what that's about?'

Morgan shrugged. 'Be nice if they had a lead on the suspect.'

'Wouldn't it? How's your head?'

'Still working, just. I was thinking as we were driving in about the fact that Jasmine's dump site was where her dad had taken his own life six months ago, and who would know this. Who did she talk to about it? It was in the papers, but for a killer to go to all the effort of driving her car there and then having to get home again, it's a lot. Emily loved where she lived, she was very proud of her beautiful apartment in the gorgeous old Georgian house where we used to be neighbours. She told me that she liked to pretend she owned the entire house and often posted photos on her Instagram outside of it, referring to it as her home. Who had she told this information to, apart from me? I think the killer knows them both on a personal level, and they weren't just randomly plucked out of a hat.'

'I think we'd already established that, Morgan,' replied Amy.

'Did we, sorry just let me get this out of my head, it's been bothering me all night. I think he's very organised, and I bet he's following the news religiously, buying the papers to see his name in print. You have to think about it, he must have known them. The CCTV at the pub shows Ben, Declan and Theo leaving, a few minutes later Emily follows. She wasn't on her phone to call a taxi when she left. Did anyone check with the taxi firms, to see if she rang for one, or if they did any drop-offs around that time?'

Cain looked at Amy. 'I'll sort that out. What about Theo? I know you're friends and you've ruled out Ben and Declan, of course, but Theo left alone. He could have taken a fancy to Emily, and she might have declined his advances and boom, he got carried away and killed her.'

Morgan felt defensive. 'That's different.'

'How is it different? He was in the area. Shouldn't we at least go question him about his movement after he left Ben's house?'

'He didn't know Jasmine for a start, and I don't think he knew Emily either. He also walked home; he doesn't have a car to transport either of them in, and as he's relatively new to the area he wouldn't know about Jasmine's dad's suicide or how much Emily adored that house.'

'Doesn't mean he hasn't killed them.'

Amy looked as if she was in pain and she held up her hand.

'Enough, we are not bringing the vicar in for questioning again with nothing substantial. The boss will have a shit fit, and besides, like Morgan said he walked home from Ben's. The vicarage is the opposite direction to Emily's address, and I doubt he would have known about Jasmine's dad. That's just clutching at straws, but, Cain, I like your enthusiasm, maybe just don't mention it to Ben.'

Cain looked deflated, and Morgan felt bad. 'We're not saying you shouldn't have an opinion, because you should always. It's just I don't think Theo has anything to do with it, and we can't afford to waste time chasing the wrong suspects while the right one is choosing his next victim.'

'Do you think that he is, choosing his next one?'

Morgan wanted to say of course not, but she knew there was a very good chance whoever it was had got a taste for killing now.

'I hate to say it, but yes. I think he will be. He's left very little forensics behind at both scenes, he's good, he's organised, he's on a roll and he is probably thinking that we haven't got a clue, so he can keep on doing what he's doing.'

'He's not wrong though, is he? We haven't got a bloody clue and we seem to be getting nowhere fast.'

Amy stood up. 'Damn it, we were supposed to go to the sixth form, Cain. Why didn't you remember?'

'Why didn't you?'

She laughed at him. 'You figure it out, Morgan, and I'll take Cain to go speak to the staff at the college so you can think in peace.'

The door opened and Ben was followed in by Marc; he looked at the three of them and frowned.

'You two were on your way to the college when I left, but I want a quick briefing while we're all here before MIT turn up tomorrow, so we're all singing off the same sheet and look like we know where we are up to and what we are doing.

'Morgan talk to me: what enquires need picking up that haven't been done?'

She picked up the list she'd been compiling and began to read from it.

'"Fingerprints." Have we heard if there was a hit on the partials from the dental surgery camera?'

Ben held up a hand. 'Actually, I just got an email and no, they don't match anything we have on file, unfortunately for us.'

Morgan nodded and continued.

'"Taxi firm for drop-offs or pickups to the pub. Check both Emily's and Jasmine's social media accounts to see if they knew each other or had mutual friends. Alternative uses for alginate." We could be completely wrong, and it didn't come from the dental surgery. "Speak to staff, students at the sixth form, to see if Emily had any issues with anyone."'

Marc glanced at Ben who was smiling.

'Good, that's good. Amy and Cain are going to the sixth form to speak to staff there, so that's another one ticked off. Morgan, can you follow up with the taxi ranks? Marc and I are going to make sure the files are in order, and everything has been updated.'

He went into his office and came out with the blue file that was the policy book, each murder investigation had one. Then they were gone, back to Marc's office, she presumed, so they wouldn't be disturbed.

Amy and Cain left her alone in the office; normally she was eager to get out there but this time she was quite happy to have some time to herself, to give her brain a rest from the constant banter and think about the murders.

She began to phone around the three taxi firms that covered Ambleside and Rydal Falls, so she could get that checked off. None of them had a drop-off or a pickup at The Black Dog all night on Friday.

Next, she logged herself into her rarely used Facebook account and typed in Emily's name; she was already friends with her, so it made sense to go through her friends list first. Morgan had a grand total of thirty-nine Facebook friends, and she had over five hundred friend requests from people she had never met in her life. Emily had over a thousand friends: it was mind blowing. They had two mutual friends: Ben Matthews and Des Black. She let out a sigh and didn't click on Des's profile, it was too upsetting. She clicked on Ben's and scrolled down his feed – his one and only post had been back in 2019. She smiled, he wasn't into Facebook or any kind of social media. Emily was going to have Ben as a friend, she dated the guy for a few weeks; she wasn't sure how she knew Des, but he wasn't here, so he was definitely not a suspect, and neither was Ben.

Next, she typed Jasmine Armer's name into the search bar. Morgan didn't know Jasmine before she saw her dead body. Emily didn't know Jasmine either: by the look of their Facebook accounts, neither of them were friends. They both had Esme Barnard as a mutual friend, which was interesting – obviously Emily and Esme were going to be Facebook friends, they were close. But Esme had denied knowing Jasmine until her husband had pointed out that she most definitely did. Morgan was scribbling this all down.

Next, she clicked on a picture of Neil and went onto his friends list, to find that he was a mutual friend of both women. Everything kept coming back to the Barnards. She saw the name 'Tobias Barnard' on Jasmine's list, and sat back. How old was he? Fifteen, maybe sixteen? She clicked on his profile and saw a picture of him standing in a pair of shorts, no T-shirt on and sweat dripping from his muscular body, which made her think he looked a lot older than the spotty fifteen-year-olds she knew at school. Apart from her friend Brad: he had been handsome and a fit rugby player until the day of his accident. A wave of sadness washed over her. She missed Brad, he'd been a good friend. Now a part of her wished she'd never logged into Facebook, to remind her of the memories of the friends who were no longer alive. She was almost tempted to go onto Brad's profile and look at his face.

'Who is that?'

She hadn't even heard Ben come back in.

'Oh, that's Tobias Barnard, he's the teenage son of Neil and Esme.'

'Get out, he looks old enough to be out drinking in the pubs.'

Morgan looked at Ben. 'Was he in The Black Dog?'

'I couldn't say. But we should get his alibi. It was only yesterday that I realised their kids weren't little boys. We have nothing to lose interviewing him. Does it say what school he goes to or college?'

'I doubt it, he won't be acting his real age on here: no respectable teenager actually writes their profile details out true to form.' She went onto his *about info* to double check. 'Well shoot me down, it says that he was a pupil at Queen Mary's.'

'I'll see if Amy can go.'

'She's gone to the sixth form with Cain. I can do it?'

'I thought we agreed office time only.'

'We did, but I know the deputy head at Queen Mary's; they're going to speak to me a bit more openly.'

'How do you know them?'

'I went to school there; they definitely know me.'

He nodded. 'Can you drive though?'

'I'm not seeing double.'

'Bloody hell, Morgan, that doesn't fill me with much hope.'

'It's five minutes away, I'll walk if you want.'

'No, I'd rather you drove. I'd come with you, but Marc wants me to give an update to Claire and a couple of detectives from MIT when they arrive. He'll be furious if I disappear without warning.'

'I'm a big girl, I can manage.'

'I know you can, don't go scaring the kids.'

She gasped and punched him in the shoulder.

'Ouch, that's assault.'

She tugged on her coat and blew him a kiss.

'Straight there and back, no messing around, Morgan, I mean it. I have not got the time to be worrying about you.'

'As if you need to worry about me, I'm fine.'

She walked out before he could change his mind, grabbing a set of car keys off the whiteboard next to the door.

FORTY

Queen Mary's Secondary School didn't look much different to the last time Morgan had walked through the gates back when she was an angry, sad and lonely teenager. She'd had friends, but none that she had been especially close to, and the ones she had were now dead. It was a sobering thought.

Morgan had known she wanted to be a police officer since the day she'd found out one of her friend's bodies had been found on a rock at Rydal Cave. She'd become a little bit reclusive, withdrawing from the friends she did have and focusing on college to get the exam results she'd needed to apply to the police.

She walked into the large airy reception area and smiled at the woman behind the desk who had a phone tucked under her ear. She put the phone down.

'Can I help you?'

'I hope so, I'm Detective Morgan Brookes. Is it possible to speak to Mr Scott?'

'I'll just check. Do you want to take a seat?' As an afterthought she asked, 'Is he expecting you?'

'No, but it's urgent.'

Morgan looked over at the three chairs, where a girl with a face that was deathly pale was sitting with a cardboard sick bowl in her hands. She smiled at her but had no intention of sitting anywhere near her, the last thing she needed on top of this pounding headache was a sickness bug. She stood, leaning against the wall a safe distance away from her, and tugged her lanyard out of her jacket so it could be clearly seen for the receptionist's benefit.

A few minutes later she heard a deep voice she recognised.

'Well, if it isn't Morgan Brookes, how are you?'

She turned to see Mr Scott and smiled; she'd always liked him. He'd been her form teacher all through school.

'Not too bad,' she replied.

She walked towards him, and he scrunched up his eyes as he stared at the side of her face.

'What happened to your face? Can I get you anything?'

'This, oh it's old news, this happened yesterday afternoon. I'm okay, thanks.'

He nodded, then opened the gate so she could get through into the school, then he led her down the corridor towards his office.

'I bet this brings back memories.'

'It does.'

She didn't elaborate and tell him it brought back dreadful memories; she followed him into his office where he pointed at a chair.

'Can I get you a drink?'

'I'm okay, thank you. It does feel strange being in here and not expecting to be told off from Mrs Robinson.'

He laughed. 'She was an old stick in the mud, wasn't she? I don't think anyone misses her. I prefer a gentler approach with the students. I think she used to forget that first and foremost they were young people with thoughts and feelings.'

'That's why everyone liked you and hated her.'

'They did?'

'Absolutely, everyone thought you were cool.'

He was grinning. 'Well, I never, thank you, Morgan, that's nice to know. Look at you though, all grown up and a detective, a brave, hardworking one too. You are such a good example to the students. How do you fancy coming in for careers week? You might be able to motivate some of this lot into realising there's more to life than being an Instagram influencer or a YouTuber.'

It was her turn to laugh. 'I really couldn't think of anything worse, sorry. I'm not into doing school talks.'

'Such a shame, but I understand. You were always so quiet, but you didn't come here to reminisce, how can I help you?'

'I'm on enquiries for two serious incidents, and I'm trying to find out some background information on Tobias Barnard.'

'You don't think he is involved, do you?'

'I don't think so, or I hope not, but the Barnard family name keeps cropping up in my investigation. I know this is difficult with confidentiality but I'm trying to find out what sort of boy he is.'

He held up his hands. 'He's cocky and arrogant.'

Morgan hadn't expected that, and he continued, 'Such great potential but completely not interested in school, not one bit. He's disruptive and, to be honest with you, I'll be glad when he leaves this year.'

'Can I ask what he's done to make you form that opinion of him? You were always the one sticking up for us all back in the day.'

'I don't know what it is but kids the last few years, they seem to have this sense of entitlement about them, they think the world owes them. Not all of them, but some of them and Tobias definitely does. I think it's because he comes from a wealthy family that he feels as if he doesn't need to do anything with his life because it's all taken care of. He's a bully too, just horrible to some of the students who come from much less fortunate backgrounds.'

'Is he mature for his age, would you say?'

'Probably far too mature, but he chooses to play the class clown to disrupt lessons.'

'What are his parents like?'

'I think his stepmum despairs of him; his dad idolises him and can see no wrong. The last time I called them in for a meeting, she was overwrought, she kept looking at Dad, who repeatedly stated that he's just a boy having fun and taking things a bit too far, and she was shaking her head in what I considered to be disbelief at him.'

'Where is he now?'

'Excluded again for hanging a year seven from their ankles in the hall by the ropes and leaving him there to have an asthma attack. If I had my way, I'd permanently exclude him, but Neil has friends on the board of governors, say no more. He is nothing like his older brother, Hugo; he was such a good student; he reminds me a lot of you, kept his head down, studied hard and caused no trouble.'

Morgan hadn't seen a Hugo Barnard on either Emily's or Jasmine's friend lists.

'Where's Hugo now?'

'I'm not sure, I think he went away to college.'

She wasn't sure if she should be asking this but did anyway.

'Is Tobias a violent person?'

He nodded. 'Unfortunately, he's always punching someone or fighting after school. No one ever complains about him though. I think they're all too scared of him. I haven't painted him in a very good light, have I? But I'm not going to sit here and tell you he's a great lad, when the reality is he's a dickhead.'

Morgan laughed. 'Mr Scott, do you always refer to your students like that?'

He grinned at her. 'Only the ones who deserve it, this is

between us by the way. If the Barnards found out they'd have me sacked.'

'I won't say a word. Do they have that much power?'

'I don't know, but Neil is almost as intolerable as his son.'

She nodded.

'You've met him then?'

'Yes, I have,' she replied. She could see him studying her intently.

'Morgan what happened to your head? Your poor face is so bruised.'

'An argument with a hammer-wielding woman. It looks that bad even under the make-up?'

'No, not that bad from a distance.'

'You are a terrible liar, Mr Scott.'

'I am? Yes, I'm not good at it, so that's why I tend to stick to the truth. Do you think Tobias is involved in your investigation?'

'I honestly don't know yet; I'm trying to rule people out.'

'As you can gather there is no love lost between us, but he really isn't a nice boy, and it would come as no surprise to me to find out that he has been up to no good out of school.'

'Thank you, I'd appreciate it if this is kept between me and you for the time being.'

'Absolutely, I'd appreciate you not letting the Barnards know I think their son is a dickhead, although to be honest they probably already know that.'

She stood up and smiled. 'I'm glad you're doing okay, Mr Scott.'

'You can call me Josh; you're all grown up now.'

She laughed. 'Oh no, I don't think I could ever do that, you'll always be Mr Scott to me.'

'And that makes me feel old.'

As she walked out of the door, he called after her, 'Morgan, I'm really proud of you, thank you for everything you do.'

Her cheeks tinged with pink. She waved at him and walked

out of the school, feeling a bit warm and fuzzy inside. She had no parents to tell her they were proud of her, so to hear that from her old teacher made her tear up a little.

By the time she reached the car she was on the verge of tears. She got inside and had to blot her eyes with a tissue as she whispered to herself, *Brookes, you're going soft in your old age.*

The girl with the sick bowl walked past with a woman who she presumed was her parent and gave a large heave, then proceeded to throw up all over the pavement, spraying pink vomit everywhere.

Morgan grimaced and drove away, before her own stomach started to churn at the sight of it.

FORTY-ONE

Morgan parked outside the front of the station and risked being told off by the Chief Super, but she really couldn't be bothered driving around the back, where the staff were supposed to leave their cars. She walked through the front entrance and past the reception desk, where Brenda was filling out forms.

'Morning, Brenda, how are you?'

'Morning Mrs, I'm probably better than you. How are you?' She stepped closer so she could take a look at her face. 'Ouch, that looks sore.'

'It is, but don't tell Ben, he thinks I'm one tough bitch.'

Brenda began to laugh. 'You are one tough bitch; your skull must be made from iron plates the number of times it's been bashed in. Why are you at work?'

She shrugged. 'What else is there to do? And the team are flat out with the murders.'

'I know, it's so terrible but you got to look after yourself, Morgan, no one else will. Hey, did Ben give you the parcel I gave to him yesterday?'

'No, he probably forgot he has it. He has a worse memory

than me and he doesn't get hit in the head with hammers, so I've no idea what his excuse is.'

'You're terrible, but funny.'

'I know, thank you. I'll get it off him later.'

She left Brenda to finish filling out her forms and wondered what parcel she had; she hadn't ordered anything to be delivered here lately.

Upstairs, the main office was empty. She wandered along the corridor and saw the glass-walled normally empty office that was kept for major incidents was lit up. As she got closer, she saw Ben, Marc, Claire from MIT, and another two women she didn't know, all sitting around the table in the corner in deep discussion. That was good, they would bring in extra staff to help them, if they needed it, and relieve some of the pressure off Ben.

She turned and went back to their dingy cramped office that was tucked away and not on display for the whole station to see. She wanted to speak to Tobias Barnard but wasn't sure how; she would have to run it by the others and get it cleared, unless she went to speak to him now, before she got her orders from above. She could do that, couldn't she? No one except for Brenda knew she was here. She could go there now... she stopped herself, no she couldn't, not if Esme was there. She would have been given bail conditions not to approach or contact Morgan. Damn it, but she wouldn't tell, if Esme didn't. She turned and left the same way she'd come in.

Brenda looked up. 'That was quick.'

'I forgot something.'

Then she was back in the car and driving towards Pine Hall, hoping to get there before Ben realised she hadn't come back, and phoned her to see where she was.

* * *

Pine Hall didn't look quite so grand the second time she approached it. She noticed that the paint was peeling in the corners and looked as if it hadn't been touched for a long time; there was a broken window, too, that she hadn't seen yesterday. A Range Rover was parked outside along with a blue moped. She hoped this meant that both Esme and Tobias were home. She knocked on the door and waited for it to open. When it did, she saw a bedraggled Esme staring back at her.

'What are you doing here?' she said.

'Can I come in?'

'I'm not supposed to be anywhere near you.'

'I know, but I won't tell and besides it was an accident, wasn't it? Or did you mean to smash my brains in?'

'No, of course I didn't. I wanted to smash Neil's in. I'm sorry I missed and got you instead. I didn't stop crying all day in those horrid cells, and my chest hurts where those tasers struck me. I didn't know it could hurt so much.'

Morgan smiled at her. 'Yeah, they're painful. I didn't think you wanted to hurt me.'

'Come inside,' Esme said, moving backwards to let Morgan in.

She did as she was asked, following her into a large lounge, where Esme closed the door behind them.

'I feel terrible about what happened to you. Are you okay? I thought I'd killed you; it was so loud, the thwack of the hammer on your head.'

'I'm good.'

'What are you doing here?'

'I know you've been interviewed, but I just can't stop wondering why you wanted to hurt Neil.'

Esme took a deep breath. 'I looked at the doorbell camera after you left, and saw that he was out when he told me he wasn't going anywhere. I told you that. I was drunk and I decided that he had something to do with Emily's murder; he's fancied her for ages. I can tell when he's flirting, he gets all boyish, if you know what I mean. It's quite sickening to watch him when he's like that.'

Morgan didn't know but nodded.

'I lost my shit, I shouldn't have, and I should never have gone into his work like that. I don't know what came over me.'

'You were in shock; I don't suppose the gin helped.'

Esme groaned. 'I'm never touching that stuff again, it's all I can taste.'

'Do you really think he could do something like this?'

'I don't know what I think. I can tell you that he's one big creepy flirt when he likes someone. I know he really liked that young dental nurse, and he definitely fancied Emily... but to think that he might have killed them? I don't know if he has the balls to do something of that nature.'

'What about your sons? Are they okay after yesterday's incident? Do they know what happened?'

'They're Neil's sons, my stepsons. Yes, they know all about it. I had to tell them when they wanted to know why we were both in custody, and why Neil couldn't come home last night.'

'How were they?'

'Hugo never said anything; he's so quiet, he doesn't really share his feelings with anyone. He's such a nice lad. He just asked if I was okay and if I needed anything. Unlike Tobias, who went mad. He was shouting and throwing a tantrum like an eight-year-old.'

She passed Morgan a school photo of both boys taken a few years earlier.

'They look so alike and handsome,' Morgan said. 'Who broke the window?'

'Tobias, he threw a chair at it in a rage because his dad couldn't come home, and he was stuck here with me. There were shards of glass everywhere; it took me forever to clean it up, and it was the last thing I felt like doing after the day I'd had. He's such a...'

'Such a what, Esme?'

A low voice came from behind her.

Morgan looked up to see him standing in a running vest and shorts, his hair damp and beads of perspiration on his forehead.

'You're such an arse, Tobias, that's what,' Esme finished.

He laughed. 'Says you, the woman who thought it was okay to drive into Windermere pissed up and smack some copper over the head with a hammer.'

He crossed his arms and arched an eyebrow at Esme, who glared at him.

Morgan stood up and turned to face him. 'Your mum had a bad day yesterday; you need to cut her some slack and be a little understanding.'

He stared at her. 'It's you, you're the one she battered and you're here sticking up for the crazy bitch. She could have killed you.'

'Yeah, well she didn't, and you need to think about how she might be feeling.'

'What about my dad? How's he feeling now she's accused him of killing two women and kicked him out?'

Morgan could see the anger blazing in his eyes, and she thought to herself that he could, with his strength and hormones, quite easily overpower and kill someone. She needed to defuse the situation.

'I'm sure your dad is okay; if he has nothing to worry about things will work out.'

He shook his head. 'Unbelievable, you're sticking up for her after what she did to you. Have you got brain damage?'

Esme growled at him. 'Go to your room.'

He shook his head, turned and walked out.

Morgan waited until she heard his footsteps as he stamped up each and every stair tread.

'I'm sorry about him, I'm sorry about everything. Thank you for defending me after everything you've been through.'

Morgan smiled at her. She felt sorry for Esme and wasn't sure that she was the killer they were looking for. Underneath all of her bravado she seemed like a nice woman, and if she felt that bad about hurting her, how would she be feeling about killing two women?

'I'll leave you to it, I just wanted you to know I was okay. One last thing, whose is the scooter?'

Esme pointed to the ceiling. 'His Lordships, I told Neil not to buy him one, to make him get a little part-time job to earn some money, to put towards it, but he completely ignored me and bought him it anyway.'

'It must be so hard trying to bring up two lads when Neil disregards your opinion.'

'You don't know the half of it. I sometimes think I'm just a cash cow for them.'

'It's your house, why don't you kick them out and tell Neil to bring them up on his own? Then he might realise how difficult it can be.'

'I would happily throw him out on his arse. I couldn't do that to Hugo though, he's such a darling; and Tobias never used to be this angry all the time. I'm hoping it's a phase and not permanent.'

Morgan smiled at her. 'They're all old enough to stand on their own two feet. I would seriously be considering it, if I was you. Especially if they can't even show you some respect when you're the one providing them with this beautiful home to live in.'

Esme nodded. 'I'm so tired of their bullshit and all the testosterone floating around. I totally get why women just pack a case and leave, to go off where no one can find them. It's too tempting just thinking about spending a week on a tropical island on my own.'

'Why don't you?'

'I'm on police bail for assault, in case you forgot.'

Morgan felt bad for her. 'Oh, yes. Look, have you ever been in trouble before?'

Esme shook her head.

'It's extenuating circumstances, you were in a state of despair after the awful news about your best friend. I'm sure you have a pretty good lawyer; they will help you and I'm not pressing charges.'

'You're not?'

'No, I can't do much about the charges for holding Neil and a patient hostage, but I won't be adding anything to the assault charge. I'm pretty sure you won't go to prison, even though it's a pretty spectacular array of offences for a first-time offender. What a way to start your foray into criminality.'

She winked at Esme who began to laugh, and Morgan joined in.

'You're pretty cool for a police officer, and I really am sorry, I would never in a million years have hurt you on purpose.'

'Thank you, and I know. When this is all over you want to think about that holiday.'

'Don't you worry, I will.'

Morgan stood up to leave, and an older boy the image of Tobias walked in the room. He smiled at her, his cheeks turning an angry red.

'You must be Hugo?'

He nodded.

'I'm Morgan and I'm just leaving, but I wanted to say hi and how sorry I am about all of this mess.'

'That's one way to describe it.' He glanced at Esme, who

was beaming at him with such fondness it made Morgan feel a little better that she had someone on her side.

Morgan wanted to get back and tell Ben they needed to bring Tobias in. He was looking like a pretty good suspect to her, and Esme was stuck in that house with him, which was the worrying part. What if he decided to hurt her?

FORTY-TWO

Amy and Cain were shown to the art department by a teenager who never spoke once. He pointed out the classrooms and then hurried away. It was a separate building to the rest of the college, built out of the same dark brown bricks and very modular in design. Amy thought it looked like a giant matchbox, not an art building; there was nothing arty about it from the outside.

'He was a chatterbox.'

Amy smirked. 'What were you like as a teenager? I bet you were one of the lads, all full of themselves on the football team and dating different girls every week.'

He laughed. 'Not even close. I was the fat boy with the man boobs who was terrified of girls, boys and the teachers. I hated school, I hated everything except rugby. I was a prop and a pretty good one.'

'You were? Sorry, Cain, I just assumed you'd always been carefree.'

'Nope, my mum, bless her, used to let me eat what I wanted because it was just me and her. She made me man-sized portions of everything, so school on the whole was pretty miserable.

'What about you, were you the moody girl who was always picking fights because they hated what they saw in the mirror?'

'Jesus, thanks a lot.' She laughed. 'Actually, that's pretty spot on. I was horrible most of the time.'

Cain stepped forward and knocked on the glass door to the art room, which was massive.

'At least you've improved slightly; you're only angry half of the time now.'

She glared at him as the door opened and a woman looked at them both.

'Yes?'

'Are you busy?'

'What does it look like to you?' She pointed to the students wandering around, some of them leaning over desks, drawing, others painting at easels.

'We're detectives, we need to talk to you about Emily Wearing.'

'Oh, I'm sorry, come in. I have a little office at the back of the room. Go down and I'll be there shortly.'

Cain led the way through the classroom. Not one kid looked up at either of them as they walked into the cramped room full of art supplies, a small desk with a kettle, microwave and assorted cutlery, mugs and plates. There were two chairs and a stool. They took a chair each, and Cain whispered, 'Well, this is cosy.'

The woman walked in and smiled at him. 'It's not much but trust me on the days you can't be bothered it's a safe haven. I can't believe that Emily is dead, that she won't be sitting in that chair you're in, complaining about her love life or lack of it ever again.'

Cain squirmed in his chair, and Amy nodded.

'It's terribly sad and so tragic.'

'I'm Nieve Hill, we worked together a lot of the time.'

'I'm Detective Amy Smith and this is my colleague, Cain Robson. We're trying to piece together Emily's last hours, and we're very sorry for your loss, but if you can help, we'd really appreciate it.'

'I don't know how I can be of much help. It was my half day Friday, so I only saw her in the afternoon for a couple of hours.'

'Well let's start with the basics. We're trying to get a general impression of her. How did she get on with the students?'

'Amazing, they all love Emily, they're not so keen on old Ms Hill,' she said, pointing to herself.

'You're not old?'

Nieve laughed. 'I am to this lot, I'm fifty-six and practically ancient.'

'What about the staff? Do you know if she had any issues with anyone here?'

'No, she was well-liked, she was quite forward in her ways, you know the kind, straight-talking, didn't take no for an answer, but sometimes that's not a bad thing, is it? I wish I had a fraction of her confidence, when I was her age.'

'Did she ever mention trouble at home? Did she have a partner or was she seeing someone?'

'Not that I know of. There was one man, a detective like yourselves. I don't think she really got over him. He broke it off quite some time ago, and it shocked her. Emily was usually the one to call it a day. She talked about him a lot at first. I don't know whether she's seen anyone since him, but she hasn't mentioned it. I think it knocked her confidence in the male department a bit.'

Amy stopped writing; she didn't want to have to show this to Ben – he was feeling guilty enough about all of this without rubbing salt in his wounds.

'What happened on Friday afternoon?'

'I came in, we had a still life class with a model for the

students to draw. Emily disappeared for a bit when I arrived, which isn't unlike her. We hide in here but there's a proper office we use down the corridor for marking and such.'

'How was her demeanour?'

'Fine, she was chatty, told me she was looking forward to meeting her friend at the pub later. Then she left a little earlier to go to a dental appointment.'

Amy's fingers gripped the pen in one hand and the notebook in the other at the mention of a dental appointment.

'Did she say which dentist she was going to?'

'There isn't much choice around here, is there? She went to New Smile in Windermere. She said she was thinking about getting one of those invisible braces, not that she needed it, but she thought she did.'

'Is there anything at all you can think of that might help, any run-ins with students or staff, any problems out of work?'

'I'm sorry, but if there was, she never mentioned it to me, and I never heard any gossip in the staff room about anything and, trust me, the staff here are the worst gossips in the world.'

Amy's phone rang and she saw Morgan's name. 'Excuse me I need to answer this.'

Nieve smiled at her.

'Morgan.'

'Are you still at the college?'

'We are.'

'Can you ask if a Tobias Barnard has ever attended any classes? He's a pupil at Queen Mary's but sometimes they send them out for courses.'

'Yes, will do. Anything else?'

'No, thanks.'

She hung up. 'Nieve, that was my colleague. She wants to know if Queen Mary's ever send students here.'

'Yes, they do. We quite often get small groups of students who are showing a gift for art. We run six-week courses covering the basic foundations of art and design, usually focused on a theme.'

'Do you recall if a Tobias Barnard ever attended?'

'Tobias, I don't think so but then again it was Emily that taught those classes.'

'What kind of things do they do?'

'The last couple of groups have done set design for the school drama groups that kind of thing. Costume making, background artwork, posters.'

Amy was scribbling it all down. 'Thank you for your time.'

'You're welcome, you will find whoever did this, won't you?'

'Absolutely, no doubt about that.'

'Good, thank you. I haven't even had the heart to tell the students. The principal is coming in soon to make an announcement, so we can send them home if they need to go. It's so sad and unexpected.'

Amy stood up, quickly followed by Cain. They left Nieve sniffing into a tissue and walked back out – still no one looked their way.

When they got outside Cain whispered, 'Talk about feeling invisible.'

'Haha, if you'd have gone in wearing your uniform, they'd have all been gawping. There are benefits to wearing plain clothes. They probably thought we were Ofsted inspectors or something. We better get back and see what Morgan's up to, and find out why she wants to know about Tobias Barnard.'

They left the college and drove back to the station, stopping for coffee on the way back.

Amy felt bad for Ben; even though he'd only briefly gone out with Emily, he must still be in shock, especially after losing Cindy then Morgan getting attacked yesterday. No wonder he had heart problems.

FORTY-THREE

Morgan made it back to the station without getting caught. This time she drove around to the back yard, not wanting to chance getting told off after getting away with it the first time. She let herself in and walked up the stairs, wondering why she hadn't called for coffees on the way in, and let out a big sigh.

She thought that Tobias Barnard was looking good as a viable suspect. They would need a strategy in place, which was where Claire and the MIT came into things, before they could bring him in. She no longer considered Esme a suspect. She wouldn't entirely rule out Neil, but Tobias was her priority now.

The lights were still on in the incident room but off in her office. She switched them on and sat back down, wondering how Amy had got on, when in walked a vision of both Amy and Cain, who was holding a carry-out tray filled with four coffee cups.

'You didn't? Oh my God, you little lifesavers. I was literally just dreaming about a latte. Please tell me one of those is mine?' She held her hands together, fingers steepled in a prayer gesture.

Cain winked at her and placed one on the desk in front of her.

'I could kiss you.'

'Don't let me stop you.'

'Haha, you're too funny.'

'Where's the boss man? We got him one too.'

'Major Incident Room with MIT and Marc.'

Cain frowned. 'Didn't get the boss's boss coffee though, because he doesn't deserve it, and what's going on?'

'I think Marc is trying to ease the strain on us all by requesting help from above, which is good, especially for Ben. They will be going through everything we've done up to now and coming up with a strategy on how to move forward but—'

'But what?' asked Amy.

'I have a strong lead.'

Ben rushed through the door and looked at her. 'You do?'

Cain offered him the coffee, and he took it smiling in appreciation.

'Yes, we need to focus on Tobias Barnard, the Barnards' youngest son. He is currently excluded from school for hanging a year seven kid up by his feet in the gym. Apparently he's violent, a bully and he knows both victims. Everything keeps coming back to the Barnards, so what if it's him? Esme said she is sick of his behaviour; he threw a chair through the window of their house last night because his dad wasn't allowed home.'

Ben was staring at her. 'How do you know this about the window?'

'I spoke to Esme.'

'Morgan, she has bail conditions not to approach you.'

'I know, I approached her. And she didn't mean it, I got in the way. She's not the killer; she was too distraught and was a right mess when I saw her compared to how she presented herself yesterday, before it all went wrong.'

'Marc will go mad if he knows you went there alone. Why did you do that? Because I'm not too happy about it myself.'

'Do we want to figure this out and get the killer in custody, or are we going to mess around taking forever while he goes and kills another woman?'

Ben took a large gulp of the coffee. 'I want you to run stuff by me, that's all. You said you were only going to the school. Morgan, do not leave this office again today. I'll share what you've told me with the others and see what they think.'

He went into his office, grabbed some files then left them all staring at each other. The door slammed loudly behind him.

'Busted again, Brookes, you are a liability.'

'Shut up, Cain, you'd have done the same.'

'Not me, I'm too scared of the boss man to piss him off like you do.'

Amy nodded. 'Can you phone your contact at Queen Mary's, and ask if Tobias attended the college for any art classes? The teacher couldn't remember off hand and said that it was Emily who taught the secondary school kids. It's definitely worth checking out. It proves they knew each other.'

'I can; they did know each other though, through Esme, and I'm sure he will have known Jasmine through Neil. She went to the house for a summer BBQ; he would have seen her then.'

'I know but it's even more of a connection, and ten quid they come in and tell us we have to do a massive house-to-house around the dentists in Windermere, to speak to everyone in the area in case they saw something when Jasmine left on Wednesday.'

'But it's already been done.'

'Morgan, you wait. They'll come in with clipboards, and every officer, PCSO and us will have to go back and canvass the entire town, so they can tick it off their checklist. It's what they do.'

Cain shook his head. 'Except for you, Morgan, because you're grounded.'

He started to laugh, and she shrugged. 'I'd rather sit here and twiddle my thumbs than spend hours freezing my pants off, knocking on doors and speaking to members of the public, which will be a complete waste of time, because if someone had witnessed something, don't you think they'd have come forward and said, "I saw that young woman get abducted"?'

Amy nodded. 'I agree with you. It will be a waste of time, but it's how it goes, and we have to keep trying, don't we?'

A few minutes later Ben came back in.

'Amy, Cain, blue room, we're going to canvass the area around New Smile again with a full team. Morgan, you're to man the phones and collate any information that comes in, follow up on leads, and under no circumstances are you allowed out of this station.'

She was furious with him; he was treating her like a child, and she could feel the rage building inside of her chest; but she wouldn't argue with him here and be disrespectful. She would save that for later.

'Right.'

He turned to leave. 'Blue room now, not in ten minutes, you two.'

'Ben.'

He looked at Morgan, and she knew he was stressed by the way his tie was skewed and his top button was undone, not to mention the darkness in his eyes.

'Did Brenda give you a parcel for me yesterday?'

'She did, sorry. I left it on the living room table and forgot to tell you when I got in.'

'That's okay, it can't be important.'

He smiled at her, but she didn't smile back. She got that he was worried about her but keeping her cooped up wasn't helping anyone.

Amy and Cain followed him out, so she rang Queen Mary's. It was going to be hours before anyone got back to her with the list of pupils who attended the college, to follow up on and that's if they even got anything. What a waste of time; she was going to be sitting here twiddling her thumbs. The receptionist told her Mr Scott was in a meeting but would phone her back at his earliest opportunity. Amy and Cain should have asked the college to check for them, but it was too late now, and she wasn't allowed out to go visit them.

She sipped her latte and began to think about the alginate and how it had got onto to Jasmine Armer's eyelash. She loaded Google on her computer and searched uses for alginate. She'd done this already, but nothing interesting had come up. It listed all the dental procedures that it was used for. She tried again with different phrasing, but even more complex dental websites loaded. She had one last go. *Alternative uses for alginate*, then she clicked on images and scrolled down, until she saw a picture saying *everlasting castings* with a picture of a baby foot. Next, she typed that into the search bar and images of hands, feet, pregnant stomachs filled the screen. She thought about the creepy mask that had turned up in the post that looked like a dead woman, and searched for death masks. That was when her whole world blew up, and she knew she had screwed up so completely she would never live it down. She had to find that mask or Barb, as Cain had referred to it. She pushed her chair back and rushed down the stairs to the front desk, where Brenda was stringing fairy lights around a wonky Christmas tree.

'Brenda when do the bins get emptied?'

'Monday, why?'

'I threw something out I shouldn't have.'

'Oh, good luck with that. Make sure you put gloves on, love. I'd help you but I'm waiting for a phone call.'

Morgan was already on her way to grab gloves out of the

report writing room, where there were shelves loaded with supplies of gloves, face masks, evidence bags. Her stomach was a mass of knots. How had she missed it? According to the YouTube video she watched, alginate could be used to take a mould of a person's face, which could then be made as a cast for a mask. Their guy was making death masks of his victims, she was sure of it, and he'd sent her his very first one. She hadn't given it more than a passing glance because it was so creepy and weird, but she needed to know if it was Jasmine Armer's face he had sent her.

Morgan didn't even put her jacket on, she ran out of the locker room exit door to the area where the bins were, hoping the fenced off area wasn't locked. She was in luck for a change, and whoever had put the rubbish out this morning hadn't snapped the padlock shut. There was a big rubbish bin, but there was also a mound of black rubbish bags. She tried to calculate how many bins there were in the station, which was like trying to guess the lottery numbers, when a deep voice asked, 'What's up?'

She turned to see a man standing there with a bin bag in each hand.

'I threw out something important by mistake.'

'Which office are you in, and when?'

'CID, it was yesterday.'

'What was it?'

'A mask, it was white.'

'Aren't you in luck.'

'I am?'

He nodded. 'Gavin thought it was funny, so he kept it to one side. It's in the cleaner's cupboard on the ground floor.'

Morgan wasn't sure whether she should cry or kiss him.

'Thank you, is it open?'

'Yep, ten minutes later and I'd have locked it and gone

home. You would have spent all day sorting through these bags and freezing your arse off for nothing.'

'You are an absolute lifesaver, thank you so much.'

She turned and ran back to the same doors she'd exited from, swiping her card to open them. Her heart was racing as she rushed to the cleaning cupboard and pushed the door, there staring at her was Barb, propped against a stack of toilet rolls. Morgan stepped inside and stared back *sorry Barb, please forgive me.*

As she looked at the serene features, she knew exactly who she was looking at now, and it made her blood run cold. She hadn't seen it before because she hadn't looked at it for longer than a passing glance. As she picked it up and turned it around she knew without a doubt that this was a death mask of Jasmine's face. Carefully carrying it, she hoped that Ben was still around. She needed to show him. But the office that MIT had taken over was in darkness, she could see from down here. The report writing room had also been empty, meaning everyone that had been available had been sent to conduct the house-to-house enquiries in Windermere.

It felt surreal, carrying a mask of Jasmine's dead face. Morgan went straight to the CSI office, wishing Wendy was back from her holidays. She wasn't sure if Claire would be here or in Barrow. It was empty, and she let out a sigh. She put the mask down on the desk and began searching for an evidence bag big enough to put it in. She had been lucky to have got the mask back, without hunting through endless bags of rubbish, so she was thankful for that, but it would have been nice to have handed it to Claire directly.

She snapped some photos of the mask from every angle and realised she should have looked for the box it got delivered in too, and let out a groan. After slipping it into a bag she wrote a note for Claire, explaining what it was and what she needed. Then she went back down to speak to Brenda.

'Did you find it?'

'I got lucky, yes. Brenda when does the recycling get picked up? Would a brown box be put in that or in the bin?'

'You're not doing too good with this old rubbish stuff, are you, lovey?'

She shook her head.

'I think they put it in the recycling skip, usually gets emptied on a Monday, too.'

Morgan was about to speak when it occurred to her that Brenda had said she'd got a parcel.

'What did the parcel look like you gave to Ben?'

'Oh, it was about the size of maybe two, three shoeboxes put together in a brown box.'

Her blood ran cold. 'I need you to suspend the rubbish collection, Brenda, please, make sure none of it gets collected.'

Once again, she rushed out of the office.

'Where are you going?'

'Need to find that parcel.'

FORTY-FOUR

The practice manager, Nancy, at New Smile Dental Surgery let out an audible groan when Ben and Claire walked in, followed by two uniforms.

'What now?'

Claire side-eyed Ben, who thought the woman staring at them in despair looked even more stressed than he was.

'We need to speak to everyone.'

'A detective has already done that, the day we got told about poor Jasmine.'

'I'm Claire Williams from the Murder Investigation Team. I appreciate that this is a difficult time for you all, but we're here and there is absolutely nothing we can do to make any of this less painful.'

'I know, I'm sorry, it's just first Jasmine, then the stand-off with Neil and his wife and that poor detective getting hurt. How is she?'

'She's okay, thank you for asking.'

Nancy nodded her head. 'Good, I'm glad she is. Who do you want to start with first?'

Ben shrugged. 'Whoever is free at the moment. Do you

know if Jasmine had any patients that needed dental impressions taken on her last day in work?'

'I can find out for you, but it's going to take a little time to check their files.'

'I'd appreciate it if you could.'

Nancy began to type on the computer in front of her.

Ben turned to the two officers.

'It's all good, we'll take it from here, if you want to crack on with the house-to-house.'

They nodded and left, passing Neil Barnard on the way in. He took one look at the officers then towards Ben and shook his head.

'This is never ending.'

Claire turned to look at him. 'You are?'

'Neil Barnard, dental surgeon.'

'Well, Mr Barnard, for your information, just in case it has slipped your mind, your colleague was murdered, and we are determined to find her killer, so if that means we have to spend all day, every day here we will.'

He stared at her in disbelief. 'Of course, I remember, how could I not?'

'Just checking before you start any bullshit. I believe you and your wife caused enough of a disturbance yesterday, resulting in one of our officers getting a serious head injury. Let's not have a repeat of that today.'

Neil Barnard's mouth had dropped open as he glared at Claire. Ben had to cup a hand over his mouth and pretend to cough, to stifle the smirk he couldn't contain. Nancy was also staring at Claire with what Ben would describe as a look of admiration.

Neil walked away, and Ben started after him.

'I'll ask him about his patients and if they had dental impressions.'

Claire smiled. 'Great.'

Ben followed Neil into the staff room, where Neil was hanging up his coat.

'Do you remember if you had any patients who needed dental impressions on Wednesday?'

Neil was pouring himself a mug of coffee from the filter machine. He didn't offer Ben one.

'I don't know, it's been a bit hectic. Nancy will be able to tell you that.'

'Do you make them often?'

'Not really, maybe one or two a day.'

'You can't remember if you did any three days ago?'

'Not off the top of my head, like I said it's been a busy three days, and I'm grieving for my wife's friend, who has also been found dead as well as Jasmine.'

Ben changed tactic. 'How are your sons coping with the news of Emily's murder? Did they know her?'

'Of course, they knew her, she was over at the house at least once a week. They're upset and devastated like the rest of us.'

'What about Jasmine, did they know her too?'

'I don't know, possibly, they may have met her at our annual summer BBQ, we have every August. Hugo may have known her; I don't think Tobias did, why unless they were friends on Facebook, everybody is friends with everyone on there.'

'Just trying to figure it out, Neil.'

'So go arrest him for having her as a friend. Have you seen how many friends people have on there? It's bloody crazy. Esme has over a thousand friends, yet if you asked her how many of them she actually met in real life and had seen them in person, I bet it wouldn't be more than ten. They go on these things and add every man, woman and dog as a friend then announce to the whole world what they're doing and where they're going. I'm surprised you don't get more murders and missing persons investigations than you already do.'

Ben thought he had a point, it was true he'd signed up to

Facebook because that was what everyone did, but he couldn't remember the last time he'd looked at it or even posted something on there. It wasn't his thing, he preferred his privacy.

'Is there anything else, I have a patient in five minutes and need to get set up?'

'Not for now, unless my colleague has some questions.'

Neil took his coffee and his attitude with him as he walked out of the staff room.

Ben went back to where Claire was waiting for Nancy to finish checking Wednesday's patient files to see if any of them had impressions taken.

FORTY-FIVE

There were no car keys on any of the whiteboards for Morgan to take. She'd come to work with Ben in his car, and he always kept his keys in his pocket. She ran back into the report writing room, hoping an officer with a vehicle had come back in, but the only person around was Mads, who was laughing loudly on the phone. She knocked on his open office door and he waved her in.

'Got to go, Robbo, see you later.' He hung up and looked at her. 'What's up?'

'Can you give me a lift, please?'

'Take a car.'

'There's no cars, everyone has been summoned to Windermere and taken all the div cars and vans.'

'Take your car then.'

'I haven't got it with me. Can you not drop me off?'

'I can't, I'm holding the fort, sorry, Morgan, no can do.'

'But it's important and relevant to the case.'

He stood up and sighed. 'Come on then and that's emotional blackmail. How's your head?'

She was so hyped up she'd forgot about the permanent headache that had lodged itself in the side of her temple.

'Been better, but it's okay.'

They walked out into the back yard where his car was parked. He began to talk about the football, and she zoned out, sports weren't her thing and football was a definite no – she didn't understand it and had no reason to.

'How come you're not on this big canvass-the-whole-of-Windermere-looking-for-witnesses job, if you're well enough to be in work?'

'What?' She realised she'd been staring out of the window and had no idea when he'd stopped talking football. Her mind was fixated on the mask of Jasmine's face that had been sitting in full view of the office, and not one of them had seen the connection to the body they had found.

'Oh, I'm supposed to be office based, in case they need anything following up on the computer, that kind of thing.'

'This is not very office based though, is it? And where am I taking you?'

'I left something at home that might be important. I only need dropping off. I'll use my car to get back then I'm not stuck.'

'Are you supposed to be driving? Did you not have concussion?'

'Yes, I can drive. The doctor never said that I couldn't, and no I haven't got concussion.'

'You were lucky then. When I saw that hammer swinging your way, I almost had a heart attack. What a sound it made when it hit your head. Your skull must be rock hard.'

He started to laugh, and she smiled. She didn't think it was very funny, but she liked his laugh, it was like a breath of fresh air after all the stress of the last forty-eight hours.

He reached Ben's street.

'No need to drive down, I'll walk from here. Thank you for the lift.'

'No problem, see you back at the station. Morgan, if you go for food can you get me a tuna or cheese savoury baguette? I forgot to pick my packed lunch up out of the fridge.'

'Of course I will, see you soon.'

She rushed towards the house. She hadn't even thought about food, she was so hyped up, but she decided she'd repay his kindness and get him some lunch on her way back. She might even throw in a packet of crisps.

She let herself into the house, not bothering to put the alarm on – she wasn't stopping long. She just needed to grab the box, have a quick look and then get back to the station, before anyone realised she'd left. Even though it was daylight, she turned on the lights in the hall as she stepped into the darkened living room. They hadn't opened the blinds this morning on their way out, which was why she hadn't seen it, and she'd taken herself up to bed before Ben got home last night.

She could make out the shape of the box on the pine chest, and her heart began to beat against her ribcage. She could feel her pulse pounding in the palms of her hands. She felt for the switch and flicked the light on, hoping to see Amazon or ASOS on the parcel, but she knew in her heart that she hadn't ordered anything online, and wasn't expecting any deliveries to her work.

Her mouth dry, she took a step forward, wondering if she should try and get a CSI here to photograph it in situ, but then again it had been handled by Brenda and Ben, thrown around on the back seat of his car most likely, where he threw everything, so it had already been contaminated forensically. She also didn't want Ben to know she'd left the station because she didn't want to upset him any further. She knew the grouchier he got, the more worried he was, and she hated that she made him feel this way.

She snapped some photos with her phone, then pulled a pair of gloves out of her pocket and put them on. She didn't want to open it where it had been taped. She would open it from the bottom. Still she didn't move forward, too scared to see what was waiting inside of the box for her.

And why her, she wondered, why had the killer sent Jasmine's mask to her? Was it some kind of challenge or was he showing off, thinking he was clever by taunting her this way? She realised she was holding her breath and released it, blowing it out through her pursed lips. Then she sat down and picked up the box.

Turning it over she saw that it wasn't taped on the bottom and managed to open it without causing any damage to the box. White foam peanuts spilled all over the sofa and carpet, and she left them where they fell, scooping more out so she could get to the contents and see if it was what she was hoping it wasn't. The little white nuggets were everywhere but she didn't care. She saw the whiteness of the mask staring back at her and thought she might be sick. Carefully picking it up by the corner she lifted it out and stared at a white, latex copy of Emily Wearing's dead face.

Her first reaction was to throw it across the room and scream, but she managed to drop it back into the box instead. She jumped up. *Fuck.*

She kept muttering over and over.

She hadn't realised her hand was shaking until she picked up her phone off the sofa. She should ring Ben, but then he would know she'd totally ignored him: it was better to get it back to the station. Scooping as many of the peanuts up as she could she put them back in the box and covered the mask. Then carried it out of the house, to her car. She realised she hadn't even picked up her car keys and had to go back inside for them, leaving a trail of those foam peanuts behind like Hansel and Gretel. This time she put the box into the boot of her car, not wanting it to get damaged or for it to be on show to anyone.

She was so distressed about what this second mask meant, she didn't notice the car parked down the street, with the driver watching her and the engine idling away.

FORTY-SIX

Nancy finally had an answer. 'The only person who took dental impressions for a new crown for a patient on Wednesday was Mr Butler, on his last patient before he finished for the day.'

Ben felt the stirring of excitement in the pit of his stomach, the kind he got when he was onto something.

'Who assisted him that day?'

'Jasmine.'

Ben looked at Claire, who asked. 'Is he in work today?'

'Nope, he phoned in sick earlier, and I've had to cancel then rearrange all his patients, which is a nightmare, but what can you do? He's rarely off sick so...' She shrugged.

'Can you give me his address? We just need a quick chat with him.'

Ben gave Nancy his best smile, trying to win her over.

'I can, but I'm telling you he wouldn't do anything like this. He wouldn't have killed Jasmine.'

It was Claire's turn to smile. 'Oh, we're not saying that at all. We just need to ask a couple of questions; it won't take long then we can get back to focusing on the killer. It's all just procedure.'

'Are you sure? I'd hate to get him in trouble, he's going through a rough patch at the moment at home with his wife.'

'Absolutely, we don't want to cause him any difficulties.'

Nancy scribbled down his address on a yellow Post-it note and passed it to Ben.

'Thank you.'

They turned and walked out of the surgery towards Ben's car. Once he was inside, he rang the office, expecting Morgan to answer. He wanted to know if there was any intelligence on the system for Butler, but the phone rang out.

'Damn it, Morgan, where are you?'

'Ladies, lunch break, making a coffee, she won't be far.'

He didn't say it, but he thought to himself *she better not be, I worry too much.*

He drove towards the address Nancy had given him.

* * *

Water's Edge was an exclusive estate of nice, detached houses on the outskirts of Rydal Falls that were built near to the River Rothay. He had thought about selling his house after Cindy died and moving there, but he hadn't had the heart to leave it, with their memories, and the guilt had consumed him so fully that he thought it was only right to stay there and torture himself daily. Which was why he'd worked such long hours after her funeral. The station had been a more welcoming place to be than his own home, or it was until Morgan came along and tipped his world upside down. He had never, ever thought he could love another woman the way he'd loved his wife, but he had slowly fallen in love with Morgan, and now that love consumed him so much, he didn't think he'd be able to carry on living if anything bad happened to her. Which was the reason he got so protective over her; he probably should explain this to her, so she understood where he was coming from, but he struggled to find the right words when he talked about Cindy, although he was getting better at it.

As the turning for the large cul-de-sac came into view he began to indicate.

'What number is Mr Butler at?'

'Twenty.'

Twenty was one of the bigger houses situated closest to the river; it was the same house he'd considered buying. Wasn't it a small world? he thought to himself as he stopped outside the drive, parking across it, where there was a small red Honda, so no one could leave if they wanted to.

'Do you think he could be our suspect?'

'I don't know, Claire; everything is pointing to the Barnards but it's all circumstantial there's nothing concrete.'

'How do you want to do this? Should we bring him in and question him under caution? He worked with her; he could have transferred the alginate to her at some point when he attacked her.'

'He seems like a nice bloke.'

'Don't they all?'

He shook his head. 'Did you ever meet Gary Marks? He was a killer and a rapist. He was not a nice bloke.'

'A couple of times, he was quite charming to me.'

'Just proves what kind of guy he was then. Let's see how Butler reacts, maybe ask him to come down for a voluntary interview.'

'I'll follow your lead, Ben, whatever you think.'

They got out of the car and walked up to the house. Ben knocked, giving it his best police knock. He knew this house was big and he didn't want to waste time.

A woman opened the door and stared at them with huge, wide eyes.

'Knock the door down, why don't you? I hope you're not selling broadband knocking on the door like that?'

Claire smirked, and Ben shook his head.

'Mrs Butler?'

She crossed her arms. 'That depends on who is asking and what you're selling.'

He pulled his warrant card out of his pocket and held it up.

'Detective Sergeant Ben Matthews from CID, and this is Detective Inspector Claire Williams from the Murder Investigation Team. Can we come inside?'

She stepped back, letting them in, then closed the door behind them.

'Go into the lounge.'

She led them to the big open lounge, with patio doors that looked out onto a garden full of paving slabs and a few pots full of dried shrivelled plants. Ben was surprised. When he'd looked at the house the garden had been all grass with sunken borders full of perennials. His own garden was overgrown, but at least it still resembled one. This was just awful, and the view to the river had been hidden behind six-foot concrete panels. There was a large shed at the back with no windows.

'Is Mr Butler here? We really need to speak to him.' Ben was hoping the poor guy was hiding in his shed.

'No, Dave is out, and I have no idea where, because he rarely tells me anything these days.'

'Oh, right. We may as well speak to you then. I'm presuming you know about Jasmine Armer?'

'Yes, I do. Dave has been very upset the last few days; in fact he's been even more unbearable than he usually is, the soft bugger.'

'How did Dave get along with Jasmine? They worked together a lot. Did he ever have anything bad to say about her, or any problems with her at work?'

She turned to look at Claire.

'He liked her. He wouldn't be upset if he didn't, would he?'

Claire gritted her teeth, and Ben took over. 'Mrs Butler.'

'Janine.'

'Janine, we need to rule everyone out who is on our list of suspects, so if you could fill me in on what happened when Dave got home from work that day, it would be really helpful.'

'He comes home early on a Wednesday; he goes to an art class at the college from six until eight and likes to freshen up and have his tea beforehand.'

'Is your husband very artistic?'

She scoffed with a loud, 'Hmph. No, in fact he's quite the opposite. There is a spare bedroom full of his artwork. I won't let him hang it on the walls because I find it too upsetting.'

Ben sat a little straighter before he asked his next question.

'Who teaches the art classes?'

She shrugged. 'Some teacher called Emily, apparently. She's wonderful, so full of life and incredibly talented.' Janine rolled her eyes. 'Dave thinks she's wasted at the college. I think he's got a bit of a mid-life crisis going on. He can't paint or draw but he's obsessed with going to art class. I don't know why the poor woman doesn't put him out of his misery and tell him he's wasting his time and hers.'

The wheels were turning in Ben's head as everything began to click together like some complicated clockwork machinery.

'Can we see his artwork?'

'You really want to see it?'

He nodded, and she stood up. 'Prepare to be completely underwhelmed.'

She led them to the stairs and up to the spare room. Opening the door she turned on the light and muttered, 'Help yourself.'

Then she turned and left them to it, going back downstairs to wait for them. Ben looked at Claire, who was standing with her head tilted to one side.

'What is that?' She was pointing to a canvas that looked as if a human torso had exploded all over it.

Ben pulled on a pair of gloves then began to go through the stacks of canvas boards leaning against the walls. He had no idea what he was looking at, but Janine was right: it was awful. He'd been hoping to see lots of paintings of women who resembled Jasmine and Emily. He didn't know how to describe what these were.

'I think Dave would be better suited to sticking with dentistry.'

Claire smiled. 'You think so?'

They went back downstairs.

Janine was smiling at them.

'Horrible, aren't they?'

'Yes, but they must mean something to Dave.'

'Are we done here?'

'We need to speak to him urgently. Can you phone him and ask him to come home?'

'He won't answer to me. You'll have more luck if you ring.'

She rhymed off his number, and Ben typed it in to his work phone. It rang out.

'When he comes home can you tell him to phone me, or if he wants, he can come down the station for a quick chat. We just need to clear a few things up. Sooner rather than later would be preferable. Oh, and have you got a photograph of Dave?'

He passed her a business card from his pocket.

She pointed to a bookcase where there were several photo frames. Ben took out his phone and snapped a couple of photos.

'He's put a lot of weight on since those were taken. I'll leave him a note. Like I said I'm going out. I can't sit around here all day waiting for him to come home. He might have gone for a walk or something, he could be hours. Or he might be at the boating club in Windermere, he sometimes goes there.'

They left Janine putting her coat on and got back in the car.

Claire was still staring at the house. 'Well, she was a bunch of laughs and not much help.'

'I don't know. We have a connection between Dave and Emily now. If she was the Emily who taught adult art, which I think she was. I vaguely remember her mentioning it. Did you see the shed?'

She moved her head up and down in slow motion.

'I think we need to get a warrant. There is a back gate next to the shed. It's the type of place you could have taken someone and kept them captive. I get the impression Janine doesn't give two hoots what her husband gets up to, as long as he keeps out of her way. You ring Marc to sort out a search warrant. Should we go to the boating club and see if he's there?'

'Let's do that then.'

Ben started the engine. He knew the boating club well. He used to cover that area when he was a beat cop out on the streets many years ago.

If they found Butler and brought him in, they might be stopping a killer from taking his next victim, and Ben wanted that more than anything in the world.

FORTY-SEVEN

Morgan pulled out of the street on auto pilot. A car horn blared at her, and she jumped. She held her hand up in apology. She needed to focus and get back to the station in one piece. She had sent Ben a message, explaining that the masks were what she believed to be death masks, and she would explain more when he came back. There were temporary traffic lights on the main road, causing long delays, so she turned off onto the narrow road that would take her past Pine Hall and the long way around, as long as it wasn't gridlocked. It shouldn't be – not many people used it as a shortcut because of how steep and narrow it was.

She drove past the entrance and wondered how Esme Barnard was doing. She could see cars coming towards her and cut off onto the single-track road. It was better than getting gridlocked on this road.

A car followed her, and she sighed, hoping they knew how narrow it was. Once it got to the top of the steep hill it opened a little wider, but it was a struggle to get two cars past each other. As the road twisted and turned she wished she'd waited it out on the main road. By the time she got over the top and down into Rydal Falls, it probably hadn't saved her any time at all.

The road opened up slightly. She heard the roar of a car engine behind her and looked in the rear-view mirror. The idiot was going to try and overtake her, so she slammed her brakes on to let them pass.

Then she felt a massive jolt as the car hit hers from behind.

It made her skid on the damp, slippery road where patches of black ice hadn't seen enough sunlight to melt it.

She felt the back end of her car begin to slide towards the steep bank leading down to the river. The car reversed. Morgan was furious. Her car was an old banger, but it did the job and served her well. But before she could do anything, the other car rushed towards her and hit her again, this time from the side. It was hard enough to push her Golf off the road, and it began rolling down the banking towards a row of pine trees, smack bang in the middle of the field.

She let out a screech and slammed her brakes on. The car couldn't gain any traction on the grass, and instead of slowing down it spun even further around, sliding down the hill at speed.

She lifted her hands to protect her face, and then with a loud crunch of metal, she was thrown so hard against the driver's side window, and with her already injured head, the force of it knocked her out cold.

Morgan knew something was terribly wrong; she couldn't open her eyes and her entire body was frozen to the core. She was shivering that much her teeth were chattering, and she could feel the sticky wetness running down the side of her head, smell the coppery tang of fresh blood. She had to get out of the car in case it exploded: it was old and running off fumes as usual, so it would probably go up. She blinked a couple of times and tried to move, but her arms and feet were stuck. She began to panic. Her seat was wedged under the steering wheel. It was hard to breathe, she had hurt her chest, what if she had a punctured lung? She didn't want to die here, on the side of a fell, in the middle of a field, all alone, scared and in pain. Everything hurt as she tried to move, feeling around for her radio to call for help.

Then she heard heavy footsteps on concrete, walking around to the side of her, and confusion washed over her. Morgan tried to open her mouth to speak, and it was then that she realised she wasn't in her car and there was a gag in her mouth. She tried to scream anyway because the panic had taken over completely. Her eyes flew open as she felt the back of an icy cold hand on her forehead, and heard a voice whisper.

'Shhh, there's no need to panic. You were in an accident, but you're safe now. I'm going to take good care of you. Lie still and it won't hurt so much. I have to go out for a little while but when I come back we'll talk some more. Maybe get to know each other a little, if you'd like that, and I'll bring back some medical supplies to treat your wounds.'

She had no idea where she was, but the cold was seeping through her bones, and his voice echoed around the space they were in. She was in a shed or a garage somewhere and nobody had a clue where she was. The pain that shot through her heart at the thought of Ben not knowing where to find her made tears form in the corner of her eyes. She blinked to wipe away the tears and found she could see a little; she would not cry in front of this man, who was wearing some kind of mask to hide his face, and give him the satisfaction of seeing her upset.

Her vision began to clear. The room was lit by a bare, dim bulb hanging from the ceiling above her head. The pain inside of her head and her heart was sharp, but it meant that she was alive. If she could feel it then she was still breathing, and as long as she was breathing she had a fighting chance.

He moved around in the shadows, keeping a distance from her.

'You stay there, and I'll be back as soon as I can, okay. I'll bring food and a first aid kit to change the dressing on your head. It's bled right through, and I'm sorry that you are in pain. I can get you some painkillers too. Be good while I'm gone, or I'll leave you here without any help.'

She heard the scrape of a door opening as a cold draught blew around her, then the door was shut. The sound of the key turning in the lock filled her with hope that she might be able to free herself before he came back, or at least she'd die trying. She wasn't going to lie here and wait for him to return and kill her, or even worse make one of those bloody awful masks of her face to send to Ben.

She began to twist her wrists first one way and then the other. It was only seconds before she felt the skin on them begin to burn from the rope, but at least she was leaving behind precious DNA, if nothing else. She began to breathe deeply, using the technique she'd taught Ben to help him destress: a long slow breath in, twist her wrists one way, then a long slow breath out and twist them the other. She couldn't move her feet, but if she could free her hands, she'd be able to pull down the gag which she was biting down hard on, to stop herself from screaming at the intense burning of her skin. Then untie her feet and find something to defend herself with when he came back.

She wasn't sure who the man in the mask was, but she would find out one way or another and she would not let him kill her.

FORTY-EIGHT

The boating club wasn't busy. They went inside to the room where there was a bar. Sitting on a bar stool was a heavyset guy with a pint glass and a shot glass in front of him. Ben knew it was Dave Butler, and he walked up to the bar. Taking the stool next to him he sat down.

'Bad day?' He pointed to the drinks, and by the way Dave Butler's eyes were glazed they weren't his first.

He nodded. 'Yes.'

'Sorry to hear that.'

Claire hung back outside the entrance, leaving Ben to deal with him, as neither of them thought he looked like a threat. His body language was one of utter defeat and sadness. His head hung low, and he was slouched over the bar with his shoulders hunched.

'Dave Butler?'

He looked at Ben, who thought that this man could have been him when Morgan first joined the team; he had been out of shape, drinking too much and depressed.

'I'm DS Ben Matthews, I need to speak to you. Have you got the time to come to the station for a voluntary interview?'

He nodded in slow motion, picked up the shot glass and downed it. Ben didn't try to stop him; somehow he didn't think that the man next to him had anything to do with Jasmine's and Emily's murders, but he still had to rule him out.

'Have you ever lost two people you really liked in the space of a few days?'

'No, but I lost someone very close to me and I know how much it hurts.'

Dave stood up. 'Have you spoken to my wife; did she tell you I was here?'

'She did.'

'She's a bitch, isn't she? Why the fuck did the mad bastard killing women who didn't deserve to die not choose her instead? No one would have missed her, not even her own mother, she's so bloody hard and cruel.'

Ben was shocked. He really hated his wife.

Dave stumbled a little as he walked towards the exit where Claire was standing. He smiled at her then turned to Ben.

'I'm a dentist, not a killer but I'd rather go with you than go home to Janine, so you can lock me up now and take as long as you want. I'm in no hurry to go back to her.'

Ben wondered how many people were actually in a relationship with someone they liked. Him and Morgan were one, Amy seemed happy enough with Jack, but he didn't know about Cain. Most of the people he dealt with didn't like each other very much. Look at Esme and Neil Barnard, she had flipped and tried to kill him.

By the time they arrived at the station, Dave was snoring so loud in the back seat Ben didn't want to wake the guy up to continue his nightmare. Claire got out first, and she slammed the door shut, which jolted Dave from his slumber.

'Where am I?'

Ben opened his door. 'Rydal Falls police station; you're here to answer some questions.'

'I am? Yes, I am I know.'

He was slurring his words, and Ben knew they couldn't interview him in this state. He was going to have to get him booked in and put in a cell where he could sleep off the worst of his day-drinking session. He led him down to custody and hammered on the door, then he walked in to see Jo and Michelle.

'Have you two even been home?'

They nodded. Jo took one look at Dave and said to Ben, 'What's this?'

'This is Dave Butler, from Water's Edge. He's here on a voluntary basis to answer questions pertaining to the two murder investigations, but he's had a little too much to drink, haven't you, Dave?'

Dave lurched forward and stuck up his thumb, letting out a loud belch.

'Have we got somewhere he can sleep it off for a little while?'

Jo rolled her eyes at Ben. 'Cell two; Michelle stick him in and show him the facilities, please.'

Michelle took hold of Dave's arm. 'Come on, Dave, you're about to enjoy the hospitality of Cumbria Constabulary's finest, although we haven't got very good reviews on TripAdvisor.'

Dave laughed and stumbled in the direction she led him. When he was out of earshot Jo turned to Ben.

'I could have done without a babysitting job.'

'I know, I'm sorry, but I need to question him and couldn't leave him in that state. I'd have had to go looking for him again and I haven't got the time.'

'The things I do for you.'

'I owe you, ring me when he's sober enough to talk. I'll be right down.'

He left them to it. They were getting nowhere fast.

Upstairs in the MIT room, Claire had made them both a coffee and managed to find some custard cream biscuits to go with it. He had sat down at the desk to update the computer, when a Response officer knocked on the door and walked in.

'All right, boss, what should we do with Morgan's car? Is she sorting out her own recovery or should we do it? Amber is asking that's all.'

Ben almost choked on the biscuit he'd shoved into his mouth. He stood up and ran for the CID office, slamming open the door hard enough that the entire wall shook, and another chunk of plaster fell to the floor.

It was empty; he checked his office – it was empty too. Her bag was still on the floor by her desk, but her coat wasn't there.

The officer had followed him down and watched him as the panic set in.

'Where is her car? Where is Morgan?'

He took out his phone as the old, yet all too familiar dread settled over his entire body as he felt his world come crashing down. Her phone went straight to voicemail.

'Morgan where are you? Ring me back now.'

He looked at the officer, whose name he didn't know.

'Someone rang it in. They found it off the road crashed into a tree near to Scandale Beck. It's a right state, but Amber couldn't find Morgan; she must have got a lift back home or to the hospital. She thought because she didn't ring it in herself, she might be sorting out her own recovery.'

'I need you to take me there now.'

The man who was young enough to be Ben's son nodded. 'No problem.'

Ben dashed down the stairs, followed by the copper.

Mads shouted, 'Where are you going, Nathan?'

Nathan pointed to Ben, and Mads shook his head. 'Tell Morgan she's a liability and she shouldn't have been driving. I knew I shouldn't have left her.'

Ben stopped in his tracks and turned to look at him. 'Where did you leave her?'

'She wanted to go home, said it was urgent, something to do with the investigation, but there were no cars, so I dropped her off. She said she was fine to drive back, when obviously she wasn't.'

Ben turned back to Nathan furious with Mads, but he also knew that Morgan was the one who had asked him for a lift, so it wasn't his fault.

Ben jumped into the van and began to talk on the radio.

'Every patrol to the RTC crash site, I want a dog handler and a drone like yesterday. We have an officer missing and most likely injured; she could have passed out somewhere in the area.'

Then he turned to Nathan. 'Blue light it.'

'Yes, Sarge.'

He turned on the lights and sirens, speeding towards Scandale Beck. Ben gripped onto the edge of the seat. Nathan was a worse driver than he was, but he was fast and sped through the traffic then out onto the road that would take them to Morgan's car.

Ben took out his phone and opened the Find My app. Morgan's phone wasn't on it, and he groaned; they had talked about setting up family sharing when she got a new phone, but she hadn't got around to sorting out a new contract yet.

Nathan glanced over to see what Ben was doing.

'Has she got Snapchat, an Apple watch, any social media?'

'She hasn't got Snapchat that I know about; she doesn't really do much social media.'

'That's a shame, Snapchat is great for location tracking.'

Nathan raced through the tight lane until he reached the spot where the other van was parked across the road blocking traffic. Ben felt his chest tighten at sight of Morgan's crumpled car at the base of the huge pine tree trunk.

He was out of the van and running down the slippery grass; he didn't care if he fell down in front of Amber and Nathan. He needed to see how much blood there was so he could gauge how desperate the search for her was. He noticed the door wide open, and as he got nearer there was a streak of red blood, smeared down the driver's side window. The airbag had deployed. He stopped and looked at the grass. It was flattened and there were clear drag marks, and he felt bile rise up his throat. The rear lights of the car were smashed, and the bumper was hanging off.

Ben lifted the radio to his mouth.

'Control I need CSI and task force here now. I want this whole area and the road cordoned off. Someone ran Morgan off the road and has dragged her from the car.'

Marc's voice answered him.

'On my way, Ben, what else do you need?'

He whispered *a miracle* but he didn't press the button so anyone could hear it. He looked in the car to see what Morgan had so urgently had to go home for and couldn't see anything on the front or back seats, then he tugged his sleeve down and opened the boot. There was the box Brenda had given him yesterday, opened from the bottom.

He turned to Amber, who was watching from a distance.

'Have you got a pair of gloves?'

She nodded and walked towards him, passing him a pair. He snapped them on and looked inside the box, to see another of those white masks. At the same time his phone vibrated, and he saw he had a new voicemail. He felt a spark of hope inside of him. It was Morgan, she was okay and had got a lift to the hospital. It had to be, and he let himself forget about the drag marks in the grass for a few moments while he listened to her voice.

'Ben, it's me. Don't be mad, I know what he's doing, he's making death masks of their faces. Look at the one I got sent a few days ago, it's Jasmine's face; and the box you had for me, it has a mask of Emily's face inside. I'm on my way back to the station with it to get it booked in, see you soon.'

She hung up, and he felt as if his insides had been torn out it hurt so much. He saved the message and ended the call. Then carefully took the mask out of the box and stared down at the dead face of Emily. Whoever had sent Morgan these masks now had Morgan, he had no doubt about it.

He stared at the drag marks: they went all the way up the hill. Whoever it was they were strong enough to drag an unconscious woman up a steep hill and then get her into a car. It clearly wasn't Dave Butler.

He began to climb back up the hill towards the vans. A killer had abducted Morgan, and Ben knew that they had to focus on the area and try to find a suitable place where he might have taken her.

FORTY-NINE

Morgan could feel the blood running down her wrists. The skin was already delicate there. She had been in this situation before and got herself out of it, and she could do it again. At least the blood helped make the rope move easier. She bit down hard on the material in her mouth and managed to rip her right arm through the rope. It hurt so bad, but she didn't waste a minute and began to tug at the binding around her left wrist, until it was loose enough to pull it out. She tore the gag out of her mouth, and it left her with numb cheeks because it had been too tight, the bastard, and sucked in huge gulps of stale air.

As she looked around she saw she was in some kind of shed or summerhouse. Sheets across the windows were making it dark and impossible to see out of, especially when you were tied to an old-fashioned dentist's chair. She knew where she was, and there was a choice of two men who could have brought her here: Neil or Tobias Barnard.

She clambered off the chair and rushed towards one of the heavy sheets, lifting a tiny corner to see where she was. In the distance she could see the back of Pine Hall. She let go and looked for something to protect herself with and saw all the art supplies on a long workbench. She wanted something heavy to knock the bastard over the head with, but there wasn't much. She tugged out the long drawer and inside saw an old-fashioned orange photograph album.

Opening it she let out a sob: she was staring at a black-and-white newspaper cut out of herself. As she turned each page she looked at news clippings about all the cases she'd worked. She dropped it back inside, wanting to be sick, and slammed the drawer shut.

Along one wall on a shelf were the moulds for the masks he had made; they were made from papier mâché and crudely resembled Jasmine and Emily.

On a shelf above it there were three plastic display cases, each one had a mobile phone inside it, and she knew then this is why they hadn't been able to find Jasmine's or Emily's phones; she could see her own with its dark green case.

She couldn't find anything heavy enough to use as a weapon, but she limped along the workbench where there were boxes of alginate powder, paints, paintbrushes, cloths, and found a box of rags. She pulled one out, about to tie it around her head, when she realised her best bet was to pretend she was still attached to the chair when he came back. He would know she had got free if she had mopped up her wound. She paused then and pulled out a few more to use. She knew she'd have to get him in the chair then tie him down, if she had any chance of escaping the room.

On the shelf was a small bottle of masking fluid. She picked it up, unscrewed the cap and sniffed. It smelled bad. It might be enough to blind him so she could make a run for it. The only way she could do that was if he got close enough to her face to make sure it went into his eyes.

She tried the handle of the door just to be sure it wasn't open. It didn't move. Then she cautiously checked the two large windows, but they didn't open at all. She wondered if she'd be able to break them. There was a possibility he would hear her. If he chased her she wouldn't stand much of a chance, the state she was in. Her heart racing she did the only thing she could, took a deep breath and forced herself to climb back into the chair.

This time she loosely tied her feet so she could get them out, then she pulled the gag back into her mouth and unscrewed the cap on the bottle of masking fluid, slipping it underneath her hip out of sight. It was uncomfortable but the pain in her head and from her wrists soon blocked it out. Then she slipped her raw, bloodied wrists back through the ropes that had bound them, hoping he wouldn't check them and see how loose they were.

She looked at the workbench and noticed a catering-sized roll of clingfilm and knew this was how he'd asphyxiated both Jasmine and Emily. He must have wrapped layers of the stuff around their faces, blocking their airways and stood watching them suffocate to death. As if to confirm this, her eyes fell onto a metal wastepaper basket on the floor that was stuffed with used clingfilm. A tear leaked from the corner of her eye for them both, for Emily and for herself. If she didn't get the better of him, she was going to end up the same, although he wouldn't be able to leave her dead in her car because that was a write-off, and she prayed that someone would have noticed it by now and phoned the police.

She couldn't think about Ben, it hurt her heart too much, so she focused on Jasmine's mask instead and kept repeating the words *I'll stop him*, over and over inside of her mind while she waited for him to come back and kill her.

FIFTY

Al arrived with four task force officers and a map of the area which he spread out on the passenger seat of Nathan's van.

'The hospitals have been checked, haven't they?' he asked, and Ben realised he didn't know if they had.

Amber, who had joined them, nodded. 'That was the first thing I did, Sarge, I rang them all to see if she'd been admitted, and she hasn't.'

'Okay, thanks. We need to look at the nearest properties that are within walking distance and go speak to the owners, to see if she has turned up there.'

'What about the drag marks in the grass?' Ben asked.

'I know, Ben, but I'm just ruling out all of the obvious first before I can ask for air support. Can you tell me again what we're dealing with so we're on the same page?'

'Morgan left me a voicemail, saying she had realised that the mask she got the other day was a death mask of Jasmine Armer. She went home to retrieve another parcel that was sent to the station that I took home for her, which contained a mask of Emily Wearing. Myself and Claire brought Dave Butler from New Smile in, but it's safe to say he's no longer a suspect because he was with us and drunk as a skunk around the time Morgan was taken. We need to locate the Barnard family because they are our other suspects. I know Morgan was particularly interested in Tobias Barnard.'

Ben knew they had to go through the motions, but he didn't want to be wasting time door knocking. Whoever had Morgan wasn't going to answer any doors and tell them she was there.

A car skidded to a halt behind the van. Cain got out of the driver's side, Amy the passenger and they came to stand next to Ben. Amy took hold of his elbow to let him know they were there, and he nodded, feeling relieved he had his team to do this with him.

'What's the plan?' Amy asked.

'Check nearest properties,' replied Al.

She bent down to look at the map. 'That's a coincidence, isn't it?'

'What is?' Ben snapped.

'Pine Hall, the home of the Barnards, is one of the closest.'

Ben was running towards the car Cain had arrived in, and both of them followed him.

Al shouted, 'Where are you going?'

'To their address. I want armed officers to follow us to Pine Hall; I want the whole Barnard family arresting and the entire house and grounds searched.'

Cain did a ten-point turn in the narrow road to get the car facing the right way, taking half of the hawthorn hedge that edged the road with him.

'Hold tight, this might be the ride of your life.'

Amy, who was in the back, scrabbled to plug her seat belt in and closed her eyes. Ben nodded at Cain. 'I don't care what you do, get me to Pine Hall.'

'Yes, boss.'

The light was fading fast as Cain manoeuvred his way along the winding roads to get to Pine Hall.

'Amy, I haven't been here before, I need you to tell me where to turn off, so open your bloody eyes.'

She did as she was told. 'At the bottom of this hill take a left onto Under Loughrigg then it's about half a mile on the left-hand side. You'll have to slow down to make the turn onto the drive though, it's quite concealed.'

Ben hoped to God another car didn't come the opposite way, or they'd all die before he could even get to save Morgan.

FIFTY-ONE

Morgan lay there listening to the sound of a tap as it dripped somewhere behind her. She tried to slow her breathing down and turned her head away from the masks. The thought of her own face being immortalised and put on that shelf made her want to scream. Then the sound of the key being turned in the lock filled her with such dread she wished she could close her eyes and forget about what was going to happen. Had Jasmine given up and let him kill her, or had she tried to escape? she wondered.

The door opened and he stepped inside, still wearing a mask.

She looked at him. He was the same height as Neil, maybe not as muscular as Tobias, but she was at an unfair advantage, so it could be either of them. Then she realised if he didn't remove the mask she'd never be able to throw the masking fluid in his eyes, which had been her plan.

He had a first aid box in his hands. He stood staring at her, his eyes moving down her body to her feet, and she wanted to scream. He must have been satisfied that she hadn't got loose because he nodded.

'I thought you would have tried to escape.' His voice was muffled through the mask. 'Jasmine tried at first but soon gave up when she realised it was hopeless; but I thought you might put up a bit more of a fight. I'm not sure if I'm pleased or disappointed that you haven't. I bet you're dying to know why you're here, why I brought Jasmine here? Emily I had no need to, as she took me to her home, which worked out far better than I could have hoped for. You see I already had a mask of her face, one which I'd made at an art class one day. It was so beautiful, so perfect, I realised that she would forever stay that age and never get older, never get lines on her forehead, crinkles around her eyes. She would always look like that, and it gave me an idea. I decided that I would take the most beautiful women I knew and make them live forever.

'Jasmine came here a few times. She was so pretty but she didn't know it, that's what made her so endearing, and then she told me about her father's untimely death, how they'd spent so many happy childhood days there, going for picnics by the water. She had nothing but beautiful memories of Thirlmere, and he'd spoiled it forever by ending his life in the very spot that she adored.

'Sad really when you think about it. That's when I knew I could make her happy again, eternally happy.

'The same with Emily. I knew she was going to end up ripping my family apart; it was only a matter of time before something happened. I could not control it, so I helped her too. She was happy to get into my car and take me back to her apartment. She took me to bed, but I didn't want that. I wanted her to live forever and in order to do that she had to die. She put up much more of a fight than Jasmine did. She was so strong, it was a proper tussle, but I managed to tie her up and suffocate her, just like I did Jasmine. I'm going to do the same for you, Morgan, once I've cleaned you up, then you can live forever too.'

He put the first aid box down on the workbench and tugged a string dangling from the ceiling. The bare bulb flickered into life, casting a cold glow over the room. He stepped forward and looked down at her wrists.

'Oh, forgive me. You did try and now look at the state of your poor wrists; they must be very painful along with your head. Would you like some painkillers to numb it a little, Morgan?'

She tried to nod her head. He would have to remove the gag so she could swallow them, and she had an idea.

'Isn't it a good job Esme keeps a well-stocked emergency kit under the sink? I think I better clean you up a little bit too. I'm worried about the injury to your head; it's going to hinder my mask making. I'm almost tempted to nurse you back to health a little before I attempt the final stage, but I think I'd be a foolish man to believe that I could keep you here like a caged animal for an extended period of time, because the longer I leave you the stronger you'll get, and it could turn quite messy. Now if I give you these tablets will you swallow them like a good girl?'

She nodded again. He took a blister of tablets out of his pocket and popped two out, then he walked behind her to where the dripping tap was and turned it on to fill a paper cup. When he came back into her field of view he placed the tablets and cup onto the workbench, and she prayed he didn't notice the missing bottle of fluid. He crossed towards her and ripped the gag out of her mouth, letting it fall down onto her chin.

'Don't bother screaming, no one can hear you.'

When he turned back to grab the pills and cup, Morgan pulled her right hand through the rope but kept it by her side. He came closer to her and bent down.

'Open wide.'

She opened her mouth, and he popped the two small white pills onto her tongue. Her arm shot up and ripped the mask off his face. He let out a roar of surprise and anger, and before he could move she grabbed the bottle and squirted the liquid into his eyes.

Hugo Barnard let out a scream so high-pitched she would have been proud of it if she could think straight. He stumbled backwards, his hands cupping his eyes. Morgan didn't waste a second; she slipped her other wrist free and tugged her feet out of the ropes. He was groaning and stumbling towards the sink to wash his eyes out. She didn't hesitate; she went behind him and kicked him as hard as she could with her right foot, her trusty Doc Marten connecting with the base of his spine, throwing him forwards, then she kicked the back of his right knee, and he went down. Grabbing the first aid box off the counter, she swung it at his head as hard as she could, and it hit with a loud thwack.

'This is for Jasmine and Emily, you arsehole.'

She hit him again and again for good measure and turned and hobbled towards the door, grabbing one of the plastic display cases with her phone inside of it. She ripped it open and held down the side button to turn it on. It was dark now and it had started to rain. She saw figures by the house and paused. What if it was Neil and he knew what Hugo had been doing all along? She picked up her pace, desperate to put space between herself and the light behind her.

FIFTY-TWO

Morgan was running to get away from the summerhouse when she heard Ben's voice call out.

'Morgan.'

'He's in the summerhouse, it's Hugo Barnard.'

She began to limp up the small incline towards him as he began to run towards her. And then she was in his arms as he scooped her up and carried her the best that he could. She closed her eyes and pressed her head against his chest. She was strong and feisty and had managed to save herself, but it was a relief to finally be in his arms. To feel truly safe.

Cain passed them going the opposite way, followed by Amy. He shouted, 'I'll be having words with you later, Brookes.'

She smiled as Ben whispered, 'Thank God you're alive, I thought I'd lost you.'

'Lost me, absolutely not. Haven't you figured it out, I'm like a bad penny I always turn up.'

The driveway to Pine Hall pulsated with flashing blue and white lights as backup arrived. Esme and Tobias Barnard had come rushing out of the front door to see what was happening. She took one look at Morgan and then glanced down towards the old summerhouse and let out a scream that pierced the cold night air.

Tobias ran to help Ben.

'Bring her inside, I'll call an ambulance.'

Al was running towards them, and he shouted. 'Ambulance on route.'

Morgan looked at Ben. 'No ambulance.'

He shook his head. 'For once in your life please let me be the one to take care of you and I say you need an ambulance.'

'Okay.'

He kissed the top of her bloodied head and gently put her down. He was out of breath and panting hard. 'Besides, if I don't put you down it will be me that needs the ambulance, Brookes.'

She smiled. 'You better not, Ben, I need you in my life. Who else would want to rescue me like you do?'

He wrapped an arm around her and helped her up the steps. Tobias had pushed an armchair out of one of the many lounges for her to sit in. His face was white as he took in the state of her, and she managed to smile at him.

Esme was sitting on the bottom stair, her arms crossed over her chest rocking.

'I'm sorry, did Hugo do this to you?' she said.

'Yes, he did,' Morgan told her.

Tobias turned to Esme, but she couldn't meet his gaze, and Morgan got the feeling that Esme had known something was wrong but hadn't realised exactly what. More police officers arrived and soon the whole house and grounds were lit up with blue lights. Finally an ambulance pulled up. Morgan, who had closed her eyes because the bright light in the hallway was hurting her head, would have placed a fifty per cent chance bet that Nick would be one of them.

'Morgan Brookes, what the hell happened to you?'

She opened one eye and smiled at him. 'Heard you were

going to go on strike, Nick, I thought I'd better get in before you did.'

He laughed. 'Well, I'm glad to see the patient is conscious and breathing although I'm not sure how the mess that is your head is. I take it you're going to actually accept a ride in my truck this time?'

'Bosses orders.'

Nick smiled at Ben. 'Glad to see you talked some sense into her. Come on, Morgan, let's get you to A&E. I'm sure they'll be stoked to see you again so soon.'

She laughed, but it hurt her head and her side, so she stopped. 'I think I cracked a rib when my car hit a tree.'

Ben looked at her in disbelief, but she knew he was grateful she was okay because the alternative didn't bear thinking about.

'You have a long night ahead of you, boss, I'll be okay don't worry about me.'

He nodded. 'Famous last words, my friend, you don't leave that hospital until the doctor agrees you are fit to go, and someone can come collect you. That's all I'm asking.'

She gave him a salute. 'Yes, boss.'

Then let Nick help her up and out into the back of the ambulance. She saw Hugo who was cuffed and complaining about his eyes burning to the two officers who were marching him up the hill. Ben called after her.

'Morgan, what did you do to him?'

'I threw some masking fluid in his eyes, it said on the back just to wash it with water. It's only like using CS gas on him.'

Ben began to laugh and Cain who was walking behind Hugo said. 'Nice one, Brookes.'

Hugo began to shout. 'I need a doctor, I'm blind, I need that ambulance now.'

Cain bent down and whispered in his ear. 'You need to get yourself into the back of the police van and a nurse will wash your eyes out when you get to the station. Quit complaining before I give you a reason to complain.'

He shoved Hugo into the van and Morgan realised just how young he looked. He was a kid, still a teenager and yet he was one of the most evil people she had ever come across.

Nick got into the back of the ambulance with her and began to dress her head wound again as his colleague slammed the doors shut. She closed her eyes and let him get on with it, grateful that she was still breathing and had not been reduced to a death mask for everyone to remember her by.

She had fought him for Jasmine and Emily, she would never forget them and the terrible deaths they had suffered. But for now she was going to let people take care of her, only for a short while until she felt better and was ready to get back to what she loved best, her job which might be one of the saddest there was dealing with murder victims and their families, but she was good at her job, and someone had to stop the bad guys so it might as well be her.

A LETTER FROM HELEN

I want to say a huge thank you for choosing to read *Hold Your Breath*. If you did enjoy it, and want to keep up-to-date with all my latest releases, just sign up at the following link. Your email address will never be shared, and you can unsubscribe at any time.

www.bookouture.com/helen-phifer

I want to thank you, my wonderful, supportive readers from the bottom of my heart for all the love you have for Morgan, Ben and the team. Without you this series wouldn't have carried on for this many stories and the team wouldn't be fighting killers to make Rydal Falls a safer place. I want you to know that your kindness makes the world a much better place and long may we go on these adventures together. Writing is my world; I love it so much and the chance to escape into a different one when my own life is hard keeps me sane. I'm sending you all a huge hug and once again a never-ending thank you.

I hope you loved *Hold Your Breath* and if you did I would be very grateful if you could write a review. I'd love to hear what you think, and it makes such a difference helping new readers to discover one of my books for the first time.

I love hearing from my readers – you can get in touch on my Facebook page, through Twitter, Goodreads or my website.

Thanks,

Helen

www.helenphifer.com

 facebook.com/Helenphifer1

twitter.com/helenphifer1

ACKNOWLEDGEMENTS

I'd like to say a huge thank you to my new editor Jennifer Hunt for stepping in and taking to Morgan, Ben and the team so brilliantly. It's been so wonderful to work with you on this book, thank you for being so lovely and here's to many more.

A tremendous thank you goes to the whole Bookouture team, there are so many wonderful people who take a story like this and turn it into the finished book that you get to read and without them it wouldn't be possible. Here's to team Bookouture!

Where would I be without my publicity gals, especially Noelle Holten who is my absolute angel, wing woman and all-round lifesaver when it comes to cover reveals and publication days. Noelle, you work so hard, and I appreciate it more than you could ever know. A big thank you to Kim Nash, Sarah Hardy and Jess Readett too.

I couldn't give my thanks without including all the other fabulous Bookouture authors who I am privileged to get to chat with, ask advice from, read their brilliant books and drink lots of Prosecco with at the parties.

As always, I owe a huge debt of gratitude to the book blogging community who are just phenomenal at what they do. You're all wonderful and so very much appreciated, that you give up your time to support us authors and share the love is so kind of you. I can't ever thank you enough.

I'd also like to thank my go to, final read through support

friend Paul O'Neill for always stepping in to save the day. Paul, I thank you from the bottom of my heart for everything.

Huge thanks to my dear friends and coffee support group Sam Thomas and Tina Sykes who seem to crop up in a lot of my books because I love them so much.

Finally, a big thank you to my family who still don't read the books, I'm not holding it against you all. I can live with that kind of rejection, just. I love you all so much and I'm so proud of you all (most of the time anyway).

Much love to you all,

Helen xx